# One by One

Helen Bridgett

*Book 1 – Professor Maxie Reddick Files*

*Stories that inspire emotions!*
www.rubyfiction.com

Published 2022 by Ruby Fiction
Penrose House, Crawley Drive, Camberley, Surrey GU15 2AB, UK
www.rubyfiction.com

ISBN: 978-1-91255-043-2

Printed and bound in Great Britain by Clays Ltd, Elcograf S.p.A.

*One by One*

*For my wonderful family and friends*
*– I'm very lucky to have you in my life x*

# Acknowledgements

First of all, I'd like to thank everyone at Choc Lit and Ruby Fiction for giving me the opportunity to share this story with you – particularly the Tasting Panel readers who passed the original manuscript and made publication possible. A special thanks to: Hilary Brown, Lucy Mouland, Katie Stevens, Dimitra Evangelou, Rosie Farrell, Alan Roberton, Ruth Nägele, Janice Butler, Wendy Stevens, Lorna Baker, Jo Osborne and Carol Dutton.

My thanks too, to my friends and family who are the best fun to be around after a day's writing. Julie and Leo get a special shout-out – thank you for always being supportive and for the use of your name! I do hope you enjoy the book. Thanks also to my fellow authors from the CBC and Crime and Publishment courses – in particular Sarah who did the first read through of this story and gave me some great advice. Finally, as ever, I thank my Mam and Dad for giving me a life-long love of books and Jason for always being there.

# Chapter One

That song meant one thing only – time for a quick exit. The wailing and flailing of drunken wedding guests erupted full force as the DJ cranked up the opening bars of "Don't Stop Believing". The dance floor came alive with guests bellowing along to the anthem which the happy couple credited with bringing them together. Georgina Pickering knew that if she didn't get out of the room immediately, she'd be dragged from her hidey-hole by some well-meaning relative and forced to join in. Too late – the father of the bride spotted her and seemed determined to round up all the single girls for one final whirl. Politely, Georgina allowed herself to be pulled into the centre of the floor.

It was an extremely unpleasant place by now: men with sweat stains and saturated shirts that strained across beer-filled bellies; women carrying high heels in their hands, dancing in bare feet on the vile, sticky floor, and everyone screeching out whatever remnants of lyrics they could remember in this state.

Georgina swung her arms from side to side and pretended to mime along with everyone else until her euphorically woozy partner found another guest to take pity on and she could escape back to the sidelines. Some people just didn't get it. She was happy watching. She didn't feel left out or lonely; she was enjoying herself – just not in the same way other people did.

'Would you like to dance?' said a voice behind her.

Georgina turned slightly towards the man addressing her. He was tall, very tall. Her face was only just level with his broad chest; she kept her head bowed, only glimpsing a small smile on a blurred face. She didn't like to have any kind of direct eye contact if she didn't have to. It led to small talk and that wasn't exactly her strong point. She shook her head, facing forwards and replied, 'No, thank you. I was just about to head home.'

'Your loss,' said the voice.

As she'd told this stranger she was going to leave, and could still feel his eyes watching her, Georgina now felt obliged to go. Her taxi wasn't booked for another forty-five minutes, but she guessed calling now to try to bring it forward would be a complete waste of time. It was Saturday night and this was a huge wedding in the middle of May, far enough from the nearest town of Lonsdale to make bringing her booking forward pretty impossible.

Instead, she decided to have a wander around the country house her former flatmate, Penny, had chosen for her wedding. It was a stunning Georgian building that had just been re-opened after renovations; in its heyday it had been known for extravagant parties and tonight, each room she walked into seemed to have been ignited with the love and abandonment of the occasion. The dance floor she'd happily left was swaying, the bar was full of animated conversations, and the cosy fireside snug was nurturing a new romance between two lovers who'd been strangers when they woke up this morning. Georgina glanced in their direction and wondered how some people seemed to find it all so easy.

As she reached the great entrance hall, her landlady, Rachel, appeared arm in arm with a guy she didn't recognise.

'Not officially the best man, but he should have been,' slurred Rachel with a big drunken smile on her face. 'Don't wait up.'

Georgina laughed and told her she was heading home. Rachel wasn't the conventional type of landlady; she was only four years older than her lodgers and partied far more than them but much to Georgina's relief, she didn't like to host them in her own flat. Rachel always said home was her sanctuary and the last thing she wanted to find when she woke up was a kitchen full of empty bottles and a floor full of strangers. Penny and Rachel went to several parties together while Georgina stayed home, happy for the peace and looking forward to the stories when they returned. She always got the tea and toast ready when she heard the key fumbling at the front door. Her flatmates often joked and called her Cinderella but they had it wrong – she was simply far happier with a book and a big armchair than she was with a crowd and a dance floor.

In fact, she'd worried for months about this day of social niceties with people she didn't know, but in the end, the wedding breakfast had been no problem at all. Penny had seated her with the singles and oddballs. Fortunately, the table was full of geeks who loved talking about their subject area and, throughout the dinner, she made a willing audience for them. Today had found her sitting next to a philosophy lecturer and the whole table joined in a lively conversation about the obsolescence, and therefore the need to eradicate binary values in society: good vs evil and male vs female. She very much doubted any other table was having a conversation like this, but Georgina could have spent all night listening to the debate. Despite their geekiness, she noticed as she was leaving that even her fellow diners seemed to have found partners by the end of the evening. She was happy for them too. As she reached the door, a member of staff approached her with a bottle of champagne.

'Courtesy of the hotel,' he said, 'as this is the first wedding since our renovations.'

Georgina opened her mouth to say that she didn't really drink but stopped herself as Rachel would probably enjoy it. Instead, she thanked him and walked out into the grounds.

It had been a beautiful summer day with the most perfect blue skies and hawthorn blossom providing the backdrop to the photographs. The weatherman had said there was a storm coming but now was the calm beforehand and the night air was welcomingly fresh as Georgina left the noise of the celebration behind and walked onto the terrace. A mature woodland, vast lawns and glistening lake stretched out before her. Georgina could see how anyone with a Jane Austen fixation, as Penny did, would pick this place for their wedding; it was very *Pride and Prejudice*. She checked her watch. It was half past midnight and the waxing moon full of folklore and new beginnings was so close to full, it cut through the darkness and lit a magical pathway across the lawn down to the water's edge. It really had been a picture-perfect day from start to finish.

Filled with the happiness that good days bring, Georgina pulled her pashmina close around her shoulders, kicked off her shoes and started walking across the lawns, cool and damp with the evening dew. Georgina mused that the new lovers, wrapped around each other in small corners of the hotel, had really missed a trick; here, outside in all the majesty of Mother Nature, that's where the memories would be made tonight.

The weight hit her like a tombstone toppling onto a grave, knocking her to the ground and crushing her chest. In a blur of time that could only have been seconds, she realised it was not rock but human; she pushed against it but the harder she fought, the greater the force holding her down. A cork popped and liquid was being poured down her throat and over her face, she had to swallow quickly to stop herself drowning in it, she coughed and spluttered as it overwhelmed her airways. Then a large gloved hand gripped both of hers tightly while the other ripped the pashmina from her, pushed it over her face and held it down tightly.

'You and I are going to have a party – aren't we?'

The hand pressed down harder and she gagged on the fine fibres that found their way down her airways but gasped for air between dry tears and a frantic nod of submission.

I'm going to die, her mind screamed as she lay too terrified to move, her entire body frozen to the core.

The hand that had rendered her voiceless was now at the hem of her dress pulling it upwards. It reached her underwear and started tearing at it. Georgina grasped at every ounce of courage she had and tried to knee the body in the groin, as she'd always thought she would do in a situation like this. Her efforts were futile, like a child smacking a naughty toy. Her legs were pulled apart and she could feel the body pulling at its own clothes as it readied itself for attack and, knowing that there was nothing now she could do, Georgina bit down on the pashmina and lay still. More than anything else right now, she wanted to live. She wanted to survive this. She focussed on the pocket of air that was reaching her lungs like a lifeboat drifting at sea. As the body pushed itself into her, she squeezed her eyes shut and pulled the rope of that lifeboat, willing it closer and closer. When he'd finished, she wanted to vomit but knew she'd choke if she let this happen, so swallowed it back, feeling poison spreading through her veins. She wanted to cut them open just to let it all out.

The body sat astride her, keeping her upper half pinned down. Her legs were numb and although the cold air hung around her nakedness, she couldn't move and wouldn't try to. It would be over soon, and she was alive.

Keep your eyes closed, don't try anything, don't look at him and if you can't identify him, then you'll live, she thought over and over again.

The body fumbled for something and after a millisecond of silence, she heard the sound of a camera clicking; he was taking pictures of her.

Horror and humiliation started to replace fear throughout her nerve endings. She clenched her back teeth, torn between surviving and doing something; she knew she should try to shrug off the pashmina and open her eyes, try to see what he was wearing, what he looked like. People would ask her; they'd ask if she'd resisted. But that would make it real, make him real. Right now, there was only darkness and pain, a numb pain that had no face, like waking up groggy from an operation. But she had to try, they would expect it; people would expect her to have tried. How could she explain herself if she didn't? They would judge her, not believe this. She had to try. Georgina scrunched her toes slightly to check that movement had returned to her legs: it had. Opening her eyes, she saw the balaclava and the red dot of the camera. She tried to pull her legs together as subtly as she could, ready to make a run for it the moment she got the chance. Her movements were deliberately slow, quiet and cautious in complete contrast to the violent pounding in her chest which seemed to want to announce her every intention to the world. Georgina steadied her heartbeat and took a breath in readiness. The hand pressing down on her thigh moved slightly and, seeing her chance, she kicked out. It was pathetic. There was no strength at all in her body; he laughed. Then slapped her.

'Fancy a dance now, do you?'

Georgina wriggled, trying so hard to get up, struggling to free herself. The body hardened and pushed her back onto the ground.

'We haven't finished.'

Georgina willed herself to die, anything to escape this. The philosopher at dinner had been very wrong; binary values were not obsolete – pure evil did exist.

# Chapter Two

Professor Maxie Reddick could hear the traffic moving on the road outside so she knew she was awake, but she simply couldn't bear to open her eyes yet and acknowledge that the morning had finally arrived. She'd got back late after editing and uploading this week's *Criminal Thoughts* podcast and Philip hadn't been in bed then. She'd tried calling and texting him but got no answer. She'd lain awake until the small hours waiting to hear his key in the lock. When it eventually happened, she listened as her husband stumbled up the staircase and fell into the spare room. At least he was safe. Maxie rolled over, burying her head into the pillow and pulling the duvet tight around herself. It was still early and although she'd only had around four hours of sleep, she could at least close and relax her eyes and that would help a little with the mountain of coursework she had to approve today. Although, she doubted she was going to get a stroke of it done.

Where had Philip been? Had Karl heard him come in? What would she tell him if he had? Maxie wasn't sure that she was doing much of a job hiding her husband's increasingly erratic behaviour from their son, but while Philip still passed-out in his own home, she could at least cover for him. Her eyes might still be closed but her mind was racing through all the scenarios that might play out today; playing the patient, understanding wife didn't come easily to her, but she thought she'd been doing a pretty good job of it since he'd been made redundant. That was over a year ago and she'd thought by now they might be back to something approaching normal. The door to the spare room clicked open, then heavy footsteps and then the front door. Where the hell was he going now? Wearily Maxie rolled herself up and grabbed the oversized dressing gown that lay draped at the end of the bed. It was his and pulling it on, she took a deep breath and inhaled happier times.

In contrast to her husband's noisy early morning flit, Maxie placed her feet carefully, avoiding the creaky step on the stairs so as not to wake her son. She tiptoed across the smooth wooden floor of the hallway, and into the kitchen where her bare feet twitched at the sudden coolness of the stone underfoot. She ran the tap slowly, quietly filled the kettle, and flicked it on gently. Silence for any length of time made her bubble with mild anxiety but she wouldn't risk music at this hour; instead she found a radio news channel to fill the space and turned the sound down low. She knew all these precautions were completely unnecessary as Karl slept like the eighteen-year-old boy he was, but keeping him safely in bed was also keeping whatever was happening in his parents' life away from him. Or so she hoped. Maxie filled the coffee pot with freshly ground soul reviving Costa Rican beans and waited for the boiling water to settle to the right temperature before adding it. She opened the fridge then cupboards and the bread bin looking for some carbohydrates to kick start the day. It certainly wasn't a morning that would get going with fruit and yoghurt. All that remained from her last shopping trip was the crust of a granary loaf; it would have to do. She squashed it into the toaster and as she did, the front door opened.

'I went out early for some croissants.' Philip held out a reconciliatory paper bag. The aroma and grease stains told her these pastries were fresh out of the oven. Not surprising really, as the deli would barely have been open.

Maxie gave him a small smile and took the bag. She was torn between relief that he seemed okay and anger that he'd simply breezed back in like that. Did he really think her that stupid? She was a Professor of Criminology, for God's sake. Her job was teaching people the power of simple observation, how to look at the evidence right in front of them. Here he stood, in last night's clothes, his shoes scuffed and dirty, his trousers creased, looking as if he'd slept in them, and his shirt buttoned up wrongly. He leaned over to kiss her good morning and his breath stank. Wherever he'd been, he'd staggered home and passed-out like this. Maxie turned her head but let him peck her cheek.

'Sorry, I got back late and didn't want to disturb you. Then I saw you were still dead to the world when I got up,' continued Philip, pouring himself a cup from the pot. Maxie knew he hadn't checked in on her at any point but said nothing; she simply put the pastries on a plate and moved to the table. Philip followed her and picked up a croissant.

'Don't you want to have a shower first?' said Maxie, looking him up and down. 'Maybe change out of last night's clothes while you're at it?'

Philip threw down the pastry and stormed out of the room, slamming the door. Maxie shredded one of the croissants in frustration. Philip didn't come back downstairs until after Karl had emerged. Maxie guessed he was looking for safety in numbers.

'So, I listened to the episode you uploaded last night.' Karl yawned.

'I hope it was more interesting than that.' Maxie said, laughing. 'I know we didn't finish it until late, but the intention isn't to send everyone to sleep.'

'No, it was cool. I wouldn't want to be on the opposite

side to you though. You know what she said, Dad? That burglars were more likely to be floored by hay fever than the police.'

As the local academic expert in crime, Maxie was often called for comments by the local media and it was a part of the job she really enjoyed. A local crime reporter – Craig Johnston had suggested they start a podcast together to talk about some of the issues in more depth and they'd been doing that now for a few months. She specialised in analysing the crime trends while Craig sourced special guests and interviewed her alongside them. It kept the format interesting, then after recording it each week, they uploaded it onto their own YouTube channel. The professor had free rein to say what she liked and during the episode that had gone out last night she'd presented the latest police rankings showing how few reported crimes actually ended in conviction. The figures were pretty appalling across the country, but their local force was particularly low in the league tables and Maxie had argued vociferously that she could probably do a better job of solving the crimes herself.

She'd been particularly proud of the sound bite Karl had mentioned: thirty-one per cent of burglars might get hay fever and only five per cent would get caught. It had come to her in the spur of the moment but she could see it being used to promote the show in the future if she worked it.

Philip looked at her with an expression of disgust or disdain, she couldn't tell which.

'Why do you wind them up like that? What happens if you get sacked for it? What will we do then? Never mind the fact that one day you might actually need the police's help.'

'Seriously? Have you forgotten that I actually did need them, and they were useless?'

'Honestly, woman, you need to get over that. It was a long time ago.'

Philip turned his back on her, and Maxie took a deep breath. If Karl hadn't been here, she would have taken her husband to pieces over that, but right now, she had to be peacekeeper. She took the remaining pastries and warmed them in the microwave before putting them on the table.

'The problem with these things is they don't really fill you up,' said Karl, wolfing them down. 'Have we got any bacon?'

Maxie shook her head. 'Sorry, mate. Why don't you two go out to a café? Get yourselves a builder's brunch or something.'

'Only round here would builders have brunch.' Philip laughed.

'Avocado on toast to get them ready for a day of demolition,' added Karl. 'Or chia seed porridge for a bit of bricklaying.'

'You could certainly lay bricks with the stuff, that's for sure,' replied her husband. 'Come on, mate, let's get ourselves to a proper caff and have a heart attack special.'

They gathered keys and wallets ready to go.

'Are you coming, Mum?' asked Karl.

'No, you two enjoy yourselves. I've got a ton of work to do so stay out as long as possible.' Maxie was relieved to have Philip out of the house so she wouldn't be tempted to start questioning him about where he'd been. She managed a smile as she watched her men leave the house, fantasising vocally about bacon, eggs, and fried bread.

Karl had inherited Maxie's dark hair and eyes but fortunately not her short stocky frame; he looked nothing like his red-headed father, which Philip always joked was a blessing. To anyone watching her boys right now everything seemed normal in their lives.

That morning, Maxie had a PhD dissertation entitled "Equality and the justice system" to review, but she simply couldn't focus on it. She thought about the show; Philip was wrong. It had been a good episode and perfectly justifiable. She'd been furious when she'd seen the latest crime stats and wasn't going to hide that. People had to wake up. She absent-mindedly switched on the small TV mounted onto the wall of the kitchen, looking for some early morning banter – wrong move. As she flicked from channel to channel, re-runs of cop shows had detective after detective solving case after case. Maxie had a love-hate relationship where the police were concerned, and these programmes just aggravated her more. Every cop was a maverick, every criminal dying to confess. It just didn't happen in real life. Even *CSI*, with its ridiculous technology that no police force on earth could afford, wouldn't get every case convicted and yet there they were, every episode, telling people that a speck of dust was all they needed. If that were the case, someone might have solved her sister's murder, but they hadn't.

'You're bloody liars, the lot of you,' she yelled at the actors.

Maxie scooped up a spoonful of jam and flicked it at the screen where it stuck, before slowly sliding onto the floor below. Philip would be thrilled about that.

Wiping the screen as carefully as she could, and the floor, Maxie gave herself a telling off and headed into the study, opening up the dissertation. The author of the paper had done a fabulous job of collating all the recent evidence on unconscious prejudice in the courtroom and would no doubt be writing a reference book on the subject in the near future. She managed to get through the synopsis before her mind started wandering again. Without the boys, the house was silent and she hated being alone, always had done; on her own, her anxieties and fears had space to roam and began hollering in her head. Her home was no longer a quiet space, it was a lonely space; it felt like a locked box that she held no key to. She didn't know how to handle Philip, how to get back the man she'd married. When he'd first lost his job, she'd suggested he needed and deserved a few weeks, even months to relax after the stress of the bank he'd worked for going under. However, there was a fine line to tread and the longer it took him to get back out there, the more it looked that he never would.

Philip had been the Director of Personnel, and therefore also the person who'd had to tell people they'd lost their jobs. He hadn't been at fault in any way, but she knew he'd taken it hard. He spent the first few weeks sleeping during the day and then he actually progressed to the sofa but not beyond daytime TV. She'd said nothing but in the second month was quietly relieved to see him buck up a little. He got showered and dressed, cleaned the house, and made dinners. He started to network and look for jobs. It had been a hopeful time and the whole family had enjoyed the flexibility of him being around but also the sense of purpose he now had. They'd had a good time together despite the circumstances. In month four he'd had some interviews, but then the rejections seemed to rain on him. Philip had nearly thirty years of experience but the sector was shrinking and he soon found that anyone with only fifteen years also had more up-to-date skills, and lower salary expectations. Maxie and Philip drank a lot in month five; having that early evening glass of wine to try to keep their spirits up seemed the right thing to do and it wasn't until month six that Maxie noticed, when she went to bed, Philip always stayed up and one by one, their bottles of craft gin soon moved from the cabinet to the recycling bin.

At the start of this year, Philip announced that with his level of experience and contacts, he was setting up a consultancy firm. Maxie had been delighted that he'd found a way out of the black mood and offered to put him in touch with the university personnel department, who she knew employed consultants. Far from being happy with the help, he'd told her to stop trying to control his life, that he was capable of doing this on his own. Maxie had been shocked but backed off and tried to focus on Karl and her job. Her own area of expertise was psychology and although it was the criminal mind she knew best, she understood enough about civilians to realise that she couldn't force Philip into anything and that it would be wrong for her to try. He needed to know she was there for him whenever he was ready. It just seemed that he'd never be ready and that the chasm between them was simply growing.

She knew that Karl had noticed the changes. How could he not? Philip said he was travelling around the country to build contacts for his new business, and although Maxie knew socialising would be part of that, it didn't seem right that her husband was always coming home, plastered. Shouldn't he be the one staying sober to seal the deal? Maxie knew she couldn't let this pass for much longer. Theirs had been a happy home once but as time marched on she was being beaten down by all this. She desperately wanted things back the way they were. They had to talk about this like adults. The time for what her American colleagues would call "an intervention" had come.

Maxie gave up all pretence of reviewing the dissertation and decided to research the correct way to hold an intervention while the house was empty, and she couldn't be caught. It relaxed her to read that careful planning was recommended. She wasn't the type of person who angered easily but she was confident and articulate, two qualities that were often mistaken as aggression whenever she found herself in an argument, and the two qualities Philip seemed to have lost recently. Maxie checked the calendar, looking for a date their son was likely to be away; there were a number of music festivals he had tickets for after the exams he'd been revising for finished but that wasn't for another month and Maxie wasn't sure she could wait that long. Maybe she should suggest that she and Philip go away for the weekend, have the discussion on neutral ground? She was working out how to persuade her husband to spend time with her when the phone rang. Picking it up, Maxie was surprised to see the name "Rachel" on the screen. While still mentally flicking through the Filofax in her head to try to remember who on earth Rachel was, she answered in as neutral a manner as possible.

'Hi,' said the voice quietly. 'I hope you don't mind me calling you on a Sunday – we met at that charity bash just before Christmas?'

That was it. Maxie's memory pinged to life as she remembered why she had this woman's number in her phone. Rachel was part of the university marketing department and the women had worked together on the annual fundraiser. They'd got together a couple of times afterwards for coffee, but since the crisis with Philip, Maxie hadn't spent much time socialising with anyone. She remembered Rachel as having a glow of positivity about her and was sure that if any of the many aura readers in Lonsdale ever got close to her, they'd say she was bathed in a bright orange glow. Maxie only knew about this colour of good-hearted souls from one of Karl's old girlfriends who'd told her that her own aura was predominantly blue; an extremely rare colour that signified intellect and intuition. It had been an odd way to butter her up, but much more original than flowers. Today Rachel didn't sound like the confident woman Maxie had met a few months ago.

'Rachel, hello – it's so good to hear from you.' Maxie wanted to reassure her, whatever the reason for her call. 'What can I do for you?'

Maxie could hear Rachel taking a deep breath before continuing. 'I need your help, but I really and truly need you to promise that you won't tell anyone else. I mean absolutely no one; not your son, your husband – no one.'

If Maxie could have explained the lack-of-speaking situation with her husband, she was sure Rachel would be relieved, but instead she simply promised her silence.

'I listen to your podcast,' whispered Rachel. 'It said you know the most up-to-date police procedures?'

'I have to know them,' Maxie replied steadily, not sure what was coming next. A million thoughts raced through her head: did Rachel want to confess that she'd committed a crime? Did she want an alibi, or help predicting how an investigation would go?

'We obviously teach them and serving officers visit us to lecture from time to time.'

'I thought so,' said Rachel, sounding relieved. She paused and the line went silent.

'Has something happened, Rachel?' prompted Maxie. 'Are you in trouble?'

Maxie heard a deep breath being taken so waited until Rachel was ready to speak again.

'It's not me,' she told her. 'Georgina – the lovely girl who lodges with me—' Rachel stopped as if steeling herself. 'Last night …' Her voice was now barely audible as if saying it out loud would invoke the crime. 'She was attacked … raped.'

'How can I help?'

'I didn't know what to do,' Rachel said. 'She's completely broken. She didn't want me to tell anyone at all, and she won't go to the police. Then I heard your show and you said you could do better than them, anyway. I thought, maybe …'

Maxie heard another deep exhalation of despair and then Rachel started crying. Maxie felt such a fraud. She'd mouthed off angrily from the safety of a recording studio but when it came down to it, when someone actually believed what she'd said, she was buckling. If she didn't help this woman, then she was no better than the people she criticised, in fact she'd be worse. She'd be a fake, a troll even. Her bluff had been called and she knew she had to grow a pair.

'I'll be right over. Stay strong.'

# Chapter Three

The Reddick family home lay on the outskirts of Lonsdale beside the park; leafy, green, hilly, and lined with modern detached houses, rather than the imposing Victorian terraces she'd find in Southsands, where most of the young people and students tended to live.

Maxie threw her briefcase onto the passenger seat and then paused, trying the think through what she'd do when she got to Rachel's flat. She pulled out her tablet and read through the notes of the Criminal Law module that covered sexual offences and their prosecution. If Georgina had been a student, then Maxie would have been obligated to report the incident under her duty of guardianship, but with the friend of a colleague, no matter how close the colleague, there was no such duty and she couldn't and wouldn't cajole the poor woman into doing anything else she didn't want to. She knew that rape cases were notoriously under-reported, although recent media coverage of the #MeToo cases had increased a victim's likelihood to speak out. However, this hadn't resulted in more convictions and in fact, things were getting worse. Universities had a responsibility to collate and publish up-to-date stats, and Maxie lamented the fact that, even now, less than seven per cent of reported cases ever resulted in conviction, while eighty per cent didn't even get as far as prosecution. One of the problems was the length of time it took to process a rape case. The longer it took for the victim to report the crime, the harder it was for the police to collect the evidence they needed and the less likely the CPS would be in thinking they had a prosecutable crime. Maxie knew she had to work with Rachel to encourage

Georgina to contact the police as trying to force her against her will was simply an extension of what had already happened.

'That'll be easier said than done though,' murmured Maxie to herself.

Maxie finished skimming her notes and started up the car; they hadn't told her anything new. Everyone who'd ever watched a crime drama knew what a rape kit contained and the importance of storing evidence effectively. She took the lesser-used back roads to the seafront and arrived more quickly than she really would have preferred. She almost felt like driving around the block once more.

The fracas with Philip was getting her down, but it wasn't just that – she was anxious and knew she had to be at her best right now. This wasn't an academic exercise, this was a young woman's life and she couldn't, and wouldn't, let her down.

At odds with the circumstances of the day, the bay was sunny and perfect. She inhaled the salty air and, tucking one of her dark curls behind her ear, took a few moments to compose herself. The building housing Rachel's flat had a fabulous view and Maxie was taken aback by the contrasts in this county as she always was when she ventured down here. Their family home gave them trees and parks that changed with the seasons as well as tiny garden birds that tweeted rather than screeched. Here, on the promenade, they had infinite sky and horizons to compensate for the menace of the enormous seagulls and their voracious appetites.

Maxie checked the address she'd been given. At one time the buildings would have been complete houses for the affluent merchants of the early twentieth century, but now they were divided into apartments. As she walked up to an enormous black front door, complete with authentic-looking heavy brass furniture, Maxie mused that its funereal solemnity seemed particularly appropriate. She looked up Rachel's name on the panel of buzzers for each flat and pressed. Rachel answered the intercom so quickly that Maxie imagined she'd been sitting by it, waiting for her to arrive. Maxie stomped her way up the stairs and by the time she'd reached the first floor where Rachel stood and beckoned her in, she'd beaten the nervousness she felt out of her system.

Rachel showed Maxie into the glorious front room where an enormous bay window made the most of the view. Maxie could see a young woman sitting on a curved window seat in the bay where the big sash window gaped open like a precarious escape route. Her face, in huge dark sunglasses, looked up to the sky, while her tiny body was wrapped up in a blanket as if preventing anyone or anything from getting close. Maxie whispered, 'Georgina?' and Rachel nodded. Maxie couldn't think of a good way to open the conversation they had to have, so simply walked up to the girl with her hand outstretched.

'Hello, Georgina. I'm Professor Reddick, call me Maxie,' she said waiting for the young woman to risk reaching out from her safety blanket. Instead Georgina wrapped herself even tighter and gave a slight nod of the head before continuing her gaze towards the sea.

Maxie sat down at the other end of the window seat and when Rachel asked if she'd like some tea, she nodded. Rachel left her with Georgina and the two of them sat in silence. Maxie knew she'd have to build trust before Georgina would be ready to talk to her, if indeed she ever would. Rachel clunked around in the background and Maxie suspected she was creating far more noise in the making of this tea than she normally would, just to break the silence. She needn't have worried. Silence was often important, and this was one of those times. Rachel brought the tea and then stood anxiously playing with her hands.

'You don't have any biscuits, do you?' asked Maxie.

'Yes, I do,' Rachel said, as if she'd passed a *Mastermind* question. 'I've got digestives in the cupboard.'

She turned on her heels, but before she could leave, Maxie took hold of her arm gently.

'They're the one biscuit I really don't like,' she said. 'Is there a shop you could pop to, maybe get something chocolatey?'

Rachel realised she was being sent out, smiled and her shoulders dropped with the relief of having someone to tell her how she could be useful. She gladly accepted the mission and left the women to their contemplation.

They continued to sit alongside each other facing forwards to the sea, each lost in their own thoughts. Maxie couldn't help but wonder who she'd tell if it had happened to her. On TV, the victim quite often broke down into hysterics, battered and bruised but still able to talk about it. That wasn't the reality for many women; research had shown that so many simply buried the crime, often ashamed and feeling complicit in some way. Maxie wasn't sure that she would be able to tell anyone. She knew Georgina didn't have a husband or partner but surely, they would be the most difficult to tell? Whenever they looked at you, they'd no longer see their partner but a victim. How did you get back into bed with someone after this had happened? Despite rationally believing in the justice system and the importance of bringing criminals to account for their actions, Maxie wasn't at all sure that she wouldn't internalise it all and pretend it had never happened. If it had been her own daughter, however, she'd have fought to find the guy and beat him to a pulp with her own hands.

Their contemplations were disturbed by yelling in the street below. They both peered over the windowsill to watch a couple trying to negotiate their car into the smallest space possible. One of them was standing on the pavement yelling instructions while the other attempted to follow them. If they could see themselves from this aerial viewpoint, they'd realise the car simply wasn't going to fit, but they persevered.

'Right – no, my right. Right hand down,' yelled the instructor.

'How many bloody rights are there?' came the reply from the car, as it attempted all of them.

'Okay … straight back now … towards me,' the instructor foolishly commanded. Maxie grimaced in readiness for what was clearly going to happen. Out of the corner of her eye she could see that Georgina was following the action too and had her mouth slightly open in disbelief. The driver did as he was told and reversed rather too quickly towards his friend. The women watching both had their hands over their faces waiting for the inevitable crunch of car against car. Astonishingly even the first crunch didn't stop the driver; he appeared to think he could somehow still get into the space and with another turn of the steering wheel tried once more, this time hitting the car on the other side whose alarm started blaring. The owners of both bumped cars must have been residents as they appeared in the street and the shouting started. Their peace shattered, Maxie signalled that they should probably get out of view and Georgina agreed. The last thing they heard as they closed the window was the instructor protesting, 'It weren't my fault. You don't know which way is right.'

The women both smiled at this and Maxie sat down on the sofa, hoping Georgina would join her now that the ice was broken slightly. Instead she stood, still tightly wrapped in the blanket, and spoke for the first time.

'I know you and Rachel mean well,' she said, 'but I just can't do this yet.'

Georgina walked out of the room and Maxie heard the door, of what she presumed was her bedroom, click shut.

Maxie noted the "yet" and her heart sunk a little. By the time Georgina gathered the courage to speak out, it might just be too late. As she paced the flat, the front door opened, and Rachel burst in overcompensating with her fake cheeriness.

'Chocolate cookies, Jaffa Cakes, and that classic favourite, the chocolate Hobnob,' she declared holding out the biscuit fest she'd bought. She looked around the room and not seeing Georgina raised her eyebrows in question.

'In her room,' Maxie whispered, and Rachel's shoulders dropped.

'I'm sorry. I thought she'd speak to you.'

'Don't worry, you did the right thing but if she's not ready to talk, we need to try to help in other ways.'

'What can I do?'

'Evidence deteriorates after three days so we need to gather what we have and make sure it's stored properly in a paper bag. And if we can persuade her to photograph any of her injuries, or take swabs right now, that would help.'

She watched as Rachel grimaced in reaction.

'I know it's horrific but if she decides to approach the police in the future, we need to be cognisant that this is what they'll need from us and the longer it takes her to go to them, the harder it will be for them to investigate. Was she wearing a dress?'

Rachel nodded.

'Yes, she'd just bought it – an original retro one from the vintage market. She stuffed it all in the bin, but I knew it would be needed so I pulled it out. It's in a bin liner though, not a paper bag.'

'Did the bin have anything in it when Georgina threw it away?'

Rachel nodded. 'It was full. I think I shook the clothes thoroughly to get rid of anything that shouldn't have been there. It was mainly eggshells which surely can't contaminate it.'

Maxie didn't like to tell her that it was the vintage market and the thorough shaking that was more the issue. It could have been handled and tried on so many times that any defence would have it dismissed as evidence, but she couldn't tell Rachel this now.

'Do you know whether she's showered since the attack? Is there any chance we might get samples from underneath her fingernails?'

'She'd scrubbed herself clean several times over before I got home.'

'She must have known she was destroying evidence by doing that. Everyone who's ever seen a cop show has seen fingernail evidence taken.' Maxie was trying not to let the frustration she felt show but from Rachel's expression, she was failing.

'I very much doubt that's what she was thinking about,' replied Rachel. 'I'd want to pour bleach over myself if it were me.'

'I'm sorry,' said Maxie. 'I'm just trying to think of things that will help convict this guy if we find him.'

'Do you think it's worth her reporting it?' asked Rachel. 'I mean, with no evidence left, is there any chance they'll find him? You said hardly anyone ever gets caught as it is.'

Maxie pulled herself upright and inhaled deeply. She was here to help, not to despair over the lack of adherence to process.

'I hate it when the odds are stacked against the victim and this is pretty much the only crime where that happens purely because people are afraid to come forward. You wouldn't not report a mugging, would you? There's the argument that unless we report this, he might do it again and that's valid. He could have a string of sexual offences to his name but if all his victims stay silent, he'll keep going and that feels wrong. It's horrific that a young woman can't report a crime because the process scares her. I'm guessing Georgina hasn't told her parents?'

Rachel shook her head.

'Does she have a boyfriend?'

'They're all quite religious,' replied Rachel. 'He's over in Africa somewhere building a nursery. There's no way she'll tell any of them about this.'

Maxie shook her head and sighed. 'The police won't investigate a rape without a first person report so we can't report it for her but equally we can't know this has happened and do nothing. Let me see if I can have a confidential word with a guy I know – Andrew Dawson. He used to be the university police liaison but he's a DS back in the force now. Andrew can advise how far we can progress things without distressing that poor woman any further. Who knows, they may have someone of interest on other assault charges. And even if Georgina doesn't think she can identify him, there are always hundreds of pictures taken at weddings and he might be in one of them.'

Rachel shrugged. 'Bit of a long shot.'

'I know but I just can't let this bastard get away with it.'

# Chapter Four

Maxie squinted as she stepped back onto the street, the sunshine blindingly brilliant after the gloomy atmosphere of the flat. She had the personal number of the university's old liaison officer in her contacts so walked along the promenade until she found an empty park bench and sat down to make the call. Andrew Dawson answered the phone cheerily.

'Long time, no hear,' he said. 'To what do I owe this honour?'

As Maxie told him broadly what had happened without mentioning names, his tone became more muted. He promised to make some enquiries and get back to her by the close of play, but she knew realistically it would take some miracle for him to find anything related. Yet another thing that didn't happen in real life – the crime wall of victims who all looked like Georgina and a connection between them all.

There was nothing more she could do here, and the only other place where evidence might exist was the scene of the crime. Maxie checked her watch. Philip and Karl would probably presume she'd gone into the university if they came back to find the house empty, so she had time to head up to Stanmer Hall.

Despite its proximity to the university, Maxie hadn't been to this country house for eighteen months or so. She thought about when the last occasion would have been and remembered a winter wedding. These grounds were beautiful at any time of year, and although most brides picked May, with its backdrop of cherry blossom for their photographs, Maxie remembered the dusting of frost and the blackness of the afternoon made magical by clear skies and fairy lights as something rather special. Of course, in December it could all have gone horribly wrong and rained all day but, on that occasion the bride was blessed.

Her tiny car crunched along the long gravel drive and as she pulled up outside the main entrance, Maxie contemplated why this always felt so luxurious – a road of rough stones. Yet it did and more than once in their *what would we do if we won the lottery* family conversations, she and Philip had said they'd have a gravel drive and huge 4x4s to scrunch along in. Well, the 4x4 was going to be hers; she'd always wanted one but simply couldn't justify one on the perfectly tarmacked roads of Lonsdale. Philip was going for a sports car. Maxie sighed, wondering when and how they would ever get back to arguing about things as trivial as which luxury car they'd each have. Those days seemed so far away now.

She walked into the hallway expecting it to be quiet, instead it was buzzing. Worker-bee waiters whizzed past her with cake stands and glasses of prosecco to queen bees waiting in the lounge for their afternoon sugar load.

'Can I help you?' called a voice from the reception desk. Her weary manner suggested the last thing she wanted to do was help.

'I didn't think the place would be so busy,' replied Maxie. 'You look run off your feet.'

'It's always the same when there's an afternoon tea offer on – we get swamped.' Her tone had softened. 'Is there anything I can help you with?'

Maxie explained that she'd been at the wedding last night and had lost a necklace. She wondered if it had been handed in. She watched as the receptionist checked a lost property log and a safe containing a random selection of trinkets; she pulled out a couple of necklaces for Maxie to look at but when Maxie shook her head, she promised to get in touch if anything else showed up.

'Could I look around myself?' asked Maxie. 'I don't want to put you to any more trouble.'

'You can, but I doubt the cleaners missed anything.'

'I'm sure they haven't.' Maxie smiled. 'Now which room was the wedding in again?'

The receptionist looked slightly puzzled by her question but pointed out the ballroom where afternoon tea was taking place.

'Wow, no wonder I didn't recognise it,' said Maxie covering her tracks. 'It's been transformed.'

'We go in as soon as people leave,' explained the receptionist. 'There are breakfasts, lunches, and this lot to serve today.'

Maxie knew she wasn't going to find anything in this freshly scrubbed interior, and that the wedding photographs would tell more of a tale; she thanked the receptionist and said she'd look around the grounds too. Rachel had told her the little she knew. The attack had happened outside by the lake while everyone else was dancing. Maxie walked back towards the front door and stood looking down across the grounds. There was an obvious route from here and she couldn't imagine any woman in their best shoes and wedding finery deciding to go off-piste just for the sake of it. She started walking, scanning the ground as she went. The promised overnight storm had washed the grass even greener, so it was beautiful to look at but yet another nail in the evidence coffin. There would be no proof of the attack to be found and although she hated the miraculous finds they made in TV shows – the alumni cufflink or discarded tissue – she was clutching at straws now but still looked. What would they prove anyway? That some of the guests of this hotel had come for a walk? The CPS would hardly be likely to jump on anything like that as a reason to proceed.

She knew that some investigators might argue that any remnants showed opportunity – the second of that holy trinity: means, opportunity and motive. Maxie had long believed and argued in her lectures that the holiest of these was motive. So many people had the chance to injure another and these days, absolutely any weapon could be bought online, yet the majority of the population chose to live peacefully. No, the difference was motive; what went on in the minds of those who took that step, those who made the decision to harm another human being. People took care to cover-up the "how" but were rarely able to disguise why they'd acted as they had. It was part of their nature.

Maxie reached the lake without finding anything helpful. She strolled along the grassy banks, wondering whether she'd find a flattened telltale patch but of course there wasn't anything like that after the wind and rain they'd had. There was an extremely romantic looking spot just ahead of her where a hawthorn tree, heavy with blossom, had scattered delicate white blooms over the grass like confetti. Even soaked into the grass, the glorious delicacy of nature seemed to tempt her towards the flowers and Maxie could imagine their beauty luring Georgina to sit down right here. Sirens in bud form calling her to her fate. Maxie shook the notion out of her head, studied the area and took a few pictures but knew she shouldn't trample through it just in case Georgina did allow them to call the police for her. She had seen the pain of the young woman and had completely empathised with her desire to say nothing, to try to pretend this had never happened. But it had happened and if no one did anything at all, then someone who had felt a compulsion to viciously attack a defenceless person, on what should have been a wonderfully happy evening, was still out there. Maxie simply wouldn't accept that. She flicked on her voice recorder and began.

'Okay,' she said aloud. 'So did you see a woman on her own, walking down here or were you here already and Georgina just fell in your lap?'

'Was it her you were interested in or was she just a random victim? And what made you decide to attack her at all? Did something happen at the wedding to make you angry? Did you have an argument with your partner? Were they dancing with someone else? Or were you the only one without a partner? Are you always the one without a partner at these bashes? Did you try it on with Georgina because she looked as if she was in the same situation as you? Did she reject you?'

Maxie stopped to play back the recording and check everything was clear. She'd transcribe this later and methodically try to answer every question. Her words sounded out perfectly, so she continued. 'I've assumed you were a guest at the wedding but maybe you weren't. Maybe you were expecting an invitation, but it never came. Did you even know either the bride or groom? Do you crash weddings? There's guaranteed to be one here most Saturdays in May, perhaps you just come along in your finery and wait until everyone is too drunk to realise you don't belong? The problem for you was that Georgina wasn't drunk.'

She looked back up at the Georgian manor house that had hosted the wedding.

'Or is it something about this place? Does it hold some bad memory for you?'

Maxie put the phone back in her pocket. She could go on listing questions for hours and would probably

*31*

be thinking of more and more throughout the day but questions were frustrating and she wanted to start getting some answers. She needed to speak to someone close to the wedding. The bride and groom had left via Gatwick airport first thing this morning, so she couldn't speak to them for another fortnight, but she could go and charm the people who worked here in the hope they'd answer a few more questions. She climbed the bank back to the entrance hall and approached the front desk, smiling at the receptionist.

'No luck, I'm afraid,' she said. 'So, I must have lost it somewhere else. But I was wondering, do you have CCTV around the building or the grounds?'

The receptionist looked puzzled and ventured, 'Just around the cellars, the front door, and the customer car park obviously, but I doubt it would spot a necklace.'

'Oh no, I've given up on that.' Maxie was smiling so much her cheeks ached. 'But this is a beautiful place so I'm thinking of organising a party but there'd be a lot of high-profile guests and I just want to be sure about the security.'

The receptionist looked mildly offended.

'We never have any problems at all here – we have a five-star rating on Tripadvisor.'

'Sorry, sorry,' said Maxie trying to recover the situation. 'That's not what I was implying at all and that five-star rating is completely justified. It's just that the paparazzi sometimes stalk the guests I'm talking about.'

The receptionist seemed placated. 'Why don't I book you some time with our events manager? He could help you with your function and reassure you about our security measures. He could fit you in on Wednesday?'

Maxie sighed but knew there was nothing more she could find out today and the events manager was the person she needed to answer the rest of her questions. She set up the meeting and once again thanked the receptionist for her help. Outside, she finally let the smile drop and massaged her cheeks. It was hard work being charming when all you wanted to do was cry.

Maxie checked her watch as she headed back to the car. It was only six o'clock, but it felt like she'd been up for a century and she still had to face the aftermath of the morning's events with Philip.

# Chapter Five

As she opened the front door, Maxie was surprised to hear raucous laughter coming from the living room and she felt her shoulders drop a little. The boys were evidently having a good time together.

'You have got to see this.' Karl grabbed her and sat her down on the sofa next to him. In the middle of the floor was a pile of clothes that Philip was "modelling" for him. 'Dad's got all these horrendous clothes from the old days.'

'I'd hardly call the nineties the *old days*,' replied Philip. 'Anyway, these were classics at the time.'

Maxie remembered the outfit her husband was wearing now, and was sure it had first appeared on one of their early dates even though it was hideously out of date, even by then. His lack of vanity and his quiet maturity had endeared him to her. He was six years older than she was and told her he just wanted a family and quiet home life. After the death of her sister, that was exactly what she needed too and so they found solace in each other. The fond memories of those first dates brightened the day she'd had, and she couldn't help but laugh along with them.

'Why on earth did you keep this stuff?' she asked. 'And where? I can't remember seeing it in the wardrobe.'

'They were in this old suitcase in the loft. He's got all these hilarious photos too.' Karl delighted in grabbing a bundle and bouncing down on the sofa next to her. 'Have you seen his hair?'

'Oh, my God.' She laughed looking at the highlighted titian locks of her husband, over a quarter of a century ago. 'I didn't know you had these. This has to have been before my time.'

Philip joined them on the sofa and took the picture from her. 'It was. I was just out of uni and quite the stud.'

'Gross,' said Karl pretending to stick two fingers down his throat. Maxie joined him pretending to vomit over the back of the sofa.

'Cheeky blinders,' said Philip, getting up and putting all the photos back in the suitcase. 'I'll have you know I was quite a catch back then.'

'I was the lucky one,' Maxie laughingly told Karl.

'You certainly were,' added Philip.

He grabbed at the clothes and stuffed them into his secret trove before closing the lid firmly. He sat on the case then picked up a sweatband he'd missed. He fiddled with it and looked contemplative.

'Penny for them?' asked Maxie.

'Just wondering where the hell all those years went.'

Maxie nodded and then jokingly shoved Karl.

'Most of them went on this ungrateful fashion critic.'

She pulled Karl towards her and forced him into a cuddle, even managing to kiss the top of his head before he could release himself from her grasp.

'So, what was all this in aid of anyway?' she asked. 'You're not taking an ancient history course as far as I can remember.'

Philip threw the sweatband at her and she caught it triumphantly.

'We went to get Dad some new gear, so he was showing me what he used to wear. The new stuff is pretty good but if I'd known about his real fashion sense before then, I'd have taken him to a charity shop or something.'

'New gear?' asked Maxie.

'For his big meetings next week,' Karl said and then seeing his dad raise his palms in caution, ran an imaginary zip across his mouth.

Maxie turned to face Philip, inviting him to explain

further, but he'd got up from the suitcase and at her glance, walked towards the window with his back to her. After a moment he turned and said, 'I've been having conversations with a company who're just starting out in the UK. It's a step on from the consultancy idea – a new model that's working superbly in the US where corporations are downsizing just like they are here. The plan is for me to reach out and establish a network of people like myself who are experts in their field. People who are good at their jobs but don't have the bandwidth to chase business. We operate under an umbrella brand which mediates fruitful business relationships by nailing the contracts. This company says if I get on board from the get-go, I could make a killing.'

Maxie found herself flinching at every word of jargon that peppered his sentence; it wasn't the way he normally spoke. Equally, she hadn't understood a word of what Philip had just said. Nevertheless, she resisted the urge to ask the million questions filling her brain and let him speak.

'I'm heading down to London this coming week to catch up with some of my old buddies to see if they'd like to be part of the programme,' he continued. 'I'll be gone for a few days and obviously wanted to look the part, so I bought a few new things. It's a fresh start.'

Maxie knew the one thing her husband hated doing was selling himself so if this company was doing the selling and he was just using his skills to find professionals who could do the work, then it might work. The word "network" niggled her and all the case studies she'd read about pyramid schemes and white-collar fraud came rushing to mind. Sometimes she wished she didn't see crime everywhere she looked.

'How is this business model different from being a recruitment agent? Do you charge for this work or take a percentage?' She couldn't stop herself and at any other time, her questions would have come across as genuine interest but even as she spoke, she knew they simply sounded suspicious. Philip flinched.

'Would you like to check my business plan?' he asked. 'Make sure I'm not doing anything stupid?'

'Woah, guys,' Karl interrupted as his mum sat back shocked. 'We're celebrating tonight. I've finally managed to update Dad's wardrobe and conned him out of a pair of trainers in the process, he's going to be a huge success and, Mum – what are we celebrating for you?'

That my husband seems to be drifting away from me, and I don't know how to stop it? That I've just met a young woman traumatised by rape on a gloriously sunny day?

Maxie shook those thoughts away and said, 'That I'm lucky enough to share a house with the two most gorgeous men in Lonsdale, nay, all of Lancashire, in fact.'

'We should definitely drink to that.' Karl leapt up and pulled out a bottle of wine from the fridge. He took two glasses from the dishwasher and poured for his parents, emptying the remains of the bottle. He handed them round and then grabbed a bottle of lager for himself and raised it in a toast.

'To us.' They clinked and took sips, Maxie very aware that Philip's wine glass had barely touched hers. She turned her attention to Karl who was trying his best to keep the mood light. They'd been laughing when she walked in, was it her fault that this was happening? What had she done to spoil things? It shouldn't be her eighteen-year-old son trying to fix this.

'Okay then,' she declared pulling herself up and heading out into the kitchen. When she came back, she had a fan of takeaway leaflets in her hand. 'If it's a celebration, then it calls for a banquet. Who fancies Thai?'

'I'd rather have something like enchiladas,' replied Philip grumpily.

'Fusion!' cried out Karl, still in peacekeeper mode. 'We'll have Mexi-Thai cuisine with Italian wine and American beer. We are truly citizens of the world.'

Maxie smiled at him, entirely grateful for his efforts. Together they read through the menus and ordered the largest selection of food imaginable. The unspoken text to their selection was that the evening had to find opportunity for laughter, and if that meant pairing guacamole with sticky rice – which turned out to be as disgusting as it sounded – then that's what they'd do.

They managed to polish off most of the unusual mezze and they all worked to keep the conversation light. When Karl eventually called time and said he was going to bed, Maxie knew there was no point in staying up with her husband, so said she needed to get her beauty sleep too. If he'd forgiven her for questioning his plans, Philip might have jokingly told her she didn't need beauty sleep, but of course he didn't.

In her room, she realised that she had, at some point, stopped thinking of it as their room. She propped herself up against the headboard and plugged her phone into the charger noting that Andrew hadn't called back. She checked the time; it was gone eleven but not technically tomorrow so she felt justified in making the call – it was close of play and he hadn't made good on his promise. Maxie listened to the phone ringing and expected to hear an answerphone message kick in but eventually Andrew answered, 'Hello?' with a yawn in his voice.

'Just wondering what the station said?' Maxie asked hearing a sigh on the other end.

'Oh, Professor. I'm sorry I didn't call you back. I thought it might be too late now.'

'Not really. I don't think I'll sleep tonight, anyway.'

'There isn't much to say,' Andrew said. 'There haven't been any other reports from that event but I can ask a female officer to visit the woman to see if she'll talk. But you know as well as I do that unless the complainant comes forward herself, there's nothing we can do.'

Maxie knew everything he was saying was true, but it wasn't what she wanted to hear so she had to bite back her frustration.

'I know and I'm trying to get her to speak to you but right now she might hate me for telling you. I need something to go on. Is there absolutely nothing? Have there been any other assaults like this? Anything at all that bears some similarity?'

'But there are no details to go on? There's no description and only the fact that it happened at a wedding to compare,' Andrew replied in the practised soft voice he probably used when meeting bereaved families.

Maxie had nothing new to tell him so sighed and rubbed her eyes tiredly. 'I'm sorry. I'll keep going. I'll try to get a description of the attacker and try to get her to come in to report it. I suppose I should also let you know that I'm asking questions at Stanmer.'

'You haven't changed, have you?' said Andrew and Maxie could hear a smile in his voice. 'Always determined to get to the bottom of things.'

'Before it was just research, now it really matters.'

Maxie's phone started buzzing with a call-waiting from Rachel, so she thanked Andrew and switched call. 'There's no joy from the police I'm afraid,' Maxie told her immediately on answering. 'But, don't worry, I'm not giving up.'

'I know you won't,' said the quiet voice on the other end. 'I just needed to hear that.'

# Chapter Six

Once again, he scoured all the days' papers and news websites, as well as the social media feeds that Georgina's friends belonged to, for any mention of his performance. There was none and there'd been nothing all weekend. On the one hand this was good news. He wasn't going to get caught before he'd finished what he'd started but on the other, his first act hadn't been recognised whatsoever. She hadn't told anyone, which meant she knew it was her fault. Even if she had, he knew the police wouldn't come knocking on his door. He'd planned everything meticulously and anyway, they'd be the last to work it out knowing their level of intelligence. They weren't much cop. He smirked at his own joke. His brother would have liked that one.

In fact, there wasn't much talk about Georgina among her so-called friends. She was barely in any of the pictures from the wedding and no one tagged her – that's how unpopular she was. It probably wasn't just him she'd offended. Her sort were all the same, like to appear all quiet and pious and that's how they catch you out, that's how they get you. You trust them and just when you're at your most vulnerable they trample all over your heart. Well this time he was doing the trampling. He felt a sour taste in his mouth at the thought of women like that. It had to be her. It wasn't his fault it had to be like that. She could have behaved differently when it mattered but she didn't. Serves her right. Maybe next time she'll think about who she hurts and the consequences of her actions a bit more. Maybe they all will.

He switched off his PC, certain he was in the clear and

picked up his camera. The footage he'd taken wasn't just a souvenir but the grand finale. He smiled to himself, pleased about this detail; not only could he share this with his brother again and again, but he still held the power to hurt that stupid bitch, to humiliate her. He just had to pick the right moment. Then the whole world would see what she was really like and the media would certainly pay attention. It would be the end of her. These pictures would be her legacy ... This is what she'd be remembered for now.

She and her ilk always thought they were holier than thou; something special, that they could screw up anyone else's life if it suited them because they were untouchable. Well, he'd soon teach them they were very wrong on that point. They were nothing special, nothing at all and as the photos showed, they were certainly not untouchable.

The memory of what started all this started to rile him. He was twitchy and now he'd sorted the first, he had to get on to the next one. He had to finish the job. He pulled up a file labelled Target2 and googled some up-to-date photographs. There it was, that smug satisfied smile borne from a life where everything must have come easily. Still, thanks to the photo he knew immediately how he'd deal with this one. It cheered him enormously to have his next plan in the incubation stage. With an overall objective in mind, he could now start planning the practical stuff, working out the tools he'd need, and the best location for the job.

'You'd be proud of me if you could see me now,' he said to the grainy photograph on the wall. 'Preparing for battle – selecting the target, choosing the weapon, deciding where and when to execute the course of action, then successfully completing the mission.'

He was particularly proud that he'd come up with

ideas which excited him almost as much as they'd hurt his offenders. Those who'd trespassed against him, one might say. On second thoughts, he'd better keep any references to religion out of his head. Only crazies quoted the Bible, and he was the sanest and most rational person he knew.

# Chapter Seven

A twinge of guilt washed over her as the smelly detritus of last night's banquet, and an unhealthily large bin of empty bottles, left on the early morning recycling truck. Maxie got into her car and pulled away quickly to start the drive to the university. She imagined the neighbours noting the increase in glass recycling they seemed to be doing. The Reddicks would certainly beat any of them at it now, if it were ever an Olympic event. It made her feel slightly ashamed of her shabby maternal skills. Surely, she should be promoting healthy eating and drinking less but as the song went "whatever gets you through the night". Anyway, by the time she got back tonight, the wonderful cleaner who'd been with them since Maxie had been promoted, would have performed her weekly magic so effectively, the slate would have well and truly been wiped clean.

This was the start of a brand-new week and after the recent surreal series of events, one that felt very different.

She looked at herself in the car mirror and noted small dark circles caused by spending the entire night searching news feeds. When Philip had come up to bed, she'd told him she had to keep working and after failing to persuade her to get some sleep, he skulked off into the spare room. Maxie had been relieved. If Andrew couldn't find a connection maybe she could so she'd spent the dark hours in the despicable world of rape and assaults. It hadn't made pleasant reading and although she now knew the names of so many other people who'd been hurt, she'd found nothing that might link to Georgina. No reports of rapes at weddings or parties at country houses. Thirty-six hours had already passed since the attack, so she needed to find a way of helping her talk about it if they wanted the police to look into the case.

The week ahead loomed large; Philip was going to London, Karl was starting his A levels, and she had to find time to focus on Georgina while teaching the last few classes of the term. It wasn't impossible and if she kept focussed, she could find time for everyone.

Maxie told herself all these upbeat clichés as she listened to the news and weather on the radio; it was going to be another glorious day and maybe that was a good omen. If the sun would just shine on everyone she loved and cared for, then that had to mean something didn't it? She'd see something she hadn't, Andrew would find a connection, and Karl would sail through his first exam. Even Philip might get the break he needed, and things would go back to normal. Although she was no longer sure what exactly that was.

'Please let this business idea, whatever it is, work for him. If you do, I promise I will never ...' she called out to whoever might be listening and then paused, wondering what she could sacrifice in return. Even for such a worthwhile trade she knew there was no chance of her giving up any of the usual vices.

'I'll never ... ask for anything else,' she decided on and then regretted it, thinking she was probably going to need something for Karl or Georgina in the near future so added, 'For myself, anyway.'

Full of purpose when she reached her office in the university, she called Rachel before her first lecture just to check in, and to reassure both women that she was still doing everything she could.

'How's Georgina? And you, how are you holding up?' she asked.

The reply of "we're okay" and little else was what she'd been expecting. Rachel told her that Georgina had stayed in her room after she'd left and then paced the floor during the night. Neither of them had slept much or was going into work today.

'I'm not surprised. I don't know how you'd ever start recovering from something like this but I'm afraid the clock is ticking and Georgina needs to report this soon if any of us want to be sure it doesn't happen to someone else. We have to help her talk about what happened, for her sake as much as anything.'

'What can I do?' asked Rachel.

'Could you see whether she'll talk to someone on the rape crisis lines? And gather all the photos you can from the wedding in case she's prepared to look at them. Tell your friends that your camera broke. On second thoughts, say your handbag was stolen.'

'Why?'

'We need a dump of every single picture taken so we can see if there's anyone in the background – and you looking for a thief is a great cover. If we don't beg for everything, all you'll get are the edited pictures where your friends look great. Who knows, they may even tell you they saw someone acting suspicious.'

Rachel agreed to give it a go and the women said their goodbyes.

Maxie had a full lecture theatre of final year students to face now and she decided to use their collective knowledge to help her think through Georgina's case. They weren't used to seeing her as anything other than the loud, lively, and controversial professor that she'd always been so she couldn't let the maelstrom in her head weigh her down. She needed to get back into character before walking in to face them.

It was time to practice what she preached. One of the techniques she'd developed to help students understand the motives and psychology of either victims or criminals was to act out the expression, *walk a mile in their shoes*. Maxie believed that if you really put yourself in another's place, you were able to step outside your own prejudices and see the world from their perspective, however uncomfortable or unpleasant that might be. It was a technique used by actors too; she'd often heard interviews where the actor said that, as soon as they put on their character's shoes, they became them. The students loved it, standing in the lecture theatre with eyes closed, she'd get them to imagine how it felt to be wronged so badly you wanted to take revenge, or to feel so angry that you needed to take a life. The students always came up with more creative work after one of these sessions. The technique helped them to think for themselves rather than simply learning from screens. Right now, Maxie needed to employ the method herself; she needed to switch off her personal life and become Professor Maxine Reddick, the beloved and indomitable force behind the success of this university's renowned criminology faculty.

She went into her office and opened the cupboard where she kept a spare outfit in case she was called upon for a last minute engagement, like attending a press conference or making up the numbers at an early evening drinks reception. Both happened often enough to warrant a smart black dress and expensive heels being permanently at the ready. Changing into the dress, she then pulled out the heels and stepped into them. Instantly she was taller, both emotionally and physically, powerful and ready to kick ass. Of course, she couldn't walk more than a few yards in them but they'd never been bought for walking in, and this morning she simply planned to put these beautifully shod feet up on the desk and get her students to do some thinking. After all, she mused, haven't I just spent three years preparing them all for a moment like this?

By the time Maxie swept into the lecture hall, she'd also applied a deep red lipstick and looked ready for business. The hall was shaped like an amphitheatre with rows of benches in several tiers. At the bottom, in the round, was a desk. Maxie's stage. The room went quiet as she took her place. Those students who'd been poised with laptops open ready to take notes, started to close them as one by one, they realised this was going to be no ordinary lecture. Excitement and anticipation began to bubble. Someone accidentally knocked their water bottle onto the floor causing many to jump but the subsequent nervous laughter eased the tension. Maxie interlinked her fingers and leant forward on the desk; she looked around the room, trying to make eye contact with each student. Some smiled, others looked away nervously.

'So, you're third years now,' she said, 'but have you actually learnt anything, or have you ignored everything I've ever said? When you go out into the world in a few months, will you be of use to anyone?'

There was a ripple of nervous laughter.

'Let's see, shall we?' Maxie continued. 'A woman has been raped at a party. She's your best friend, there are no witnesses, she doesn't know the perpetrator, and she's too scared to come forward. What are we going to do about that? Four teams – left back, left front, right back, right front.' She divided the room with hand gestures to indicate the teams.

'Team One, why won't she come forward? What do we know about victim psychology? And how are we going to use what we know to persuade her to report this? Or perhaps you'll decide that we shouldn't persuade her – your choice.' Those at the back of the hall on the left-hand side scribbled furiously. 'Team Two, we as her friends are first on the scene. What should we be advising? What procedures will we recommend to her? And what evidence is most useful and what if we don't have it? Team Three, profiling – it's one offence so we don't have much to go on but who might we be looking for? Team Four, you're the CPS – you're going to tell us if we have enough to prosecute, but also get ready with what you'll need. What are the statistics around rape? Why do prosecutions fail so often?

'You've got forty minutes and then I want you all back here, presenting your best knowledge and instinct. I am the victim and you can ask me questions, but I won't tell you much. Now get going.'

The students gathered into their teams and huddled together, some within the lecture theatre and others to rooms outside. Maxie pulled another chair over and put her feet up – she needed this time to think too. Now and then a student would come up and ask a question, but she gave them as little as she had, to work on. One student even encountered her bursting into tears at the ferocity of his questioning. He retreated to his teammates soon after that. It was one thing learning about the impact of crime on victims, but it was quite another when faced with the full force of it, as Maxie had seen since getting Rachel's call.

The forty-minute alarm sounded on Maxie's phone and she looked up to see the rows of students buzzing and ready to speak.

'Team One,' Maxie called, stepping away from her desk and joining the other students on the front row to allow the team to take centre stage.

Team One outlined the many reasons rape victims don't come forward; the shame they feel, as if somehow they'd invited the attack, the fear they won't be believed, and the dread of any court case, where they're sure their lives will be pulled apart and shown to the world by the rapist's defendant.

'Even the helplines use language that isn't helpful – crisis. Who'd go to a crisis centre for help? It's like a downward spiral,' said the speaker from Team One. 'Once the victim has it in their head that it will be a hideous journey, they start building in more and more reasons to stay silent. They won't want to ruin their friend's party by forever associating it with an attack.'

This got a murmur of despair, but Maxie knew it was perfectly true.

'If this was an important party, like an engagement or a twenty-first,' persisted Team One, 'then the victim doesn't want people reminded of the attack every time they reminisce, or see photographs from the event. Five years' time, she's sitting in a bar and she gets a Facebook reminder, or someone says, "Do you remember so and so's birthday?" or "That was such a brilliant gig", and then they stop in their tracks and go all awkward because they remember that it was the day she was raped. It would never go away unless you left all your friends behind.'

'So, are you recommending she doesn't report it?' asked Maxie.

'Not at all. Even if some of us would never report it in real life we decided as a group that for this exercise, we'd try to persuade her.'

Another speaker took over with their solution. 'We have to turn a downward spiral around. We have to change the language and persuade our friend that she's not a victim, but she's part of the team who will track this bastard down. She's a warrior. We know that some people are terrified about telling their parents or boyfriends but saying "I want to stop this swine" sounds far more positive than admitting to being attacked. We're not going to mollycoddle our friend, instead we're going to tell her that he picked on the wrong person this time because *she will* get him convicted.'

The team were high on their positive psychology solution and got a round of applause from the other students. Maxie nodded her approval and although she wondered how long it would take Georgina, or any other victim, to move from scared witless to superhero, the language used to describe crime was extremely powerful and there was something in this.

Team Two were playing the role of a friend, the first person the victim had confided in. They were more sedate in their presentation as they reminded everyone that CSI teams regard the victim as one of the crime scenes because of the evidence on their bodies and then went on to outline the well-known police procedures and what the victim should be prepared for.

'But she won't go to the police,' Maxie interrupted. 'What are you going to do to help?'

They promised that they were coming to that and then did so stating that they'd ask their friend to bag her clothing, ask her to comb through her hair, including her pubic hair, and bag that. There was a snort from the audience and Maxie wondered how she'd feel if one of her friends asked her to do that. The team mentioned getting hold of every photograph they could from the party and a guest list if there was one. They talked about subtly interviewing as many guests as possible to see if anyone remembered the victim talking to someone or seeing her heading for the scene of the crime. They finished by saying they'd try to visit the crime scene but doubted anyone would tell them anything.

'Without the access and authority the police have,' they concluded, 'this will be tough to prove, but perhaps if we can narrow things down it will help them if our friend eventually reports it. Also, if we find out who did it, but there isn't enough evidence, we can name and shame him even if she doesn't.'

Maxie raised her eyebrows; so far she had a roomful of senior criminology students ready to take the law into their own hands but it had been her first instinct too. Perhaps that was the inevitable result of all the cutbacks and scrutiny the criminal justice system had faced in recent years, but it was also down to the anonymity of digital connectivity. Anyone could say anything about anyone. She'd pick a jury of her peers over trial by social media any day. Maxie signalled the next group to begin and the speaker for Team Three leapt up to centre stage with cocksure confidence.

'And we can help you do that,' he began in response to the previous team's closing comments. 'Now, as the good professor said, we've been getting into the minds of criminals for three years now so we probably all know what we're looking for here. We only have one crime so we can't catalogue the dates and times of various assaults, or the type of victim he goes for in order to build a profile, so we have to rely on typical profiles.

'It is said that rape doesn't have a sexual motive but is instead a means of dominating the victim, showing power and strength. It's sometimes borne out of difficulty in forming relationships and that's why we've often read about the socially awkward perpetrator. However, there are other options: the sadist – the person who enjoys the act and then enjoys the fact that the victim will continue to suffer after the act; then there's the narcissist. This guy doesn't think he's the problem. The victim was coming on to him or was asking for it in some way. To him, there hasn't even been a crime.'

Maxie thought for a second that her student had put himself in the criminal's shoes rather too well with that last sentence. He seemed to be enjoying himself and that riled her. He wasn't taking this seriously.

'So, we're looking for a loner, a sadist, or a narcissist?' she snapped. 'That doesn't really narrow things down for us. In real life we don't exactly wear our profile in big letters on a T-shirt, you know.'

The speaker held a palm up to say "wait for it" and then continued when the laughter from his audience had subsided. Maxie swallowed and calmed herself.

'This guy has gone voluntarily to a party, so he's not that awkward. We believe he probably tried to chat a few people up and they turned him down. This continued rejection turned to anger, and he wouldn't have been prepared to leave the party without scoring. After all, he's made an effort. Maybe our victim was being polite and he thought he had a chance, but then, when he asked to walk her home or get her a drink, she said no. I would recommend asking other women at the party if someone kept pestering them, someone might have tried it on with a few people, and that's the person we should be talking to because ladies and gentlemen – I think we're looking for a narcissist.'

He bowed and from the back of the room someone shouted, 'We won't have to look far, will we?'

Maxie knew some of what he'd said had merit, but they'd concluded too quickly and conveniently built a scenario to fit the profile. People were never that easy to classify. She invited Team Four up and their female team leader strode up to the podium with poise and confidence. Despite now feeling uncomfortable that she'd used

Georgina's case today, she was pleased to note that each team had somehow inhabited the roles they'd been given as they'd been taught. This woman put her hands on her hips and looked around, shaking her head. After a few sighs she spoke quietly to make the room lean in towards her.

'With you lot on this case, it has absolutely no chance of getting to court.' A murmur of laughter rippled around the room, but she kept a straight and serious face.

'There are eleven rapes an hour in this country: eleven. Think about that. While we've been sitting here, eleven people – mainly women and mainly young – have been going through their worst nightmare. Ninety per cent of them know their attacker in some way and only a tiny per cent of those bastards will be prosecuted for what they've done.

'So, we all need to act quickly,' she continued. 'But let's face it, a system that lets down ninety per cent of people isn't going to be fixed with a few tweaks. So, we're going for something radical.'

Maxie's curiosity was definitely piqued.

'Remember a while back, the academic who said we should decriminalise rape? Yeah, she had a book to promote, but she was on to something. It ties into your ideas about warriors vs victims. If you are brave enough to come forward and give us such personal evidence, then we, the CPS, are going to believe you – period. No trial, no cross-examination, we'll convict the guy. First offence, it's a small sentence like community service but his name is known, and it'll be three strikes and he's out – prison.'

'He gets to offend three times?' yelled someone.

'Beats two hundred or whatever the latest serial attacker got away with,' replied the team leader. 'So, change the system because it just doesn't work.'

As the speaker returned to her seat, Maxie got up and applauded everyone.

'Great session, everyone,' she said. 'I'd be glad to have you fighting my corner and I'll have a word with the Justice Secretary when they're next here, shall I?'

As the students left the hall, buzzing, Maxie reflected that they'd learnt well but her students simply couldn't imagine how this would feel for real. The session had helped clarify her thinking and harden her resolve; when it came down to it, she might know all the police protocols but her hands weren't bound by them and she could take this investigation any way she liked. What she wouldn't do was sit back and wait for Andrew. She had too much experience of waiting around for news from the police when the crime had actually been reported – and then getting nothing.

She had to do this herself.

# Chapter Eight

Having spent all morning of this warm day in unsuitable heels, the balls of Maxie's feet protested in pain on any exertion. She hobbled from the lecture theatre back to her office and groaned with relief as she cast off her shoes, giving her toes some much needed freedom even though they still bore the swelling and redness of their recent captivity. She wriggled and flexed them, trying to get the circulation flowing as she dialled the number of Chief Inspector Heather McAlister. They'd met at a conference on Policing and Criminological Research shortly after the new chief had been appointed and through their conversation Maxie recognised her desire to make a difference quickly. However, like everyone else, her budgets were being squeezed and with the rankings standing the way they did, Maxie guessed she couldn't look a gift horse in the mouth.

'Hello, Chief Inspector,' she said, hoping her tone said she respected the chief's rank but regarded her as a friendly acquaintance. 'It's Professor Reddick from Lonsdale University. Are the criminals keeping you busy?'

McAlister snorted with laughter. 'Professor, good to hear from you. I've been meaning to call you.'

For the past two years, Maxie had been trying to persuade the previous chief inspector to establish a formal collaboration, sharing research and testing innovative approaches to policing as soon as they'd been developed at the university. McAlister was a fresh broom and willing to do things differently so Maxie listened and nodded along as McAlister played back the proposal Maxie had presented to the force all that time ago, as if it were the chief inspector's own.

'Other forces and universities are ahead of the game

on this. We've both got some catching up to do,' said McAlister. 'We need to be open to new ideas.'

Maxie did a silent fist punch on her end of the phone, relieved that they might actually get this up and running. The force's road to Damascus moment couldn't have come at a better time.

'I completely agree and would be delighted to lead a working party on this,' replied Maxie. 'And it gives me a great excuse to ask you for a favour in return.'

Maxie told her about her quandary, that a close personal friend had been attacked, but was afraid to come forward.

'We're not the dinosaurs we used to be you know,' McAlister replied. 'If you can get her to call us or even come in, tell her we'll just listen to begin with – nothing scary. Then if she wants to take it forward, we'll handle her report with care and sensitivity.'

'I know that, and I'll try again to get her to come in but, to be honest, I'm not sure it's going to happen. I'm hoping to persuade her to write down as many details as she can and if she does, I'll bring them in along with her clothes from the night. I know you can't do anything unless she reports this herself but if you're looking at any other cases and there are similarities ...'

Maxie heard a heavy sigh on the other end of the line; another case that couldn't be solved would be bad for the rankings and both of them knew that.

'In the spirit of collaboration?' she added.

'You know we're clutching at straws with no first person,' replied McAlister. 'But bring me what you've got, and I'll get DS Dawson to look into it.'

They ended the call with platitudes, then, happy to at least have this tiny glimmer of light, Maxie leapt up with her hands in the air. Her feet yelped sharply – they hadn't been ready for that level of activity.

On a roll, Maxie's next stop was the PhD lounge – a quiet area on the first floor where her doctoral students isolated themselves from the rest of the world. She knew she'd find her student, Leo Turner, there with his head buried in academic papers; she wasn't wrong.

'Leo,' she declared, startling everyone in the hushed space. 'Come with me. I need you.'

If she couldn't get some facts about this attack, there would really be no point in going back to the chief inspector and it was simply too good an opportunity to miss. And all the research she'd read suggested that if Georgina didn't tell someone at least some of the details, she'd suffer for longer, bearing them all by herself. Maxie knew it would be a fine balance though; recalling the night in detail was probably the last thing Georgina wanted to do, but there was a technique Leo was working on that might help her. Dissociative Recall was a well-established procedure in NLP, and although Neuro-Linguistic Programming was frequently dismissed in the mainstream media as being all about manipulation, Maxie was an expert practitioner and had used it on several occasions to help students get over exam anxiety. This technique had only recently been used in criminal cases, and she was supervising Leo's research into the potential of the technique in interviewing victims of distressing crimes. She believed it could help Georgina, and Leo was only too willing to talk about it.

'I really believe it will help victims to talk about the incident without reliving it,' he gushed when she sat him down in a spare pod. 'As you know, it involves hypnotising the subject to relax them, and then asking them to imagine they're floating above a cinema watching themselves, watching a movie of the trauma so they aren't in the movie or experiencing the emotion of watching a movie – they're distanced but able to observe.'

Maxie knew all this and knew the procedure had to end by embedding a happy or calm memory that had occurred after the attack; it was vital to bring the subject back to a safe place so they could move past the moments of the attack. Leo was still talking as Maxie spun her pen around in her fingers, wondering whether Georgina would allow her to try this out.

'How far have you got with your research?' she asked.

'I'm almost through the desk element, collating all the studies that have gone before,' he replied, ruffling his hair with his fingers and looking even more the socially unaware boffin. 'I really think we'll have something quite special by the end of the study and then we could start developing the police training.'

Maxie knew the end of the study was about two years away which was absolutely no use to her. She interrupted Leo and explained that she wanted to try a more informal version of the technique right now – he looked dismayed.

'You wouldn't be publishing it, would you?'

She reassured him that it wouldn't impact his study or his PhD; he had to show his work was original to get the award and realised that she'd probably waded into the discussion with size nines by suggesting she shortcut his research.

'I imagine my efforts would be laughed out of the university so I wouldn't worry.'

This seemed to appease Leo and he started to discuss the merits of various adaptations of the technique, oblivious to Maxie drumming on the table as she thought through her likely approach. Suddenly she slapped both hands down looking triumphant.

'I'm sorry, Leo, I have to go,' she said, waving her goodbye to the startled student.

As she left the building, Maxie got a text from Leo. *Soz. Forgot to say good luck. Brain freeze*!

She snorted affectionately; he was a good guy and she was sure he'd make a good research student. She could imagine him one day becoming a TV professor, the Attenborough of Criminology. He was photogenic enough but just had to get over that compulsion of his to bamboozle everyone he met within the first five minutes. He hadn't seemed to notice that she was finding the pace of academia unhelpful right now.

The afternoon faculty meeting started at three and was pure torture for no other reason than it was stopping Maxie speaking to Georgina, and right now every hour counted. As soon as she could, she darted out of the building and into her car. It wasn't peak commuting time so the drive to Rachel's was painless and the parking easy. After the sleepless night and the full-on day, Maxie suddenly realised she was absolutely shattered. She pulled a hairbrush out of her bag and then opened her mouth wide, stretching her face into a more awake expression. Getting out of the car, a slight but welcome breeze enveloped her, and she took a deep breath allowing it to refresh and rejuvenate her. The seafront was once again glorious; the ripples on the surface of the water glittered in the sun and stretched for miles to the horizon. From here it was easy to see why their ancestors had believed the earth was flat; it looked as if you could sail out there and just disappear over the edge, away from everything.

Maxie turned away from the sea towards Rachel's flat. By the time her friend had answered the door, there was no sign of Maxie's tiredness and instead she stood there wearing a positive, optimistic mask; she guessed from Rachel's demeanour that she'd done exactly the same.

'Oh, hello, good to see you,' said Rachel overly cheerfully and loudly. Maxie smiled gently at her and squeezed her hand. Rachel reciprocated and the physical connection seemed to steel both women; they nodded at each other and went inside. Georgina wasn't in the living room and Rachel signalled towards the bathroom from where a shower started up on full force.

'Has she said any more?' asked Maxie. Rachel shook her head. 'Told her parents or boyfriend yet?'

'I can't imagine her ever doing that,' replied Rachel.

'I'm sure they'd want to support her.'

'I just think she doesn't want to upset them.'

'What about the wedding photos?'

'I've asked and they're starting to come in, but it could be a while before we have them all.'

'Ask them to hurry up. We haven't got a while.'

They heard the shower stop, a door open and another door being firmly closed. Georgina obviously wasn't going to join them.

'Could you make us some tea?' asked Maxie before getting up and heading to the bathroom. Steam filled the room so completely that the shower must have been scalding hot. Maxie wafted her way through it and noted several empty shower-gel bottles in the wastebasket; she wondered how many times she'd scrubbed herself since the attack and if she were starting to feel clean again yet. As she left, she met Rachel bringing a tray of tea and cake for Georgina; Maxie noted the cup she'd chosen with its "Hug in a Mug" design in soft, plump typography. It was a small but loving gesture. Maxie took the tray and gently tapped on Georgina's door.

'Can I come in? I have cake.'

The door opened but Georgina went straight back to her bed; Maxie sat on the edge and handed over the cup and plate. Georgina put the plate on her bedside table, nudging out of the way more cups and another plate – both still full of their contents. Maxie saw that on the floor beside the table there were others lying, their contents similarly untouched. Georgina sipped at the tea and Maxie made no attempt at conversation but waited quietly, aware with the rise and fall of her chest, that her breathing now matched the young woman's. The silence wasn't awkward, the way it felt at home after one of the rows with Philip, and Maxie knew not to break it, especially not with any platitudes like "I know how you must be feeling". No, if either were to speak, it should be Georgina, even if she simply asked the professor to leave her alone.

'Have you found him?'

By the time Georgina spoke, Maxie was almost relaxed, as if in a meditative state. She shook her head gently.

'But Rachel is getting hold of pictures from the wedding to see if we can spot anyone we don't know. You could take a look at them if you're ready?'

Georgina picked at the seams of her duvet cover and shook her head. 'I didn't see him.' She closed her eyes tightly as she continued. 'He … he was big, tall.'

Maxie was delighted to hear her give some detail about her attacker and couldn't hide the hopeful tone in her voice. 'That's good, it's something and pictures might prompt a memory of something else, perhaps what he was wearing.'

Georgina lifted her gaze and looked directly at Maxie. 'I never want to remember more than I already do. I don't want to look at photos and realise I do know who he is. Can you not understand that?' Her voice rose from brittle to angry by the end of the sentence.

Maxie was relieved to hear something other than defeat from her; she reached out and took Georgina's hands in hers. 'I'm not going to sit here and say I understand what you're going through because I don't, and although I think I can imagine how I'd feel, we're different people. But I have to be truthful with you, and I'd like to tell you what I think if you want to hear it?'

She paused and waited for Georgina to nod her agreement.

'I think if you bottle this up, you won't get over it. You say you don't want to know who he is but, what if at some level you already do remember a detail? What if you're walking along the street one day, maybe in a few years from now, and something happens? Maybe you get a whiff of an aftershave or hear a laugh that somehow you recall? What if you bump into him when you're not expecting it?'

Maxie saw Georgina flinch and realised she was tightening her grip on the poor girl's hands. She let go and softened her tone. 'That might be far harder to cope with than working through the pain right now with people who care about you.'

'I'm not going to the police.'

'And that's your choice.'

They fell silent again although Maxie could hear her own heartbeat as it sat in her throat pounding away. Given what Georgina had just said, her next actions could go terribly wrong. Maxie allowed the silence to settle them both, and as they regained that contemplative state, she kept her gaze straight ahead and asked, 'Did they have trout for the main course at the wedding?'

'Err, no, salmon,' replied Georgina confused.

'And what colour were the bridesmaids' dresses? Were they salmon too?'

'No, they were blue.'

'And was he wearing blue?'

'No, a dark green hoodie.'

'And did Rachel make you toast and honey for breakfast this morning?'

'Marmalade.'

It had taken a few seconds, but Maxie had a new fact. Just one, but she now knew part of what he was wearing. She kept her gaze straight and waited for Georgina to speak.

'Thank you,' Georgina said quietly, and Maxie relaxed knowing that she'd found a way of talking about what had happened. They continued these bizarre conversations until Maxie had four facts: he wore a green hoodie, nitrile gloves, a balaclava with a head torch, and had a local accent. After each fact was revealed, she brought Georgina back to a safe environment, showing her that it was in the past and that her life needn't be dominated by this, she'd survived and one day, she would be okay.

Maxie knew that asking any more would be pushing it on a first session, so she called it a day.

'I'll come back tomorrow,' she promised as she left Georgina's bedroom. The young woman nodded and snuggled down into her bed sighing. It was a sigh of someone who'd had a small weight lifted from their shoulders. Maxie knew it was only the start, but that's all she needed tonight.

# Chapter Nine

Maxie was relieved when the alarm finally sounded. She'd been awake all night mentally working through her game plan. Although Georgina had protested otherwise during their first session, on some level she obviously wanted her attacker to be identified and caught. She could have stopped the question and answer routine at any time, but she didn't, and she'd looked relieved at the end. Maxie still had doubts about what she was doing; did she only want to find this man to prove she could? Somewhere in the back of her mind she still felt she could have tried harder to find out what happened to her sister who had been killed during a home burglary many years ago. But she'd been young and naïve then, had trusted the system. Had believed they'd find the killer and lock him up forever. Thinking about how stupid she'd been infuriated her. She threw back the duvet and stomped around the room. How ridiculous were police protocols which prevented them even looking at crimes? How insane was it that an attack couldn't be investigated if the traumatised victim didn't come forward and subject herself to police questioning?

She heard Karl heading into the bathroom. He'd been bullied and beaten up when he first went to secondary school for simply being skinny. He hadn't wanted to tell his teachers and had begged her not to march up to school, as she'd been determined to do. On recalling those days, Maxie instinctively clenched her hand to her heart, the memory of him crying and feeling trapped still very vivid to her. Bullies preyed on the loners, the quiet ones, and they kept going until they were stopped or simply got bored. Georgina was evidently on her own at that wedding, was easy to take advantage of and that thought infuriated Maxie. Why should they get away with it?

Breakfast took longer than its usual twenty minutes; Philip was leaving for London and couldn't decide which tie went best with which of his new shirts while Karl was pretending not to fret over that day's exam.

'You'll both be fine,' said Maxie picking out a tie and handing it to Philip. 'You both know your subject so just keep calm and knock 'em dead. Are you sure you don't want me to make you a special dinner?'

'Deffo,' replied Karl. 'I'm going for a Nando's straight after. You didn't want me home or something did you? With Dad not being here?'

'Deffo – not,' said Maxie. 'I'm going to be late back if you're certain that doesn't make me a neglectful parent.'

Karl ducked to avoid the ruffle of the hair that was coming his way and told her he was certain. Maxie gave both her men a kiss for luck and headed out.

Although she'd known Karl's exams started this week, she had completely forgotten about the first of them being today and was relieved Karl didn't want her around tonight. She had the meeting with the Events Manager at Stanmer Hall and her head was so full of questions for him, she didn't want to have to cancel it but would have done if Karl had asked her to. Before Stanmer she had a full day of work ahead. And she owed it to her students to focus entirely on them for the next eight hours. Fortunately, that wouldn't be hard, as the highlight of the day was an undergrad tutorial on criminalisation and the definition of crime; these sessions were always lively ones.

In previous years they'd resulted in fabulous debates as her students tackled a core question in criminology – who decides that one act is criminal, and another isn't? She always ended this tutorial by asking students to write a paper on the activity that they would criminalise, and the punishment they'd propose. It had to be well argued but it could be anything, and historically the activities they'd chosen reflected the issues of the day and their lives in particular: companies using packaging they knew wasn't recyclable, landlords charging rent for sub-standard accommodation and not using your right to vote. Their punishments tended to be quite inventive too, and she couldn't help smiling to herself as she imagined courts telling the CEO of an offending company that until he sorted out the recyclability issue, every single packet with his logo would be posted back through his letter box. She couldn't deny that it would probably get the issue sorted a lot more quickly than the pitiful fines that were handed out.

After dumping her briefcase in her office, Maxie went straight to the tutorial room where her students were waiting.

'Okay,' she said tapping her palm on the table. 'Let's discuss our society today – in fact, the society that your generation will inhabit and create rather than mine. In this future society, what do you think we will eventually re-classify as a criminal act?'

The tutorial passed with a genial discussion about age discrimination; with the boomer generations taking the flak for the ills that would be faced by the young.

'When a person reaches forty or fifty,' asserted one student, 'they should be forced to retire and enable a young person to take that job or get promoted. Job-blocking should be punished through increased taxation so that it's not actually worth the elderly working.'

Maxie didn't know whether to feel flattered that they

hadn't realised she was forty herself, or terrified that they were about to go all *Lord of the Flies* on her. She wondered how Philip would rise to this debate but doubted that genial banter on the subject would go down well given the struggles he'd faced recently. She dismissed the group who were now jokingly taking the job-blocking penalties to the extreme; Maxie tried to imagine her students' reaction when the parents they'd incarcerated couldn't afford to fund their gap years.

After a morning that had been entertaining enough to keep her distracted, the afternoon was hijacked by a committee meeting with a project group who were trying to attract a sponsor or funding for a new cybercrime research facility. The issue wasn't in finding a company interested in the work or the profile it would create for them rather it was in finding someone with neutral politics that the university could partner with. The company currently offering the most funding was also unfortunately associated with influencing elections, an accusation obviously denied.

'Surely the important thing is to get this off the ground – we're lagging behind,' said one of her colleagues. 'And what happened to innocent until proven guilty?'

'It would be absolutely useless to have a facility which prospective students and clients had no respect for. The research would carry no weight whatsoever,' argued another.

Maxie found herself once again seeing both sides of an argument but since meeting Georgina, her appetite for simply debating crime and criminal psychology was waning. What use was it having all this knowledge and insight if it couldn't be put to use? She'd always loved the law and if it hadn't been for their complete failure to find her sister's killers, she'd have joined the police. She lost all respect for them the day they announced the case was no longer active. Focussing on criminology was her way of staying close but having the freedom to criticise from the sidelines. Now that didn't feel enough and the itch to use what she knew was growing; she wanted to get this day over with so she could follow up the enquiries that were spinning around her head. She had to get this room to stop debating and simply make the decision.

'Do the right thing now or we'll forever be wishing we had,' said Maxie standing up to signal the meeting was ending. 'Set up the facility and do as much as we can by offering internships to our most talented students. Then when we have a prototype, look for paying clients who'll help it grow organically until we find a sponsor that doesn't cost us our souls.'

She scampered out of the room as quickly as possible to avoid any of the post-committee lobbying that usually happened. Finally she could get out of here and get back to doing something useful.

'Is the Events Manager ready to see me yet?' asked Maxie. He was late, and her need to get this conversation started was threatening to override her usual sense of politeness. The receptionist rang an internal extension and called her colleague. After a few minutes a stylish young guy approached her with a folder of brochures and his hand outstretched.

'Hello, there, I'm Josh,' he said.

They looked each other up and down. He held himself tall with a professional stance and was quite handsome with dark curls framing his face, and dimples when he smiled. He had a firm handshake that said *competence* and a dress sense that said *flair*. Maxie wondered whether he was like this at home or whether it was his work persona;

either way, if she were really here about a stylish event, she'd have been reassured so far.

'So, Professor, I've googled you I'm afraid and know how famous you are, so let's see what we can do for you.'

He led her through to a quiet corner of the lounge. 'Is it a graduation party or perhaps an awards party for the podcast?' he asked coyly, notepad poised.

Maxie weighed him up deciding which tactic would be most likely to make him open up, without having to reveal what had happened; if he realised she was asking about a real crime, then he might just clam up if he sensed there was a threat to his venue. Maxie decided that he looked like a man who enjoyed a gossip so she decided to butter him up.

'I'm sorry, I've misled you,' she said as coyly as she could. 'I'm not organising an event at all but you're on the right track. I'm working on an episode of *Criminal Thoughts*, doing some research about relationships and weddings and I couldn't think of anyone who would know more about them.'

Josh's expression moved from slightly miffed to puffed-up during that short sentence. Maxie kept going. 'I'm looking at what tips people over the edge and thought I'd see if you had any stories about jilted brides or bridegrooms. If we use any material you have, I could pay for sharing your expertise or give you a credit on the show.'

She watched him smile at the word "expertise" and his eyes practically pop at the suggestion of a credit.

'How exciting,' he said settling back in his chair. 'Tell me what you need to know.'

Maxie took out her voice recorder and notepad, as much to make this seem official as anything else.

'My personal field of study is psychology,' she said not

lying completely. 'Trying to understand why some people carry out criminal acts while others in the same situation don't.'

Josh leaned in enthusiastically and nodded.

'In other areas of life, the amount a person has invested in a situation can be the trigger and I wondered whether this could apply to weddings.'

Maxie was grasping at straws as this didn't sound anything like an interesting idea for one of her episodes, but she was counting on Josh wanting to know more.

'You mean if they've spent more on the wedding then they're more likely to go off the rails if it goes wrong?' asked Josh. 'In my experience they just ask for a refund, but they can get pretty nasty with that.'

'I meant emotional investment. Have you ever had a wedding here where it seemed to matter more to either the bride or the groom? You might have been able to sense the imbalance.'

'Oh definitely,' enthused Josh getting into his subject. He opened his files and started telling her about some of the weddings he'd arranged, and the disasters that had befallen them, as well as the ones he'd known from the start were "the start of a truly magical journey". To her delight, the folders contained photographs of each couple during their initial consultation and he confessed to creating a little nickname for them so he could differentiate them later.

'Brunette with bossy mother just doesn't distinguish.' He laughed. 'But I will always remember the Kim and Kanye wannabes.'

Maxie smiled but wondered what the hell her nickname would have been. Josh continued talking, so she went back to nodding, taking notes that she'd never look at again and probing further at times to make it seem genuine. When he'd finished going through all the weddings he had records of, Maxie thanked him and then asked what she really wanted to know.

'What about the ones that don't happen? Have you ever arranged a wedding here and then it fell through, maybe the groom was jilted at the altar?'

Josh sat back and sighed, as if recalling a great tragedy.

'There was one, around this time last year. It wasn't pretty. The groom standing there full of hope; it should have been the happiest day of his life. He was nervous already but then the best man had to go up and tell him she wasn't coming, that she didn't want to marry him. It was awful.'

'What did he do?'

'Well, you'd think he'd crumble, wouldn't you? But no, he insisted on everyone going ahead with the party. The bride's family didn't stay but his did, and his friends got absolutely plastered on the champagne – after all, they weren't paying for it.'

'Do you remember how the groom behaved that night?'

Josh nodded. 'Not likely to forget. He tried to shag half the staff, got quite nasty when they turned him down.'

'And have you seen him since, or did you take a photo of him?'

Josh replied that he hadn't seen him but must have a picture although if he still had it, it would be filed away. There was no point showing that picture to prospective happy couples.

'Did he have a nickname?' asked Maxie hoping it was something telling like Vlad or Norman Bates. 'And can you check the date to see when exactly the anniversary of the wedding would have been? Sorry – lots of questions but it sounds interesting.'

'I can look it all up,' replied Josh. 'Do you think the anniversary might stir up some pent-up emotion? Would you try to get him on the show? I can't imagine he'd want to relive it.'

'Just exploring options at this stage,' replied Maxie. 'But while I'm here, can I change the subject completely and ask you about wedding crashers?'

Josh smiled broadly and Maxie saw that, although he was definitely wearing his work persona, he just loved to talk and was sure that if she ever needed to speak to this man again, she'd found herself a fabulous source of information. She was also certain that if she could ever reveal the real reason for her questions, he'd understand the initial deception.

'I know I shouldn't,' he delighted, 'but I think they're hilarious. Imagine deciding to put on your best togs and spending every Saturday night dancing to "Time of My Life" with a bunch of strangers – it's mad. Honestly, if I didn't do this job, then I might just take it up.'

He started singing and despite herself, Maxie couldn't help but laugh. It was strange to hear; she couldn't remember having a moment of spontaneous fun for a long time, but she had to get back on track.

'Do you get many crashers here?' she asked.

'No, unfortunately, we're just that bit too far out. They stick to the hotels on the seafront and then they can move from one to the other if things get boring. It's a shame in a way because we always throw a good party here. Have you ever been to one?'

'No,' replied Maxie before remembering she'd told the receptionist that she had been at the wedding. She had to keep going and hope they didn't talk. 'But a friend of a friend got married here at the weekend.'

Josh frowned at her and closed his folder with a snap.

'So, that's what this is about. The incident at the evening do? You're not really here to discuss a show are you?'

'What do you mean? What incident?' asked Maxie.

He sat silently for a moment or two weighing her up. She put down her notebook and pen, holding her hands up in the air.

'I have no idea what you're talking about but I'd really like to hear about it,' she persisted.

'There was a bloke,' said Josh with reluctance. 'Absolutely plastered and pestering women to dance. He got a bit shirty when they said no – you know the type, thinks he's God's gift and can't understand why everyone doesn't fall at his feet.'

'A narcissist,' murmured Maxie nodding along. 'What happened?'

'He picked on the wrong woman. Her other half was built like a centre prop – and it all threatened to kick off. The bar team had to separate them and get him out of the building. It was okay in the end, the drunk left and the couple got a free bottle of wine.'

'Did the drunk bloke leave the premises? I mean the grounds too?'

'I presume so. No one saw him again.'

'Do you have a description?'

Josh shook his head. 'Sorry, I wasn't there but the night team might remember. Why do you want to know?'

'Just wondering if it was one of my students. There were a few here and I'd hate to find out one of them was behaving that way. What about your CCTV? The receptionist says it covers most of the function rooms and corridors. That would have captured him, wouldn't it?'

'It was out that night everywhere but the car park.' He shook his head sheepishly. 'Management don't want anyone to know.'

Maxie sighed in despair. It was one step forward and two – or maybe even three – back.

'It's fixed now,' offered Josh. 'Look, I'll ask the night team what he looked like or if they got his name.'

'If I had a photo of the students who were here, would you show it around – discreetly of course?' asked Maxie.

'Yes, I promise. I'll help however I can.' Josh held his hand to his heart. 'But don't give us a bad review on your show, will you?'

'I won't,' replied Maxie. Keeping Josh happy meant access to the venue and that seemed a fair exchange.

# Chapter Ten

*Thursday, 21 May*

Finally, it felt as if that light had started to appear at the end of the tunnel and Maxie wanted to rush full speed towards it. A message from Rachel that morning said the photos had started flooding in from the guests, and Maxie was planning to head round immediately after work. There was no denying her husband's absence was extremely useful right now. She wasn't sure how he'd react if he knew what she was doing and was happier not to have to explain herself.

Karl also seemed focussed on his exams and getting through them with the support of his friends rather than her. He'd reminded her on several occasions that maths and graphic design weren't exactly her strong point so as long as she kept paying for the takeaways, she was mother of the year.

She had a couple of days now where she could concentrate her efforts entirely on Georgina and selfishly hoped Philip would continue to find this new role as completely absorbing when he got back. She wasn't at all sure how she'd manage to keep it all going if he didn't.

Arriving at Rachel's flat later that evening, it felt oddly peaceful. Rachel led her to the table where her laptop stood and clicked the mouse, opening up a file of photographs; hundreds of them. Maxie's jaw dropped as the little thumbnails turned into pictures of people and just kept going, on and on. Eventually they'd all opened and they could scroll down the enormous task ahead.

'I did what you suggested,' said Rachel seeing the

expression on Maxie's face, 'and got the unedited files. That's the problem with digital, you can snap away as much as you want and then delete ninety-nine point nine per cent of them later. And this lot are only from a few friends; there were nearly a hundred guests at that wedding.'

Maxie puffed out her cheeks then clicked on the first image. 'Then we'd better get started.'

Rachel talked Maxie through every picture and together they wrote down the names of the people she recognised and who they'd come to the wedding with. They studied any unknowns and created a separate file containing photographs of people Rachel couldn't identify or men she knew had come alone. Georgina hardly featured in any images and when she did, it was in the background.

'Could we take this file of people we don't know to the police and get them to use that facial recognition software? Is it real?' asked Rachel.

'It is real but they can't give us that resource yet and the face would have to be on their database,' Maxie replied. 'Unfortunately, we can't just rock up and say – here's thousands of pictures of people we don't recognise, could you look them up please?'

Rachel buried her chin in her hand and sighed.

'I'm sorry I snapped, it was a good suggestion,' continued Maxie, rubbing Rachel's back supportively. 'And if this were an active investigation, then maybe they'd look at them, but until then we have to do the legwork. We have to eliminate as many of these as we can. I heard there was a bit of a fight at the wedding but there aren't any pictures of it. Did you see it?'

'No,' replied Rachel. 'But I might have disappeared upstairs by then.'

Maxie's stomach suddenly rumbled loudly and they

both laughed. Maxie raised her arms above her head, yawning. She looked at the time; they'd been hunched over this laptop for more than two-and-a-half hours.

'We need a break,' she said getting up and stretching. This had left her whole body aching, right the way from the tight curve of her lower back, to her gritty and bloodshot eyeballs. Rachel vanished into the kitchen and re-emerged with two glasses of wine and a bowl of crisps.

'Not exactly a balanced diet,' she said apologetically.

'Oh, I don't know,' replied Maxie. 'You've a glass in each hand.'

She took one of them and swallowed a soul reviving sip. Sighing with satisfaction she said, 'Georgina's not around tonight, is she?'

Rachel shook her head. 'She went to church. One of her friends there is giving her a lift back.'

'But that's brilliant,' said Maxie. 'Do they know what happened yet?'

'God no,' replied Rachel and they both laughed a little at the blasphemy.

'Getting back out there is a good sign, even if it is only to church.'

'I know. I've still got everything crossed, but it gives you hope doesn't it?' said Rachel. 'I mean that she might eventually get over it.'

Maxie shook her head. 'I doubt she'll really ever get over it but maybe she can learn that it needn't define her.'

They clinked a toast to Georgina and got back to work.

They ploughed on through another sixty images; Maxie thought that by now, she probably knew this wedding party more intimately than anyone who'd been there. She'd seen teenage guests sneaking forbidden sips of wine from abandoned glasses, husbands with their hands on thighs that didn't belong to their wives, and wives paying very close attention to the rear ends of certain waiters. All pretty much what she'd expect from a boozy do, but quite entertaining to see it captured in such uninhibited detail. Rachel had been horrified to see her wild and unrestrained dancing in all its glory.

'I look positively insane,' she'd said deleting it from the collection immediately. Finally, they came across a picture with Georgina clearly in the background.

'Who's the guy standing beside her in this one?' asked Maxie. The photo showed Georgina, her head cowed, standing at the bar next to an extremely tall man, so tall in fact that his head hadn't been captured at all. One of the few facts they had about the attacker was that he was tall.

'It's just a plain white shirt so not exactly helpful. Do you remember anyone dressed like that?'

Rachel studied it but shrugged. 'I'm the world's worst witness, Professor. I really wasn't paying that much attention to the men's clothes. I was too busy taking them off. Christ, if only I hadn't ...'

'It's not your fault any more than it's Georgina's,' said Maxie. 'But we both need to ask people about this guy.'

They noted the number of the picture and Maxie scribbled a huge asterisk beside it; it felt like something to be going on at the least. Neither woman wanted to give up until they'd been through the whole file, so it was dark by the time Maxie said goodbye. They had around a dozen men to identify, including the "Headless Tall Man" as he was now known. Rachel would ask her friends about them and Maxie would get the pictures to Josh to see if any of them was the guy who'd started the fight.

When Maxie left, the sky had turned a clear deep indigo, and the edge of the world was no longer visible; only a sliver of moonlight on the sea gave the blackness some perspective. A car pulled up outside Rachel's flat and Maxie saw an older man get out, walk round to the passenger door and open it. Georgina emerged and shook his hand; the man waited until Georgina walked to her front door and waved him off. As she watched the car drive away and a light go on in the flat above, Maxie exhaled deeply, realising that she'd been holding her breath until she could see the young woman was safe.

She turned toward the sea and listened to the sound of the tide rushing up over the pebbles and then retreating back. She timed each wave, counting how long it would stay ashore. It was hypnotic. Maxie hoped that Georgina could hear this from her room, and that tonight it would lull her into a restful sleep. She probably hadn't had one of them since the attack. Taking one final breath to fill her own lungs and soul with this deep peace, Maxie got into her car and set off for home.

He'd seen her go out earlier, looking like she didn't have a care in the world. Yeah, she'd looked behind her a few times, and jumped when a group of drunks came towards her, but that was hardly enough. He'd sat here in his van, waiting for her to come home and here she was – nearly fucking midnight, sauntering back with a man for Christ's sake. All his efforts meant nothing to her. She was laughing in their faces yet again. He hadn't ruined her life at all, not like she'd ruined his. Well, he wasn't finished yet. He gripped the steering wheel and turned the key, revving the engine hard so it roared out his anger. It was time to move on to the next phase.

# Chapter Eleven

*Friday, 22 May*

Despite the high from the previous day, Maxie now felt an unwelcome uneasiness as she remembered this was the day Philip would be getting back from London. She stood at the kitchen window staring out at nothing, unable to focus and not wanting to admit her feelings but they wouldn't leave. With everything they'd gone through over the past year, it would be natural to be anxious that things had gone well for him or excited that he was coming back but, although those emotions gave rise to the same tightness in the stomach, what she felt wasn't either of these. She hated herself for acknowledging it – but it was dread. She'd spent so long walking on eggshells, afraid to share anything she was working on or tell him about a good day at the university, just because it felt like rubbing salt into the wound of his redundancy. There had been a time when she could have asked his opinion on the police collaboration or even Georgina's case – without mentioning her name of course. Maxie slapped her cheeks to drive away this feeling; she wasn't being fair on him. He'd reacted badly to her questions about the new business but it was in its infancy so what did she expect? He was just anxious. Hopefully today would be her husband's turning point and this new opportunity would give him back social engagement, intellectual stimulation and an income, all the things she knew he'd really missed over these past months. Her husband would probably seem reborn by the time he got home.

She had a lot of urgent work today but she was doing

it at home so she could be here when Philip got back; despite her anxiety, she didn't want to show him how she was feeling. Dragging herself back to the present and grabbing a coffee, she parked herself in the study, turned up the radio for company and started tidying piles of paper so she'd have the space she needed. They all used this room for studying or working so it was out of bounds to the cleaner and the boys had filled the space with clutter; Maxie needed to make it look less like the site of a jumble sale before she got started. She stacked their paperwork neatly and scrubbed away a coffee stain with a tissue, ensuring she sat down to a spotless workspace. She noticed an unfamiliar company logo on a letterhead and guessing this was the umbrella consultancy brand Philip had talked about put it to one side. The uncomfortable feelings returned as Maxie realised she'd never seen the logo before because he'd blocked any efforts she'd made to find out what he was doing and she hadn't tried too hard, anyway. She had to change that, to show a real interest and to get him to confide in her like he used to. The letterhead had a website address, so she made a personal pledge to visit them after she'd pursued the lead from the photograph and done her work. Then tonight, she'd put on her best welcoming face and be ready with intelligent, open questions as well as a bottle of his favourite Pinot Noir when he got back.

'Make a bloody effort, woman,' she said to herself, as she Blu-Tacked the letterhead to the wall behind the computer.

Opening her emails she saw that Josh had already sent the picture of the jilted bridegroom. That was good – he was keeping his end of their bargain. Maxie returned the email with a copy of Rachel's Headless Tall Man, telling Josh he'd been at a wedding recently and asking if this could be the one who was pestering people or if he recognised him "despite the photographical decapitation". Josh responded immediately asking "shouldn't he be riding a horse" and promising to get back to her as soon as. Maxie smiled at his enthusiasm then turned her attention to the scanned image of the jilted man and the woman he thought would be his bride. Maxie was slightly saddened to see Josh had written "was never going to happen between these two #leaguesapart" in his email and yes, on the surface, she was beautiful and he was simply average. She could imagine Josh's sentiment on the tongues of other guests, almost ignoring the fact that here was a guy who'd suffered, not only intense humiliation on what should have been the happiest day of his life but also heartbreak. How would it feel waking up the day after? On the morning you should have been starting your honeymoon and remembering that it was never going to happen? It could make you angry for a start and she remembered Josh telling her that he'd gone wild afterwards. It was nearly a year since that day, so it was possible that he'd come back to the scene of his humiliation to get some kind of revenge and if Georgina had rejected his advances too ... but it was such a long shot.

'I somehow doubt you would attack a random woman,' she said to the picture. 'You'd be more likely to try to wreck your ex's life wouldn't you?'

Although she was sure Josh would have contact details for the runaway bride, she didn't think this line of enquiry was really worth following up. This guy didn't match the pictures of the unidentified people from the wedding. He wasn't large the way Georgina had described, and Josh's file said he'd come from Dublin so he wasn't local either. His girlfriend had been the Lancashire girl. If all else failed, Maxie might try to find out if she'd heard from him since the wedding-that-didn't-happen, but for now it was low priority. Maxie played the voice recording she'd made at Stanmer listing the questions she needed to answer and then began working through her responses.

'Were you jilted here?' she heard her recorded voice say.

'No,' she replied out loud as she stood staring out of the study window. 'We don't think so unless it happened before Josh's time, but that was long enough ago as not to make sense.'

'Were you a guest?' asked the recording.

'We haven't found you yet but we're still looking. You made all the effort to come to Stanmer and you brought a balaclava. Why did no one see you? How were you invisible until then? Are you staff? That's more likely and I still don't have that list. You might have hidden in the grounds knowing you were safe from the camera phones until someone came out.'

'... was she a random victim?'

'Now this, I do not know. Maybe you chose her specifically.'

Maxie stopped recording and dialled Rachel's number. 'Are there any angry ex-boyfriends lurking around in Georgina's past or people she may have turned down? Not just romantically, maybe for a job?'

Maxie could hear Rachel breathing while she thought. 'I don't think so,' she eventually replied. 'It's only a small children's nursery she works at and she's not in charge of recruitment and on the love front, she kept herself to herself. If there had been an ex, it would have been someone else from her church. I could try to ask her but it seems unlikely.'

'They move in mysterious ways,' replied Maxie, knowing of so many case studies where the criminal had believed he was doing the work of the so-called Lord. They ended the call and Maxie googled the church Georgina attended.

"We accept without reservation the complete teachings of Holy Scripture and the inspired and infallible Word of God ..." the website declared, before going on to explain the importance of purity before marriage and confining sexual relations to the purpose of procreation.

Maxie personally found it hard to accept that anyone still thought like this, but it might explain why Georgina was so afraid to talk about the attack. To her, and no doubt some others in the church, it had been a violation of their beliefs and not simply one of their congregation's. Maxie took down the address on Ditchfield Road and made a mental note to visit them soon.

Her eyelids suddenly felt heavy; she needed more coffee before doing anything else so strode back into the kitchen and ground some fresh beans. She felt no further forward despite eliminating some of her questions from the voice recording even if only on the basis of logic. What did she have left? Someone from the church? Headless Man? Staff? She jotted each possibility on a separate Post-it note and stuck it on the metallic noticeboard alongside a reminder to book a dental appointment. When she'd finished, she took a step back and looked at the incongruously cheerful neon-pink notes. The coffee grinder stopped and her nostrils instinctively flared slightly taking in the rich earthy aroma of the freshly ground beans.

As the caffeine started coursing through her veins, she gave herself a shake. It was now nearly a week since the attack and getting justice of any kind was still so far away. She had to plough on until she got a glimmer, a spark to show her which direction to look and it wasn't going to happen by staring at Post-it notes. She had to find out more about Georgina's life.

Maxie took her coffee back into the study. An email from Heather McAlister asking how the proposal was going popped into her inbox. *Damn*, thought Maxie. She hadn't finished the proposal she'd promised the chief inspector but still really wanted the unit to get off the ground and moreover, now Maxie knew just how much she wanted to head it. Maxie replied that it was nearly ready and then, spinning the plate that represented her career, she put aside her questions about the case and tried to concentrate on finishing the chief inspector's proposal. Even while doing it she was thinking two steps ahead; she'd ask Josh about the staff working the wedding when he called about the headless man. If there was merit in investigating either the staff or their decapitated guest, she'd take them back to McAlister when they met to go through the proposal.

The paper had to be perfect, giving McAlister an oven-ready solution – after all, it was the carrot Maxie hoped to dangle in return for favours on this case.

When the phone rang, Maxie looked up and was surprised to see she'd been ploughing her ideas into this proposal for over four hours. It was past five and there'd been no word from Philip – he had to be on the train home by now.

Rachel was on the line. 'Can you come over?' she said. 'Georgina said she has something to tell us both. I think it's important.'

Maxie's mind went straight to the spinning plate of her marriage which had been wobbling a little too much in recent days. She wanted to be home when Philip got back from London, she wanted to be ready with the wine and the constructive conversation but she just couldn't say no to Rachel or Georgina. She remembered that she actually needed to go out to get the wine anyway and there was an off-licence on the sea front. A perfect excuse. She gave her marriage plate a quick spin and told Rachel she'd be there in ten minutes.

They paced the floor waiting for Georgina to emerge from her bedroom. When she did, she had a weak smile on her face as if trying to cheer the room up. She wore layers of jumpers but even they couldn't hide how gaunt and pale she'd become in a very short time. She sat down on the sofa, sinking down like a child in a giant's house and said nothing but picked at her fingernails, already red and worn from constant biting. Maxie hunched down at her feet and tried to take the woman's hand in hers but Georgina pulled it away and hugged herself tighter.

'Is there something you want to tell us?' asked Maxie, very softly.

Georgina gulped and steeled herself for her announcement. Maxie guessed it was something she'd practised before coming out.

'I've written everything down that I know,' she managed to say, 'and I've spoken to the pastor. He says it wasn't my fault at all and he agrees with you, that I should try to stop him doing this to anyone else.'

Maxie took the envelope handed to her and let Georgina find the words she'd probably practised.

'I want to report it,' she said exhaling heavily as she got those last words out.

'Well done,' said Maxie. 'I'm so proud of you. This is incredibly brave and your pastor is right, we should try to stop him.'

Georgina bit her lip as if holding back tears. It didn't work and one solitary drop ran down her cheek.

'I'd like you to come with me,' she said. 'And you need to find him quickly … I've remembered something else …'

Maxie leaned in as the woman's voice was getting softer and softer with each syllable.

'It wasn't a head torch he was wearing' – her breathing was getting rapid – 'It was a camera.'

With that, Georgina buried her face in her hands, digging them into her skull. Rachel looked panic-stricken at Maxie.

'Are you saying you think he filmed the attack?' Maxie's voice was barely a whisper but she needed to be absolutely sure what Georgina was saying. The young woman nodded before rushing out of the room. Maxie heard the sound of dry retching coming from the bathroom, and then the bedroom door slam shut.

'Shit,' said Rachel. 'Do you think he's going to put it online or something? That would destroy her.'

Maxie shrugged. 'It may be a trophy of sorts. The sick pig ... She'll need to delete all her social media accounts so if it's uploaded, she can't be directly tagged in it. That will help a little in reducing who sees it. You should do the same.' She shivered in disgust at the thought of a mind that enjoyed reliving such a violent attack, but she knew there were many people out there like that. The irony of the legal situation hit her hard and she snorted.

'The ridiculous thing is that if he posts any pictures without Georgina's consent, the police can pursue him without that first-person testimony. They could go after him for that, even if she hadn't reported it.'

'We're not going to let him get that far, are we?'

'No, we're bloody well not.'

# Chapter Twelve

As she stepped back onto the street, Maxie stabbed at the numbers of both Josh and Andrew several times but every time, she simply got their voicemails. She left forceful messages telling them she urgently needed to speak to them both and that they were to call her at any time. Staring frustrated at the phone she saw the text from Karl: *Get here, Dad cooking!*

Shit, that marriage plate was surely about to crash to the ground now. She'd missed Philip's arrival and that's the time she'd wanted to use. That half hour where it was more natural that she would perch on the bed while he unpacked and ask him how his trip had gone. Conversations didn't feel as strained if they didn't take place face to face over a table. She'd always hated dinner dates in her younger years for that reason. It felt like an interview.

She hadn't done anything she'd planned, she hadn't found out about this company he now worked for and she hadn't bought that bottle of his favourite wine. It all seemed irrelevant given what she'd just heard, but it wasn't – this was Philip's big day. It was important to him and she wouldn't let the case ruin it for him. She was starting to realise why most detectives on TV had troubled personal lives. She took a breath and put herself into wife and mother mode before replying to Karl: *On my way, bringing wine.*

Maxie jumped into her car and went to turn the key. She couldn't do it, she couldn't just go home now. She couldn't simply ignore what she'd just heard. The bastard had photos of that poor girl. There was a chance they were for his own pleasure, which was bad enough, but there were websites. Places online that loved this kind of footage and the thought was nauseating.

Who the hell did she know who could access these sites?

'Andrew, answer your bloody phone,' she yelled as she stabbed at his number for the umpteenth time. Fortunately, this time he answered.

'I was just about to return your call,' he began.

'Look,' said Maxie. 'This case has just taken a hideous turn. Georgina thinks he may have taken photos of her. Could your web guys see if anything is out there? On revenge or sadist sites? I'm going to speak to the university cyber team too – please, I know I'm asking a lot but this would destroy her. And, she's coming forward. She's making a statement.'

Maxie paused for breath, not sure what more she could say.

'Christ, that's awful,' replied Andrew calmly. 'I'll see what I can do but just promise me you won't start searching for those kinds of websites yourself. They're not something you'd ever forget.'

Maxie promised and for once she meant it. She messaged him a photo of Georgina she'd got from Rachel, arranged to come into the station tomorrow, and then rang the department head for cybercrime to ask for his help too. Again she got an exclamation of horror but a promise to investigate. Sending Georgina's photo out felt like a violation in itself but it was the only way.

*Where r u?* said the text from Karl.

Maxie sighed. There was nothing more she could do and she had the best people on the job. She had to compartmentalise herself and be Mum and wife again.

A smoke alarm was blaring across the house as she opened the front door. Philip had finished pulling one alarm apart to get the batteries out and was now rushing to the next one. She dumped her bag in the hall then ran towards the smell of carbon coming from the kitchen. Karl was wafting smoke out of the window with a tea towel and Philip returned to scrape black bits from a skewer of prawns. Maxie put her hand over her mouth and moved in closer.

'I think they're dead now,' said Philip. 'Couldn't risk giving you underdone prawns.'

'Good thinking,' she replied. 'And I like them well done, anyway.'

Karl brought a saucepan of rice towards them, stirring the top half with a spoon while the blackened bottom half was stuck firmly. 'Hope you like the rice well done too.'

'At least the wine will take away the taste. Where is it, Max?'

'Sh—ugar, I forgot. I'm sorry.'

'No problem,' replied Philip but the words didn't match the expression on his face.

'Never mind, I think we can still rescue this,' she said, hoping to recover the situation.

Maxie nudged the men aside, told them there were a couple of beers in the fridge then reached into a cupboard and pulled out some jars.

She edged the prawns and pepper from the skewer, cutting off the worst offending parts, then tipped them into a jar of curry sauce. The rice was beyond rescue, so Maxie pulled naan bread from the freezer, warmed them through, and they sat down to eat.

'Now that's why your mum is a professor and we are but mere mortals,' said Philip to Karl. 'Calm in the face of adversity.'

'You can still taste the burnt bits though, can't you?' Karl replied.

Maxie grimaced and took a sip of beer after forcing down a mouthful of food. 'Shall we give up on it now?'

They all pushed their plates away instantly.

'Thank God for that,' said Philip. 'It was awful.'

'Maybe why you never see napalmed crustaceans on the takeaway menu,' added Maxie, heading to the freezer and bringing out a tub of ice cream. She plonked it on the table with three spoons. 'Something to take the taste away?'

'Thank heavens for ice-cream,' said Philip as they finished the tub. 'Though a good glass of wine would have gone down even better.'

Maxie could feel his eyes on her but didn't look up.

'So what have you been up to while I've been away?' He reached across and rubbed her arm, but his touch caught her by surprise, and she flinched.

'Just work,' she said, hoping he wouldn't ask any more. Fortunately, her son intervened.

'Talking of which ...' said Karl. 'How did it go, Dad?'

Philip shuffled in his chair but nodded. 'Fingers crossed but, yeah, looking good.'

'So when this takes off will you be getting like megabucks? My mate's dad works for this consultancy ...'

Maxie watched her husband as Karl enthused about the extortionate day rates his friend's father charged, and how he'd bought him a new car and put it down as a company expense. Philip started fidgeting the way he always did when he was uncomfortable; first he held his hand over his mouth then rubbed the back of his neck. The evening had gone smoothly so far, but she could see he wasn't ready to cope with anything beyond the pleasantries. They both needed time to absorb whatever it was they were coping with.

'Oh, we get it now,' she said. 'Our son isn't really interested in the job at all, just the company car. Well, you're way behind me and my Jeep on this waiting list.'

She stood up, cleared the empty ice cream tub away and stretched her arms above her head.

'I'm bushed, I'm afraid. I might just head up if no one minds?'

'Oh, come on, we haven't been together for days,' said Philip. 'I thought we'd watch something together – something that doesn't take too much brainpower, like an old comedy or something.'

'He means Monty Python doesn't he,' said Karl to his mum.

'I'm afraid I think you're right,' she replied.

'Nothing wrong with a bit of *Life of Brian* after a hard week,' said Philip.

'You know every line in that film,' mocked Karl. 'And your accents are awful.'

'You're a very naughty boy,' sqwarked Philip quoting a famous line from the film. They found the film on Netflix and relaxed into it, laughing at the parts they knew and listening to Philip doing impressions of each character. After about half an hour they each drifted towards their various screens. Maxie could see from the light reflected in Karl's face that he was scrolling through social media feeds whereas Philip's slight frown came from an inbox that he constantly refreshed. It was probably safe for her to get back to the case now without any questions.

'I'm going to head up now,' she said to two nods but no glances.

She closed the bedroom door, taking out her phone and tablet; there were no messages from the men but there was one from Rachel saying she'd scoured social media and could see no mention of Georgina so they'd both deleted their accounts now. It was a slight relief, but Maxie still checked the local news sites, the nursery where Georgina worked, and looked on the church's website again. If he wanted to cause her embarrassment rather than keep things to himself, he'd try to spread the images among people she knew. There was nothing on any platform she could access.

She was about to give up for the night when she remembered Georgina's letter. She tried to tear it open gently, unsure if she actually wanted to read it tonight but then Philip walked in and she knew she couldn't. Maxie secreted the letter into her bag as he got into bed beside her.

'Okay if I read for an hour?' he asked.

Maxie nodded. It felt strange to have someone taking up space again. She opened her paperback to a page folded at the corner but couldn't relax. At one time they'd have lain here quietly, each absorbed in a different story but still together; she was relieved when he eventually suggested turning off the lights.

'Oh, by the way,' said Philip as she lay in the dark with her back to him. 'I borrowed a bit of money from the joint account.'

'Okay,' she replied, but lost in thoughts about the investigation, she had no idea what he'd said.

# Chapter Thirteen

The Killers' song playing through his earphones seemed to suit his mood perfectly. He sang louder and louder, along with the chorus until he was bellowing the words out and amusing passers-by. He and Brandon Flowers were the same, they had soul, but they weren't soldiers.

Today, he noted, he felt utterly content again. He wasn't going to be distracted from his plan; he had a purpose and was pursuing it with all the wit and guile he possessed. He imagined this must be how Einstein, or even Elon Musk, must have felt at some time; they had a vision and although the world might not appreciate them, they knew what had to be achieved even if the means of achieving it was complex and required intelligent thought. And it was such fun! More than he'd ever imagined. If people out there knew how gratified they'd feel, actually planning and plotting the perfect revenge, then they'd give up all that mindfulness rubbish every time someone wronged them. They wouldn't turn the other cheek. But most people were lazy; they'd rather whinge on social media than actually do something about it. Well fortunately he wasn't most people. A traffic warden walked past and checked the meters of cars where other drivers had taken stupid, stupid risks.

'You won't get me that way,' he murmured as he smiled at the warden. Nope, they'd never find him on as simple a mistake as a parking charge or a broken tail light, the way they did on films. Imagine the great Al Capone being caught out by a stupid tax return. Nope, his number plate would never go through any cameras and his shoeprint would never be found at any scene. Anyone caught out by these things nowadays pretty much deserved captivity. These people were so dim they wouldn't exactly be contributing to society in any other way if they were free. Target2 was still sitting outside the pub where he'd been for over two hours now; one of his group got up to buy the next round but he held his hand up to decline another drink. At last, that meant Target2 had to be leaving the bar soon and the reconnaissance mission could begin properly.

He planned to follow Target2 home and check out the streets nearby. It was this sort of attention to detail that would protect him. From the opposite side of the street he watched his prey walk to the bus stop and check his phone; this was good. It would be easy to follow a bus unnoticed, and at this time of night he wouldn't have a million drivers behind him screeching their horns every time he stopped behind the bus or allowed it to go in front of him. It was almost too easy, he thought as he got back into his van.

He followed the bus through the streets of the city until it stopped at the edge of a 1950s housing estate in the eastern suburbs; tourists never got to see this end of town, where locals actually lived. The style of house with its well-tended garden and flowery curtains suggested that Target2 probably lived with his parents – not such a big shot after all are you? Still, this was a good spot. It had real potential. He parked up and, keeping his distance, followed his prey. An elderly man walked past with his dog, so he struck up a polite conversation and strolled with him asking about the area. If his prey turned round now, he'd see nothing more than two geezers and a mongrel chewing the fat about local history and picking up dog shit. His prey turned off into an alleyway.

'Where does that lead to?' he asked his dog-owning accomplice. The man explained it was just a shortcut to the other side of the estate, but he'd never risk going down there alone.

'The kids keep smashing the street lights and the council never bother fixing them. You can't see a thing down there.'

'Well, he looked as if he could handle himself anyway,' he replied wondering how much more perfect tonight could get; he had his target, location and getaway route. A bike would fit easily down that alleyway; now he just needed to acquire his weapon of choice. He had one more stop-off to make and then it would be back to the bedsit and time for a bit of online shopping.

# Chapter Fourteen

*Saturday, 23 May*

Waking with Philip alongside her felt odd; a bit like when you first wake up in a hotel room and know that the windows are in the wrong place and the bed isn't yours but you can't quite work it out. At first it just seemed that the space in her bed had shrunk, and it wasn't until Philip slung his arm over her and pulled her closer that she remembered why. She gave his hand an affectionate squeeze and crept out from under his hold.

Taking her clothes into the bathroom, she got dressed in the "uniform" she preferred when it started to get hot, a free flowing linen tunic that Karl had once called her tent-dress – so cheeky. She smoothed the fabric down, wondering whether the clothes Karl had chosen for Philip had worked, whether he'd looked the part. She wondered what the women he was networking with were like and what they wore. Did they wear those impossibly high heels and shift dresses that hugged every curve? Did they worry about losing their figures? She'd never been thin, so didn't really have a figure to lose. Figures required some level of self-restraint that she'd never enjoyed or practiced.

Her husband used to admire her love of life; voluptuous in every way – that's how he'd described her: gloriously, abundantly voluptuous. She recalled those words and wondered whether his taste had changed since then. And for that matter, whether hers had.

There'd been no response from Josh last night so Maxie planned to drive straight to Stanmer and then to the station where she'd arranged a meeting with McAlister.

Georgina was going to join her after that to make her statement. Philip didn't stir as she whispered a goodbye then crept down the stairs. She was glad of that as she hadn't quite decided whether to tell him the truth about her day's agenda if he asked. She looked at him, still dead to the world. He was probably exhausted after all that networking – being nice to people all day would have worn her out that's for sure.

To her relief, a text came through just as she was starting up the car: *Have info on hdlss man.*

There was a chance she'd have a name and Georgina's statement by this afternoon. Her heart seemed to have taken residence in her throat as she paced the reception waiting for Josh to emerge. She recognised the receptionist as having been on duty the last time she was here and asked politely where Josh was. The receptionist told her that he was "rushed off his little tootsies" with last minute wedding crises. Maxie could imagine him using those exact words but really needed him to hurry up so sent him a message to say she was waiting.

She fidgeted in her seat in the calm foyer as waiters and bar staff zigzagged across her on autopilot. She couldn't help but scan each of them, but there was no one she'd describe as particularly tall – despite everyone's obsession with being unique and different, she found it amazing how many people would just be described as "average" when push came to shove. When Josh appeared, rushing towards her with his folders tucked under his arm, the flush of excitement on his face told her she'd been right, that he'd thoroughly enjoyed his crisis.

'Talk about bridezillas,' he declared as he approached her.

'I'd rather not if you don't mind,' replied Maxie.

He took the hint and led her to a quiet corner of the

hotel bar, pulling out the photograph Maxie had emailed over. 'Okay, your Headless Tall Man – I'm sorry but he wasn't the one who started the fight.'

'You know this for sure?' asked Maxie getting a nod in response.

'Who is he then?' she continued. 'The guest I've spoken to from that wedding doesn't recognise him.'

Josh frowned. 'Why are you so interested in him? He wasn't the jilted guy and he didn't start the fight.'

Maxie decided it was time to confide in Josh so told him most of the truth leaving out Georgina's identity and the exact nature of the attack, after all, now that Georgina was officially reporting it, he'd be getting a visit from the police, anyway.

'I didn't imagine this was about something so awful,' he said sadly. 'I've worked in this hotel for over seven years, as a waiter and barman before I eventually got this job. I've seen so many aspects of human nature play out but never anything like this.'

Maxie had to prompt Josh out of his thoughts. 'Headless Man?' He shook himself back to the moment.

'He's one of the casual staff brought in for the event. We usually need extra people so call them in as and when. They have to wear their own white shirt but we give them that tie you can just see stuffed in his pocket. He shouldn't really have been on that side of the bar so I imagine his shift had finished.'

Maxie hadn't noticed the tiny scarp of tie before but was grateful Josh had.

'Tell me you know who he is,' she said.

'One of these.' Josh handed her half a dozen job applications. It wasn't a huge number of people to look through but Maxie wished for once, someone could give her a straight answer. She started skimming the pages.

'There are a lot of students here.'

'That's where our casual staff generally come from, especially after the exams which is great because that's usually when all the weddings are.'

Maxie pulled out one of the applications. 'What do these little squiggles and numbers mean on this guy's?'

'It's his outstanding info. Technically they're employed by the temp agency so they do the passport checks but we ask to see them when they arrive for duty, just to be sure.'

'And this one didn't bring ID?'

'It looks like he had a railcard but that's not enough for the rules.'

'So, on the night of the wedding, there was someone here who no one knew? Does that happen often? Surely it's illegal?'

'We do our best, but people get ill or don't turn up when they've said they will. We have to find replacements at the last moment and if they don't bring their ID on the night, we turn a blind eye. They don't get paid until we see it so they usually bring it in the next day. There's rarely a problem.'

'Did you eventually get this guy's ID?'

Josh promised to check with HR and her mind moved to the next question forming.

'How do casual staff get to and from the hotel?' she asked. 'I don't imagine they can all afford a car and buses don't come all the way up here.'

Josh explained that they had a minibus to ferry evening staff to and from the city centre. After that they had to make their own way home.

'So, when does this bus leave?' Maxie pounced. 'And was he on it?'

She imagined she was pushing things with Josh but she had to keep going. He knew now that this wasn't just an episode of *Criminal Thoughts* and that he wasn't going to be on the podcast. Worse than that, his venue might be investigated for employing people illegally as well as the attack. He'd lost the spark he had when it was all just gossip and she could see he knew this was serious.

'I'm sorry,' he muttered. 'I just don't check on them when they finish their shift.'

'I know, and it's not your fault,' said Maxie. 'But didn't you say that the CCTV in the car park was still working that night? Why don't I look through it and see if I can spot this guy getting on the bus when it leaves?'

'I'm not sure I should be doing that?' he replied.

'I'm only looking for that one person,' said Maxie. 'I have a meeting with the police later today and if I can rule him out, it'll save them going through it. What would you rather? Me having a little look, nice and private, or the police turning mob-handed with warrants for all your guests to see?'

Josh shrugged and led her to a small room where the CCTV screens were displayed on a large desk.

'If I get into trouble for this ...'

'You'll be in more trouble if they find out you're employing people without the right ID. I'm sorry, Josh, but you know how serious this attack is. If I can rule the staff member out before the police are properly involved, then you'll be in the clear. I won't tell anyone about seeing the CCTV,' replied Maxie crossing her heart.

He found the footage from the night of the wedding then left the room and Maxie started going through it. By God, it was tedious. Even fast forwarding through the grainy images was enough to have her eyeballs bulging from their sockets. And it had been of no help either. She watched the minibus load with cheerful men and women at least twenty minutes before Georgina was attacked. It wasn't hard to spot the now not headless man; he had to duck to get into the van but he definitely did get in and so wasn't on the grounds when it had happened. Unless he'd got off the bus and run back to the hotel, which was highly unlikely as he'd have drawn too much attention to himself. A dead end. Short of quizzing every single man at the wedding, she wasn't sure where she could go next. Maybe Andrew had something for her? It was time to leave for her appointment with McAlister, so she left Josh a note, thanking him, and headed out of the building.

When Maxie arrived at the station later that afternoon, she was told the chief inspector had been delayed and was invited to rearrange their session for the following day or to wait. Maxie silently screamed at yet another person on a different speed to herself, but she had no choice so chose the latter and loitered around the reception. She tried Andrew's number to let him know she was in the building but again there was no answer. There was nothing to do but wait.

As she sat, she noticed the rhythm of the place and wondered whether their two worlds could find a harmony of sorts, whether a collaboration could get results. There was a pace and bonhomie between the officers that appealed to her and convinced her even more that she could make this work – it seemed to match the urgency that she felt right now. McAlister's secretary eventually approached her and led her to a waiting area directly outside the chief inspector's office, saying she was just finishing a call and would be out shortly. Maxie used the time to send a text to Rachel, checking that Georgina was still coming in today. The reply said she was, but that she was stopping off at the church first to get some strength. A believer's version of Dutch courage, thought Maxie.

The door opened and McAlister appeared with hand outstretched.

'So, you have the first draft of the collaboration proposal?' she said, showing Maxie into her office and sitting down at an enormous meeting table, directing her to a chair on the opposite side. The set-up was almost a cliché in power play. Everyone had to know by now that where you sat in a meeting revealed your attitude and McAlister had them sitting in what was known in behavioural studies as the "competitive position". The desk was a barrier between them, designed to show that she was in charge and negotiating would only happen under her rules. As long as she knew the game, she could play it.

'I do, but I came here today to get your views so that the final draft is in itself collaborative. There's no point this just being my thoughts – you are, after all, the expert in catching criminals and I'm just the academic. Please tell me everything you want this to be.'

She knew that someone of McAlister's intelligence could see this flattery for what it was but knowing the person in front of you was keen never did anyone any harm. Maxie moved her chair to sit alongside the chief inspector – the co-operator position – and taking out a notepad and pen from her briefcase, sat poised ready to write. McAlister raised her perfectly arched eyebrows but then laughed and pushed back in the chair, crossing her legs – towards Maxie, she noted.

'That would be extremely helpful, thank you.'

McAlister proceeded to list the elements she was particularly looking for. Maxie scribbled her notes but knew as she wrote that her proposal covered pretty much all of this – the data analysis, the training and the cybercrime research in particular. When the chief inspector finished speaking, she stood up and held out her hand. Maxie promised to have the whole package ready for her approval by the end of summer.

'Then we can start collaborating,' she added as she held the chief inspector's grip.

'Talking of which, how is the young woman you mentioned?' McAlister asked, beginning to nudge Maxie towards the door.

'Good news, she's coming in to report it, but we still need your help and expertise and it's rather urgent now,' Maxie replied. 'It's come to light the rapist may have filmed the attack and I've asked Andrew if he could see if there's a chance your digital team picked it up anywhere? If there is, it might be our best chance of finding him after so much time has lapsed. I just can't rest knowing there's someone out there who might do it again. I imagine you hate that feeling too?'

'We have to get used to it – if that doesn't sound too defeatist – but it's harder when we know they've done it, and we just don't have the evidence to convict,' she replied pointedly.

'And this might not be enough evidence to find the attacker never mind convict him,' Maxie conceded. 'But I'm clinging on to the hope that this guy is already on your radar and maybe it will be that final nail in his coffin. Is there anything else you can do, Chief Inspector, anything at all?'

Maxie stood like an immoveable object until McAlister nodded and went back to her desk to call her secretary in. At her request she called for Andrew who appeared in less than ten minutes looking as if he'd been summoned to see the headmaster.

'As DS Dawson has already started an investigation,' said McAlister making it very clear that he shouldn't have done this, 'then he has permission to continue. When the young woman comes in to make her statement, we can formalise it.'

McAlister then made some noises about offering the professor "their full support" before politely dismissing the duo.

Maxie followed Andrew back to his desk and pulled up a chair to sit alongside him. She watched as he showed her the email he'd sent to his colleague with details of the attack.

'An email? Is that it?'

'You heard the chief – I shouldn't have even done that, and they'll get back to me if there's anything,' replied Andrew.

Maxie instantly regretted what she'd said and dug her fingernails into the palms of her hands rather than scream out her frustration.

'I'm sorry. I know how swamped you all are here, I'm just afraid for her. When do you think they'll reply?' she asked, sighing.

'I've told the team it's urgent and asked them to prioritise it as a favour. Trust me, they will investigate it and we'll know by tomorrow if they've found anything.'

Maxie calmed herself down.

'There is another angle,' she said. 'The hotel weren't checking the temp staff before they began their shifts. I don't suppose you've got a wave of crime linked to waiters or bar staff, have you?'

'Only wage docking.'

They sat quietly for a couple of minutes as an unspoken truce formed.

'Look,' said Andrew. 'The first thing we need is that statement and I promise you, I will give this everything I have. I'll let everyone know the chief has fast-tracked this one and we'll throw all we can behind it.'

Maxie nodded her thanks as one of Andrew's colleagues approached him and told him he was needed urgently. He leant over to whisper in Andrew's ear and the almost imperceptible glance in Maxie's direction told her this was something she needed to know about.

'There's been an incident at a church in Southsands,' he explained, turning to look at her.

Maxie's entire body went cold. 'Which church?'

'The very orthodox one on Ditchfield Road.'

The room was spinning, and Maxie felt sick with dread. Andrew stood up, grabbing his jacket and badge.

'I'm sorry,' he said. 'I have to go.'

'Please, that's Georgina's church. You have to take me with you,' begged Maxie, stumbling to her feet.

# Chapter Fifteen

The blue lights and crime scene tape told her that the incident was serious. Maxie knew when she heard the address that this was Georgina's church and although she was praying that whatever had happened was not related to the young woman, it was simply too much of a coincidence for them to be unrelated. A constable stood outside the modern church building where apart from the throng of curious onlookers, a small group of people stood around a man dressed soberly in corduroys and a V-necked jumper. Maxie presumed that he had to be the pastor Georgina had talked about; he was managing to look every inch the churchman, even without a dog collar.

The professor scanned the crowd, but Georgina wasn't among them and anger started to replace the terror thrashing around her head. Why hadn't they persuaded her to report all this sooner? Why hadn't they found her attacker? Maxie knew instinctively that inside this church was more bad news and the knowledge that she'd almost certainly failed was tearing at her.

Once he'd signed them in on the crime scene log, Andrew headed straight into the church and Maxie followed close behind. He turned as if to stop her from going further but she pleaded with him, and given the chief's words earlier, he decided to let her in.

There was something about churches that made you almost tiptoe when you entered them, and despite this being no more than a large whitewashed hall with wooden chairs arranged facing a lectern, it had the same effect. The cold air seemed to shroud her body as she followed the officer up the central aisle towards the altar, behind the lectern; the vaulted ceiling stretched high above her and the enormity of the space it created added to the sensation that she was being watched. Maxie wondered if He knew she didn't believe in Him.

Andrew stopped in front of her. She watched his shoulders drop in despair. She couldn't see what he was looking at. Until he squatted down to get a closer look at the body.

Maxie screamed out and rushed towards Georgina, lying lifeless. Despite all her training and supposed objectivity, Maxie reached out to try to hold her close. Andrew grabbed her before she had a chance to destroy any evidence.

'I'm sorry,' she wept. 'I'm so sorry.'

Maxie buried her head into Andrew's chest unable to stop the tears. She could feel his arm resting awkwardly on her shoulder and knew she had to pull herself together. Maxie pulled a handkerchief from her pocket and wiped her eyes.

'He really wanted to make her suffer didn't he?' said Andrew.

Maxie looked up and to the direction he was staring. Her mind simply couldn't process what she was seeing. The altar was covered in multiple photos of the original attack, but the images chosen didn't look like a violent assault. One showed Georgina's face with her eyes closed and her mouth open in what could have been agony or ecstasy; another her bare legs and exposed body; yet another her underwear discarded among the confetti of blossom petals. Maxie was horrified as her eyes flew from one picture to the next: Georgina with a champagne bottle in her hand, Georgina lying down with her arm above her head looking almost relaxed. Misleading images repeated over and over again, and across the horizontal beam of the crucifix, the words "Every harlot was a virgin once".

Maxie collapsed onto a chair as the very will to live left her body and her mind was overwhelmed by a sensation that this was all her fault.

Andrew put his arm around her and said she'd have to leave the scene while it was processed but that he'd keep her up to date.

Outside, Maxie was introduced to the pastor, who mentioned having to speak to Georgina's parents and boyfriend. Maxie's heart sank even further with the thought of all Georgina's efforts to keep her suffering from them being in vain. The last thing she wanted was for everyone who mattered to know what she'd been through, and here it was happening. The pastor, the congregation, her boyfriend, and now her parents would see these images. There could be no question that the attack had been random now; this was highly personal. It was such a depraved act of vengeance by someone and there was no chance of the media not picking up on it.

He'd been clever enough not to post anything online as that would have left an easier trail for an experienced cyber team and besides, this was far more impactful. The images would be international news within minutes, if they weren't already. The tragedy was that no one would be focussing on the real crime. Georgina's death would be the addendum to these horrific pictures.

Maxie couldn't just stand here wallowing, she had to pull herself together and finish what she started. Around her, the police and crime scene teams were processing the church and she was of no use.

If this was an act of vengeance, as she believed, then there had to be something about Georgina they didn't know. Maxie had once heard an old adage about murder investigations: find out how they lived, and you'll find out why they died. The churchgoing nursery teacher couldn't be all there was to the young woman who'd been mercilessly killed and humiliated.

'I'm sorry you had to see this,' said Andrew. 'Her parents will need to make the formal identification but from the photo you gave me, it's the woman you came to us about, isn't it?'

Maxie snorted her disdain and then lifted her head to look him directly in the eyes. 'The one we all completely failed,' she said, anger filling every inch of her.

'I'm sorry.'

Maxie needed someone to lash out at right now so if he'd protested resources or the lack of a first-person report, or any of the garbage she could imagine coming from an official spokesperson's mouth, she'd have lain into him, venting every ounce of rage in her body but deep down, she knew this wasn't his fault. It wasn't really her fault, or Rachel's, or Georgina's or even the system, if she were being really truthful. There was only one person to blame and he was still out there. They'd all done their jobs – it just wasn't enough.

'What happens now?' she asked.

'We'll get it confirmed but it looks to me as if she's been strangled. So it's a murder scene and we'll give it everything we have. Then there's the revenge porn too. We'll get him, Professor.'

Maxie's whole body had seized as the words "revenge porn" left his lips. It was the term the media would undoubtedly use; the words that would, from now on, always be associated with Georgina's name. Maxie almost felt relieved that the young woman would never see this, her worst nightmare come true.

'Has anyone told Rachel?' asked Maxie.

Andrew shook his head. 'That's the landlady you mentioned? No but her parents are being told now.' A uniformed officer tapped Andrew on the shoulder and nodded for him to follow her. The detective turned to Maxie.

'Look, I need to get to work and I'm sorry, but you can't be here. Why don't you grab a coffee over the road, and I'll come and get you when I can?'

'I'll wait for Rachel to get back from work,' murmured Maxie. 'She should hear about this from a friend not a policeman or religious nut.'

'Good idea,' Andrew replied leading her gently but firmly out of the cordoned off area.

Maxie tried Rachel's number expecting no answer and there was none. She walked into the café and ordered a coffee. She was the only one in the place not rubbernecking the incident over the road. She knew what was inside that church and doubted that image would ever leave her. Sitting at the laminated table farthest away from the door, she took a sip; it was overly milky and only lukewarm. It was the type of drink you pile three teaspoons of sugar in and give someone when they're suffering from shock. The café might not have known her circumstances, but they'd guessed what she needed. She dialled Rachel's number again and listened to her cheery voice asking her to leave a message.

'Call me, Rachel. As soon as you get this, as soon as you come in. Ignore all other messages and call me first – please, it's really important.'

Then she remembered she still had Georgina's letter. She dug around in her bag until she found the still-sealed envelope. She paused before opening it, almost as if she were about to open someone's diary. She'd been given permission – well, more than that, the envelope was addressed to her – but she still couldn't help but feel like an intruder, especially after today. Maxie opened it carefully and unfolded the sheet of paper, noting that it was handwritten. It was in neat, careful handwriting that looked practised as if the writer had drafted it once, then again as beautifully as she could. Not that the content was beautiful. Maxie read through the details of the evening as if reading a horror story, knowing that at the end, a crime would be committed.

Dear Professor Reddick,

I want to thank you for everything you've done for me. I know that I haven't exactly helped myself or you. Everything happened so quickly and yet it didn't, it lasted forever but it was as if I weren't in my own body – it was me but it wasn't, if that makes sense. I suppose it was my fault in some way, I know I shouldn't have walked alone in the grounds, but the evening was beautiful ...

Maxie laid the letter out on the table and sat for a moment with her head in her hands, covering her eyes, not wanting to read further. Thanks to the photographs in the church, Maxie knew some of the details Georgina alluded to: she'd suffered twice and he took his time. Georgina had been right; the light she'd initially thought was a torch was indeed a camera.

I can't bear the thought that one day someone will turn up with a picture of me like that so after I make my formal statement, I've decided to leave this place behind and go somewhere safe. I can't simply wait around for that knock on the door. I realise you might not agree with what I'm doing but I'm sure you'll understand.

This would have well and truly broken you, thought Maxie. She wondered whether that safe place was Africa and her boyfriend; Maxie doubted even that would be far enough away to hide from this now.

The one tiny shard of light that Maxie clung to in this blackest of days was the fact that by doing this, Georgina's attacker had shown his cards just a little more. This gave her and ultimately the police a little more to go on. The police would tell her whether he'd spread these images through cyberspace, maybe on some bragging forum the way that big-game hunters like to display the latest endangered species they've slaughtered. But he probably knew he didn't need to now because someone would leak them eventually. This vile creature had known exactly where to display them to hurt Georgina most. The drink, the photos – they told of someone who'd enjoyed violating her. This wasn't simple aggression or a random attack, Georgina was the intended victim and Maxie had been right when she'd asserted that it had been carefully planned.

Maxie read through the letter again. She had to find out how this man had known Georgina because he obviously wanted to destroy the very thing that made her who she was. It wasn't about rape or porn ... It was about revenge. If he'd attacked her in any other way, she'd have been able to turn to her parents, her boyfriend, or her church for comfort but this act carried with it shame and suspicion. It was the one thing he could do to make sure Georgina would be isolated from everything she knew. Her family, her community, and her job – he knew she'd have to walk away from all of these to recover from that one night.

'You fucking bastard,' she uttered out loud.

An old man on the table opposite lifted his walking stick up unsteadily and punched the air with it. 'You tell him, love.'

Her phone buzzed with Philip's name on the screen.

'Where are you?' he asked when she answered it. 'I know you had a meeting with the chief inspector but you can't still be there.'

'I've been trying to help someone. She was attacked last week but now she's dead.' Maxie didn't have the strength to sugar-coat it.

'Christ, that's awful,' he replied. 'Come home, I'll fix you a drink and you can tell me the details.'

'No, I can't. I have to tell her best friend. She has to hear it from me.'

'I'm sure the police have people who can do that. Come home, Maxie.'

'No, you don't understand, I can't.' She ended the call abruptly then dialled Rachel's number again only to hear the voicemail message for what felt like the hundredth time that night.

Sitting there doing nothing wasn't an option so Maxie decided to drive to Rachel's flat and wait outside. The last thing she wanted to happen was for Rachel to find out what had happened through local news or WhatsApp.

Maxie stood, scraping back the plastic chair against the wipe-clean vinyl flooring. She drained the cold dregs and took the cup back to the counter where the assistant took it and lethargically threw it in the dishwasher tray without looking up. Maxie took a fiver from her purse and put it in the tips jar; finally, he looked up and smiled. She crossed the road and walked back towards the church where her car was parked. The crowd around the church had swelled and she could see people who were obviously members of the congregation talking to people who equally obviously weren't – the media had arrived. She wondered whether they'd also made their way to Rachel's flat – she had to move quickly. Walking with her head down, she reached the constable on duty at the church door.

'Is Andrew still here?' she asked. 'I need to tell him that I have to leave.'

'He's gone,' replied the constable.

Maxie threw her hands in the air and then simply lost it with the poor guy.

'Would it have been too much effort for him just to let

me know? I've been sitting over there like a lemon and meanwhile this lot,' she threw her arm out in the direction of the journalists, 'have probably told everyone in the world what's happened before we've had the chance to tell Rachel.'

'Woah there, he had to go … Official business. This is a crime scene ma'am.'

Maxie stormed off and throwing herself into her car, screeched away almost daring them to come after her for speeding. She tore along towards the seafront and parked on double yellow lines. She calmed down slightly when she saw that she'd at least reached Rachel's building before any of the media. She walked up to the door and pressed several times on the bell. There was no answer. Frustrated, Maxie returned to her car and reclined the driver's seat ready to wait it out until Rachel got home.

She was awakened by her phone ringing – it was Rachel. Noting the time and peering up to Rachel's flat as she answered the call, Maxie realised she'd been asleep for twenty minutes and there was now a light on in Rachel's window.

'Rachel?' said Maxie. 'I'm outside your flat. Don't answer any other calls – I'll be one minute.'

Maxie rushed across the street and was buzzed in straight away.

'Hi there, Professor, sorry I missed your calls, phone was dead,' said the young woman as she opened the door. 'How did it go at the police station?'

Maxie explained only the simplest fact, that she was sorry, but the police had found Georgina's body and that she'd been murdered.

The guttural wail of pain and horror that came from Rachel was one that only ever happened when getting this kind of news and was one that Maxie knew far too well.

# Chapter Sixteen

Nathan Hadley slung his rucksack over his shoulder and closed his locker on another shift; it was the weekend at last and he wouldn't have to put on the uniform again for two whole days. He'd still have an early start – on Sunday morning he would be coaching the local youth football team as he always did, but that was something he loved. Beyond that he didn't have to do a single thing. He'd be back in on Bank Holiday Monday but until then the days were his to do as he pleased and he intended to relax as much as possible.

He ran his fingers through his hair and checked himself out in the gent's room mirror as he walked past. Christ, he looked wrecked. He needed this time; he might love the job, but it wasn't loving him back.

As he walked out of the door, the noise levels were rising. The city felt like a volcano ready to erupt; it had been bubbling along all day long and now as dusk fell, it would spew molten lava of people along the promenade and through the narrow lanes. Summer in Southsands attracted pleasure seekers of every nuance, and the A&E waiting room would be heaving later on this evening. Day-tripper shiny red bonces and heatstroke, plus plenty with a bellyful of beer, a gashed knee, and a hankering for a fight; and that was just the women. He used that line often, especially when reassuring terrified locals with a genuine reason for being there, but there was certainly truth in his joke. The women down here on hen parties were a nightmare thanks to the constant marketing of gin and prosecco.

Gym o'clock, that's what they should invent instead of the gin o'clock or wine o'clock, like his colleagues talked about. Again he felt more than a bit pleased with his play on words; he'd wanted to be a PE teacher when he was young and still had a dream of leaving nursing and becoming a Personal Trainer one day. He could picture himself being interviewed on TV like one of those celebrity trainers – "It's Gym o'clock!" could be one of his catchphrases. It would be the title of his YouTube channel or DVD, if anyone still made or used them. It would go down well in the US. He imagined leading a class of hard-core gym-bunnies. He'd be yelling 'What time is it, suckers?' and they'd yell back "Gym o'clock". It could definitely work but it was just a fantasy and he knew it.

Maybe one day he'd actually do it. A background serving the public as a male nurse would only work in his favour. If he didn't get so much satisfaction from what he did now, he'd probably give it some serious thought.

He passed a shop window and took a discreet look in, holding himself taller and pulling in his already flat stomach; he really tried to take care of himself and always got enough attention in any bar he went in to know that on a good day, he was quite good looking; Pretty Boy they'd called him when he first started work. They couldn't now, at least they couldn't in the hospital anyway, not because he'd lost his looks completely but because they were afraid it could be taken as homophobic or sexist or whatever other politically correct bollocks the bosses were worrying about this week. The other staff still ribbed him when they went out but he was glad to be free of it at work because it made him sound like an airhead which he most definitely wasn't. His colleague Shrek had also been relieved when the order came round for the name-calling to stop. Nathan laughed a little remembering the poor orderly's joyous reaction.

He pushed open the door of the gym and those familiar smells welcomed him; the sweat on bodies and towels, the rubber of the treadmill at full pace and, making a comeback for summer, the remnants of coconut oil. In this city the body beautiful needed to be tanned as well as buff despite all the cancer warnings. Nathan changed into his racerback top and shorts, picked up his towel and water bottle then strode towards the rowing machine for a warm up. The news was on a constant loop on the screens around the room. He really didn't want to be distracted by whatever was going on outside so walked to a quiet part of the studio and put in his headphones. Nathan clipped his feet into the straps and tightened them up, holding his body upright and flexing his biceps as they reached out towards the handle. He set the machine to maximum resistance and yanked the handle back hard, sending the flywheel whirring round furiously. He kept going, all the time watching himself. Now that the oxygen was flowing and his cheeks were a little flushed, he looked less haggard. He pulled back his shoulders to make his chest wider. He hadn't lost it yet – he could definitely see himself on one of those morning shows giving viewers advice on looking better. Checking that no one was behind him, he mouthed "Gym o'clock" in what would be his presenter persona and then winked at the imaginary camera with a cheesy grin.

After forty minutes of intensive workout, Nathan left the rower, wiping the sweat from the handles and the seat; he took more time than usual doing it for a couple of reasons: number one, he was a bit pleased with himself that he'd worked so hard and built up so much sweat, but second because he was now thinking of his future stardom and he didn't want anyone dissing him saying he never cleaned up his own mess even before he got famous. His brand would be polite, respectful and hard-working; mothers would just love him. Heading to the weights area he sat on the bench and picked up a bar, adding thirty kilos to each end. He lay back and pushed the barbell to the ceiling, his jaw locked and contorted at the effort. He strained until it felt as if his chest muscles were being ripped from his sternum.

He stopped and took a long drink from his water bottle, pouring a little over his head and then wiping it with his towel; he had to be careful not to injure himself before his fantasy career had even started. Nathan sat up on the bench, his arms resting on his knees and looked around; the place was quiet as it often was on a Friday night, but he recognised some of the diehards and wondered if they had anything in their lives other than this place.

There was a funny-looking bloke in a hoodie and a baseball cap on the cross trainer who he hadn't seen in here before. He was a big enough bloke, but the guy's posture was all wrong. Nathan wanted to tell him that scrunching your body up and keeping your head low didn't allow the oxygen to circulate, that it didn't help the body's aerobic throughput. Nathan could offer him some tips but when he tried to make eye contact, the bloke curled up on himself even tighter. Yep, every inch of the guy's body was just screaming out "do not approach".

Nathan showered, sprayed himself with deodorant and pulled out a fresh T-shirt from the rucksack before stuffing the sweaty gear in and squashing the bag up in his locker – he didn't want to be dragging that stink around the bars so would pick it up tomorrow. The T-shirt was a bit crumpled but he stretched it over his body and smoothed it down. He doubted they'd be looking at the creases tonight. He moisturised and dried his hair, perfecting the casual look with a tiny bit of gel. Another quick look and he was good to go. He'd meet the boys at the pub for a couple of shorts but then get home before ten. They'd take the piss out of him for being a lightweight but he didn't want to waste all that effort he'd put in tonight for the sake of a few pints. And beside which, he was knackered. The working week was always tough but recently he'd also been covering for holidays and would be taking on extra shifts throughout the whole of summer, while those with kids took some time off. Nope, the idea of a quiet night on the sofa with some healthy homemade pasta, and the extreme sports channel on the box was pretty appealing.

The bar they were meeting in was a fifteen-minute walk from the gym with a stop at the cash machine on the way so he'd have enough for the kitty. He walked slowly along the promenade, letting the light breeze of the evening cool his body temperature and calm down the adrenaline spike of the working week; he felt good after that session and wanted to stay like this.

'Nate,' came the cry as he walked into the door and adjusted his eyes to the dim light. The Cask & Keg was as designer as they came with its stripped wooden walls and lumberjack decor. Old black and white photos of loggers hung alongside inspirational chalkings; the ones urging "Explore", "Run Wild" and "Don't Get Caught in a Trap" seemed to leap out at him tonight. It was still fairly empty as this bar didn't have a happy hour and that kept the tourists out for at least the first part of the evening.

Nathan approached his friends seated at the long high-level oak benches that ran the length of the room and gave one a friendly pat on the back. The kitty was pushed towards him.

'While you're standing there, Pretty Boy,' said one of the guys. Nathan pretended to protest but took the order and headed for the bar; as ever, he wasn't waiting long before being served by one of the female bartenders. He ordered the round that had been recited to him and got a slimline tonic. At least if he was getting the orders in, he could disguise the fact that he wasn't drinking. He picked up all four drinks at once and carried them over to the bench where the conversation was about the Grand Prix. He knew enough to agree and disagree with the main arguments about which driver or which team might win, but he preferred active sports like mountain biking and surfing.

'It's hardly a sport,' he teased. 'Getting in a car and sitting there? Might as well have the Uber World Cup if that's all it takes.'

'Like to see you give it a go,' came the reply. 'All that G-force tearing through your body, they're as much athletes as your skateboarders or whatever it is you watch.'

Nathan knew this, but the banter was all good fun and it started up a loud debate about which activity that had no right whatsoever to be called a sport. After insulting darts (fat blokes with paper planes), curling (basically mopping the floor), and the ribbon twirling thing in gymnastics (no one could contemplate how that even got into the Olympics but they had to admit the athletes were pretty muscular), they all agreed they hated dressage most of all, saying it might be a sport for the horse, but not the rider who just sat there in a top hat. Nathan joined in with the laughter as one of the gang started prancing around the table, demanding a gold medal for his efforts. Nathan picked up one of the golden coloured beer mats and formally awarded the guy his trophy. At the next round Nathan shook his head and said he had to be going. The guys protested, but he pleaded exhaustion after a day on his feet and said his goodbyes.

Outside the light was drifting away and the birds that swooped over the crests of the waves at dusk had begun their air show. Tourists and locals alike stood on the promenade, transfixed by the elegance of the starlings, hundreds of them perfectly synchronised, never bumping, barging or arguing with each other. Nathan watched for a brief moment and while the murmuration was undeniably mesmerising, he'd seen it before and would see it again. It was a metaphor for how life could be. We could all get along together if we chose to – and starlings didn't drink lager either of course. As he walked slowly towards the bus stop, checking the time on his phone, one of his friends ran out of the bar towards him and asked if he fancied sharing a cab.

'You not staying?' asked Nathan. His friend explained that he had an early start in the morning. 'Then definitely. I normally get the bus but no problem travelling in style for a change.'

They changed tack and headed towards the taxi rank where the cars would soon be lined up waiting for the late night onslaught, but for now the queue was only three to four people long. The promenade was busy with groups out to enjoy themselves but still quite cheery and civilised at the moment; a few gangs of women dressed in hen-party sashes with slogans such as "Bride to Be" and "Maid of Honour" over their outfits, and carrying giant inflatable penises, were the only hint at what might lie ahead for the city. Nathan nodded over towards them.

'Glad you're not on duty tonight?'

'Too right,' replied his mate. 'Who'd want to be out in this?'

# Chapter Seventeen

'I was sorry to hear about that girl,' said the manager at the studio.

Maxie nodded. More than a fortnight had passed and now Georgina was only "that girl". Her death had coincided with some political scandal later in the evening so although the local media were still interested, it hadn't even made national news; she was gone and forgotten. Not if Maxie could help it. Craig persuaded her that the best way to keep the case in the public eye was to go with the revenge porn angle.

Although she detested the fact that everyone seemed obsessed with this, she knew her co-presenter was probably right and she could only remind the population what had actually happened if she kept talking and they kept listening.

A cauldron of emotions was still swirling around in her brain and her gut but there was only one in her heart and that was deep, deep sadness. She'd wanted to help Georgina so badly and now she'd failed. Whoever did this had been clever in not distributing the images online. The sophisticated systems the police use would have led them to the perpetrator by now and although they'd deny it, the force loved nothing better than showcasing their cybercrime techniques. They certainly seemed to enjoy tracking online criminals more than a bloke with a Polaroid – even if he was a murderer.

She had to dig deeper into Georgina's past to find this person, but she couldn't contact the family. Andrew had warned her that Georgina's parents had asked for complete privacy so that their daughter could rest in peace and they hadn't made any statements at all. Maxie could understand that in one way, but she was frustrated by not being able to talk to them. Andrew had assured her that the investigation would be thorough and with McAlister's approval, had promised to keep her completely in the loop if they had any news.

Maxie's temples were pounding with the frustration that seemed lodged there. A heavy thought was weighing her down. She knew it was wrong but she just couldn't help herself from thinking it. That the system seemed to have failed Georgina and all she wanted to do right now was find the bastard who'd hurt that girl and deliver some people's justice of her own.

Philip now knew what she was involved in but despite his protests that she was out of her depth, Maxie was not going to give up any time soon. She rang Andrew several times a day for an update on the official investigation and refused to stop her own line of enquiry.

Tonight, although her heart wasn't really in it, the professor knew she had an outlet here so she cleared her mind ready to sit in front of the mic. She could at least get everyone in the county looking for this bastard.

She walked into the studio which was quite a grand name for a poky box room.

'Evening, Professor,' said the sound technician as she walked up to join Craig.

Their podcast was growing and more and more listeners were tuning in each week. The technician had been a godsend, teaching them both so much about creating a format that was professional and entertaining. Thanks to Craig's contacts, they'd been featured in the local press as one to listen to and although they were both learning as they went, the listeners seemed to enjoy it. Interest in the criminology course also seemed to be growing, so the university encouraged the podcast and shared it on all their social media accounts. Maxie couldn't believe how much interest people around her seemed to show in it although it was yet another bone of contention between her and Philip, coming as it had when he'd been at a real low spot.

'So, you're a "podcast star" now, are you? Is being an esteemed university professor not enough for you? It's as if the gods have decided to shine on you as much as they're shitting on me,' he'd said when one of the papers had featured the show.

'Things come in three's,' she'd replied. 'Karl got his place at university, I've got this, and now it's your turn. I'm sure you'll get a huge fabulous job offer but then maybe you'll just win the lottery as well and tell them all to sod off.'

He'd stormed out of the room, leaving her wondering what to do. The university would expect her to keep it going and when his mood improved, Philip would claim he hadn't meant her to stop. Maxie kept working with Craig to make the podcast more popular but didn't talk about it at home and although Karl told her what he thought about each episode, she knew Philip never listened to any of them.

Craig Johnston had covered the crime desk of the local paper for years and knew who to call upon whatever crime they were discussing. Now in his late fifties, he'd built his career alongside many of the police force so had a few contacts among retired cops. He occasionally got the inside story on investigations for the podcast but that was rare now as the police force worked harder to control the information that reached the public. Craig, like Maxie, had been surprised by the audience figures the show was getting and had transformed his appearance in the months she'd known him. He volunteered for any interviews they were asked to do and, eager to capitalise on his position as a local celebrity, he'd had his teeth whitened and his hair darkened.

As Maxie approached him, she noticed that his eyebrows had been plucked and his eyelashes seemed to frame his bright blues eyes a little more. She smiled to herself. Why the hell not make the most of it, life was short. For some people, far too short.

'You look well,' she said and watched him subconsciously smooth his eyebrows. 'Who have we got tonight?'

'Let's just say this one is going to get them listening,' he replied.

Then, as if on cue, their guest marched onto the set. The tall, uptight woman, her blonde hair in a tight bun and her trouser suit immaculate, walked like someone who intended to give orders and be obeyed. Maxie saw the technician subconsciously retreat a step and tip his head a little, as if doffing a cap, when she passed by.

Lucy Bauken, an ex-politician who'd been forced to resign from her own right-wing party, was well known for her black and white view of life. She now made a living by offending practically everyone she came across, particularly anyone she regarded as having "wet liberal values" or what another person might call a "balanced perspective on life". It was bad enough listening to Bauken's opinions when you weren't personally involved in the case but tonight Maxie would have to use all her strength and reserve to resist throttling the woman.

All three took their places, the studio hushed, and the show began with Craig saying how he was as horrified as everyone else by what had happened especially since someone had gained crime-scene footage and had tweeted an image of Georgina's dead body but with her face pixelated out. Maxie hadn't known about this and could have screamed out loud there and then. She wanted to rush to the computer and tear out every cable so they couldn't broadcast this poor woman's life as entertainment to the world but that would make no difference, it was already out there. She dug her fingernails hard into the palms of her hands until their sharpness left tiny wounds; she could look at them at any time during the recording and seeing the scars, feeling that pain, she'd remember the real purpose of tonight's show.

'So, let's start with our resident expert, Professor Reddick,' said Craig. 'Can you remind us what the law actually states with regard to revenge porn? It's not strictly a new law is it?'

Maxie cleared her throat and began calmly. 'I think we all need to remember that the real crime here is the horrific murder of a young woman and we need to find out who was responsible.'

'That's very true and I know the police have committed their full resources to that – but what about the revenge porn? It's been a crime for some time, hasn't it?'

Craig had said he was going to stick to the subject of the show until the end when she could make her real point. She nodded at him and answered his question.

'Yes it has. We do tend to think of this as a new offence but it's been illegal to distribute private material without the other person's consent since the 1998 Malicious Communications Act but in 2015, the law went a step further by making the sharing of images without consent a specific sexual offence.'

She reached down and took a drink of water, willing the prickle behind her eyes to quell. If she stuck to the facts, she might just be okay.

'Under this new legislation – and by the way, I think

calling it porn is entirely inappropriate – the sharing of private sexual materials without consent and with the purpose of causing embarrassment or distress can result in up to two years in prison.'

She had said the whole sentence without breathing once and now exhaled, relieved to have got through the opening of the show. She lifted her head to see Bauken shaking hers in disgust.

'Absolute twaddle,' said Bauken in her clipped voice. 'That we should waste taxpayer's money and overburden the prison service even further because someone has a change of mind. What sort of person allows themselves to be photographed in that position in the first place?'

'Surely, you understand that when some pictures are taken, the person is usually in a relationship and isn't thinking of what's going to happen when the relationship ends,' replied Craig, looking quite excited about the controversial debate inflaming the show.

'And that's what we've come to, is it? A nation that puts people in prison when their girlfriend or boyfriend change their mind? In my view we should be imprisoning the so-called victim for being so stupid as to have their privates filmed in the first place. All actions have consequences and if this country brought back national service for young people, they might start to understand that.'

'Imprison the victim?' Craig leaned into the mic and lowered his voice. 'Okay, everyone out there, let's hear what you all have to say about that. Get onto Twitter and give us your views. Professor, what do you think?'

Maxie sat silently for a millisecond knowing that on radio or podcasts, silence was terrifying for the production team. Craig watched her and she saw the panic forming behind his eyes as he opened his mouth to speak. She held up the palm of her hand to stop him.

'It is completely unacceptable for us to use this case as an example of revenge porn as this was a violent attack and then murder.'

Craig opened his mouth to interrupt her. She leaned over and switched off his mic.

'Let me finish. If you insist that it is what we are here to discuss then I will say this. I may not understand why people take private pictures of each other, but I completely respect their right to do so. I also know that some images and videos exist because they were taken without consent in the first place – it isn't difficult to do. How and why they exist is not the issue. The issue is that the images were never intended to be circulated because they were *private.*'

'Private?' barked Bauken. 'There's grass in the background of these, how can it be private to display yourself in a public park or somewhere similar? There could never be a set of pornographic images of me out there for people to balk at – simply because I wouldn't do something like that. I repeat, do we have to legislate for stupidity?'

For a fleeting moment, Maxie couldn't help but wish Georgina's attacker would find his way to Bauken and make her regret her words. She shook the thought away. No matter how horrific this woman and her views, no one deserved that. She continued to try to give the reasoned argument without being drawn into Bauken's agenda.

'When a person decides to distribute private pictures without consent, their sole intent is to hurt their victim. It's no different to picking up a knife and plunging it into them, they've chosen a weapon and they've used it to destroy another human being.'

'Oh poppycock. If you'd been at the other end of a knife in combat like our brave forces ...'

'Will you shut your mouth and listen,' snapped Maxie,

getting silence from Bauken and a solitary handclap from the technician in his booth. 'It's obvious there was no consent here. A person's life has been destroyed. We live in a world where this act can never go away. It will live on in cyberspace forever. If the perpetrator had stabbed his victim, the wound would be sewn up, it could heal eventually. People would visit them in hospital … they'd take flowers and grapes.'

Maxie saw Craig switching his mic back on but nodding for her to continue.

'But with this, victims feel shame and that they have to hide away. They listen to people like you and blame themselves for the crime. I've known people take their own lives, unable to cope with the fallout. It is wrong, utterly, utterly wrong. It's a violation as disgusting as any other and I would urge everyone out there watching; don't think this couldn't happen to you. If you know the person who did this, or think you may have seen something relevant, then for God's sake call it in and let's get justice for … her.'

Maxie caught herself just in time, not wanting to share Georgina's name despite everyone knowing now.

'And I'll say one more thing,' Maxie continued, 'which Ms Bauken may or may not agree with. If you've got a problem with someone and you face them in a fair fight, that's one thing. If you go behind their backs with something like this, then hide – you're a coward. A loathsome coward and you will be despised for the rest of your life.'

It wasn't until she stopped speaking that Maxie realised that she'd lost the demeanour of a calm, balanced professional some time ago. She was glaring at the mic, pointing at it as if it could force Georgina's attacker to come out of hiding and face her.

*

In one of the many rented bedsits that filled the city, he lay on his bed, hands on head listening to her voice. He smiled.

'You can think what you want of me, Professor – it won't help them. Any of them.'

# Chapter Eighteen

After that show, the podcast listener numbers grew and the Twitter account started to be bombarded with topics they wanted Maxie to cover. More importantly, a dozen or more listeners had come forward with potential leads. Most of them were women whose boyfriends had released pictures or videos of them. Others got in touch to say that they'd seen someone behaving suspiciously at the church, or knew Georgina from years ago – it didn't matter what their connection was, Maxie had taken down the details of every potential lead. She had given her list to Andrew who said he'd follow them up, but she wasn't prepared to wait for that.

Maxie had moved into their spare room and filled the walls with a note of any and every lead she obtained. Only when she'd personally followed each one up could they move to the "eliminated" folder.

'What on earth is all this?' Philip had asked on seeing the collage of strangers' faces. 'This isn't your job, Maxie. You need to let it go.'

'How the hell can I? Would you let it go if it had been me?'

Philip had slammed the door on his way out and never entered the room again. That was fine by her. She didn't have time to pander to him right now. Each morning over the next few weeks she'd pick a couple of names from the wall and take them into work. While supervising the students' end-of-year exams she'd search online for every detail she could find and work out from their social media feeds if they were near the wedding on the night in question. Some were on holiday that week, others had pictures and posts that showed they couldn't have been there. Some were too short or too fat. But for those who fit the bill, those she couldn't "alibi" for the night of, she found out where they worked and where they were likely to be that week. She'd find out about their friends and the places they socialised. Then she'd go and find them, following them into bars and clubs. She'd get them alone and show them a beautiful picture of Georgina, asking if they knew her and watching for a reaction. The ones who got shirty with her stayed on the list and were followed for another day.

It was just past six but Philip had called her at least twenty times in the past hour and she'd ignored each call. She was sitting at a table outside a café-bar waiting for one of her suspects, Mitch Ferris, to finish his shift and this one looked promising. He was registered with the temp agency who supplied Stanmer Hall but as the phone rang yet again, she knew she had to pick up.

'Are you coming home tonight? Only, we were supposed to be celebrating tonight – remember, Karl's last exam was today? He'll be home soon.'

'Of course I remember,' replied Maxie, hoping her husband hadn't noticed the delayed reaction while she tried to recall what day it was. 'I'll be there soon.'

Damn. Time seemed to have evaporated recently and there wasn't enough of it to do everything. Maxie could see through the window of the café-bar that the guy she was investigating was taking off the apron that all the waiters wore. She stood up and loitered by the door.

'Excuse me, could you look at this photo and tell me if you know this woman?' she asked as soon as he appeared.

Mitch smirked at her. 'Nice try. It's that revenge-porn girl isn't it? You're not going to get me on that one.'

He went on his way with a self-satisfied look on his face. Maxie walked into the cafe and approached someone who looked like a manager. She told him she was Mitch Ferris's aunt and she needed to talk to him.

'You've just missed him,' replied the manager. 'Had to go and run an errand but he'll be back in an hour for the rest of his shift.'

'I can't hang around,' replied Maxie. 'When does the shift finish?'

'Not till eleven.'

'Thanks,' replied Maxie. 'I'll probably just call him then. Don't tell him I was here – it'll only worry him.'

The manager shrugged and Maxie couldn't tell whether or not he would tell Mitch that his aunt had called in – but it didn't matter. She knew where and when she could speak to him and she would be back.

When Maxie arrived back at the house, Philip had put banners up in the garden and chilled some beers in an ice bucket. Karl was already home, the barbecue was lit, and the burgers were on standby. Philip handed her the spatula.

'I didn't think you'd want me cooking these after my last attempt.'

Maxie made an effort to smile and then gave Karl a big hug.

'Well done, you, for getting through everything. I'm sorry I haven't been around much.'

Her son shrugged a "no problem" and clinked beer bottles with her.

After the burgers had been devoured, Karl went to the pub with his mates leaving Maxie and Philip alone in the same space for what seemed like the first time in ages. The silence was uncomfortable, but Maxie couldn't think of anything to say to her husband. The only thing on her mind was getting back out there to question Mitch. Eventually Philip spoke.

'Did you get the chance to speak to your procurement team?'

Another damn. Philip had finally asked her to follow up that lead she'd mentioned ages ago, with the university. She'd promised to find out how they selected consultants, but she'd forgotten all about it.

'I'm sorry, with end of term and the exams and everything, it just slipped my mind.'

Philip shook his head. 'It wasn't the exams that made you forget was it? You haven't thought about me or what I'm going through for weeks. Well, there's probably still time. Promise me you'll focus on us for just one day and find out what I need to do.'

'I'm sorry,' replied Maxie. 'There isn't much time now. The procurement window shuts at the end of June so they can read the tenders over the summer. You'd have to get the full proposal in by Tuesday.'

Maxie couldn't even bring herself to sugar-coat that information. She knew she'd failed him yet again. She'd gotten used to his disapproving looks and remarks and knew she looked ragged from all the times he'd told her that recently – but he wasn't doing much better himself now she actually looked at him properly.

'You know that's next to impossible. You're a complete waste of space.'

He marched off into the house leaving Maxie alone in the garden where she sat with her thoughts until it was time to go back to the café-bar. She walked through the kitchen to pick up her keys. She could hear the TV in the living room so walked in and told Philip she was going out for a short while.

'Do what you like,' came the response.

Maxie drove to the café-bar and waited outside until Mitch appeared. She waited until he was a little way ahead then got out of the car and started following him. He was evidently going for a drink rather than straight home. Maxie tried to keep a discreet distance behind as she watched him going into a snooker club. He hadn't spotted her yet but if she went in there, she'd stand out like a sore thumb. No matter, that's what she had to do.

There was a bouncer on the door who didn't look as surprised as she'd thought he would when she approached the door. Maxie walked straight into the dimly-lit room, filled with green baize tables and the sound of the balls hitting against each other and tumbling into the pockets. The clientele hung around the room like worn prison jumpsuits on coat hooks. They all looked as if they'd either been inside or were planning a trip there soon. Mitch had gone to a table at the far end, so Maxie sat at the bar and ordered a beer. The barmaid who served her seemed fairly friendly so after ordering another and telling the barmaid to have one herself, Maxie decided it was time to start asking questions.

'Do you know much about Mitch over there?' she asked, nodding her head discreetly in his direction.

'Well, I know he comes in here a lot.'

'Does he have a girlfriend? Do you think he's ever violent with them?'

'What sort of question is that?'

'Can you look at this picture? Have you ever seen him with this girl?'

'Woah,' said the barmaid backing away from Maxie who was now leaning over the bar. 'I don't know what this is all about, but you need to ask him this stuff yourself.'

'Mitch,' she called out. 'Get over here.'

Maxie got off the bar stool and squared up against Mitch who approached with his entourage.

'You again. What the fuck are you doing following me around?'

'Tell me what you know about this girl!' she yelled in his face. 'Tell me or so help me God, I'll pick up one of those cues and smack that stupid grin off your face.'

Mitch simply laughed and threw his pint over her.

'That's all you're getting from me, you dozy cow.'

'Madam,' the bouncer had arrived. 'Come on, let's get you out of here.'

He dragged her kicking and screaming out threats, to the front door.

'You don't want to be threatening Mitch here,' said the bouncer when they were outside, and she'd calmed down. 'Now, can I get you a cab?'

'I've got my car.'

'I don't think you should be driving – you're angry, you've had a drink. Let me call someone for you.'

'There is no one,' replied Maxie. She looked up at the enormous muscled skinhead who was being kinder to her than she deserved. 'But, thank you. I'll be fine.'

She steadied herself and walked off. It was true, she wasn't in any state to drive and besides which, she didn't want to go home. She called Andrew.

'Maxie, what's the matter? Has something happened?'

From the sound of his voice he'd obviously been asleep and at the thought of having ruined yet another person's day, Maxie just broke down in tears.

'I blew it,' she wept.

'Stay where you are,' said Andrew. 'I'll come and get you.'

*

Later, in his neat kitchen over a milky coffee, she wiped herself down with the towel he'd given her and explained what she'd been doing.

'I did tell you to leave the investigation to us.'

'But you're no further forward. It's been five weeks and you have nothing.'

'Chasing every lead you get on social media isn't going to get you anywhere.'

'At least I'm trying.'

'We all are, Professor, but you need to let us get on with our jobs. It's obviously getting to you.'

He drove her home and as she kicked her shoes off in the hall, she glanced in the mirror and saw what Andrew meant. She was wearing every moment of these agonising weeks on her face. A bag lady with sallow skin, frazzled greying hair, and a crazed expression was staring back. No wonder she hadn't looked out of place in that club.

# Chapter Nineteen

Maxie's face felt swollen, as if the grief she'd felt over the past month had punched her repeatedly in the face. Yesterday she'd accompanied Rachel to Georgina's funeral as there'd been an independent post-mortem to allow her body to be released to her parents. Their church had pushed for it on their behalf but to Maxie it seemed like an admission of defeat. As she sat with the other mourners while the pastor recounted stories from the short life of a twenty-seven-year-old young woman, the reality of the tragedy hit Maxie hard.

During the service she'd stayed at the back of the church, trying to hold back the shock and disbelief in order to study the expressions of everyone there. Arsonists like to return and watch the building burning so there was a chance that someone here was enjoying the spectacle rather than mourning a loss. Afterwards, as they stood outside the church, Maxie had made a point of approaching every tall man to give her condolences and asking them how they knew Georgina; then she either mentally eliminated them or put them on the shortlist she was drawing up in her head, ready to add to her wall.

In the week since that night at the snooker club, when she realised how obsessed she'd become, she'd made a real effort. She'd had her hair done, put on make-up every day, and made an effort at mealtimes. But it was all a show. She was bone-tired and when she'd arrived home after the funeral, her body gave in and she simply couldn't face the world. She'd gone straight to bed and cried herself to sleep.

Now, this morning, the muscles holding her lungs inside her ribcage bore a heavy ache from having spent all night curled up weeping. She was still wearing the dress she'd worn to the funeral, the one she'd also slept in, but she felt somehow stronger and realised it was no longer defeat she felt in the pit of her stomach – it was bloody-minded determination. She was going to find this guy if she had to track down everyone who'd ever as much glanced at Georgina the wrong way.

Andrew had checked up on Mitch and eliminated him from the enquiry. He'd also reiterated that she had to let them get on with their job, but she couldn't do that any more than she could focus on her own job or family right now.

As she walked down the stairs, she could hear a talk radio show coming from the study. Her body dropped a little remembering that she'd be sharing this space today, but she'd been making a real effort and had to continue. She took a deep breath and walked towards the room where Philip was now arguing with the radio presenter. She stood in the doorway unnoticed as he ranted about the relative values of work satisfaction versus salary levels. Maxie watched him getting more and more animated and she remembered the debates they used to have. Sometimes she picked the opposing argument just to wind him up. She used to love to hear him talk passionately about a subject he cared about. It would be nice to think that one day they could both be like that again. She cleared her throat and he spun round in complete surprise.

'How long have you been standing there?'

'Long enough to hear you assert that self-actualisation can't happen if the man's primary needs are not met.' She attempted a smile.

Philip turned the radio off. He tidied up his papers and closed the computer screen down abruptly.

'Don't stop because of me,' said Maxie. 'I need a shower and then I'll take my laptop into the kitchen. What are you working on? Was that an old school photo?'

'You don't miss a trick do you?' replied Philip taking the papers off the desk, putting them into a drawer, and locking it.

'I'm sorry. I didn't mean to pry, I was just …'

Well, seeing as I'm not going to get a university contract then yes, I'm going through old companies and school friends, listing where they work now to see if they would benefit from what I'm offering. The parent company are encouraging business leaders like me to mine our contacts and create a sales funnel – when I list the places my old friends work nowadays it's amazing how many companies I could have an inroad to.'

'And then what happens? You call them and get them to employ the consultants on your books?'

'It's more complicated than that. You wouldn't understand.'

Philip stood, put his hand on her back, and guided her firmly out of the room. 'Why don't you go and have that shower. You look terrible,' he said nudging her back into the hallway and closing down the conversation – as he seemed to be doing every time she tried to show an interest. He didn't seem to have forgiven her for "losing him" the university contract as he saw it, but he seemed to have forgotten that he was the one who'd turned it down when she'd first mentioned it.

Feeling more than slightly wounded by the rejection, despite her efforts, Maxie retreated upstairs and grabbing the biggest, softest bath towel she could find, locked herself in the bathroom. She stepped out of her funeral clothes, leaving them in a pile on the floor. She looked at them wondering if she'd ever want to wear them again, then gathered the lot up and stuffed them in the little pedal bin. They didn't fit and unfolding themselves started spilling back out. Maxie sighed – it seemed as if she couldn't even throw things away properly today. She waited for the water to reach a scalding-hot temperature and stepped inside the shower cubicle, turning her face towards the spray and willing it to take the outer layer from her body; the layer that had stood beside Georgina's grave. Her heart still felt as if someone was holding it in their fist and gripping it hard, but she'd run out of tears. Pouring a handful of shampoo into her palm she scrubbed her hair, digging her fingernails into her skull. It felt good so she did it again and again until the shampoo bottle was empty, and her fingers had started wrinkling.

Stepping out of the shower, twenty minutes later, she wrapped herself up in the towel, and patted herself dry.

She was ready. It was time to get back to work.

'You took long enough,' said Philip as she walked back into the kitchen. 'Feel any better?'

Maxie nodded and opened her laptop.

'Do you want to tell me about it?' asked her husband. The truth was that she didn't. She didn't want to keep talking about what had happened. She wanted to be doing something about it, but to get back to how things were between them, they had to start to let each other back into their own space. Philip was defending his territory, so she had to be the one to make the first move.

'The young woman I was helping …' Maxie couldn't say the words. 'It was her funeral yesterday. There are no clear leads and I honestly don't think the police are going to find the guy who did it.'

Philip put his arm around her shoulder and pulled her towards him in a hug. Maxie flinched slightly at his touch but he didn't seem to notice. She pulled herself away and walked over to the kettle, flicking it on and staring at it, not wanting to face Philip.

'I'm sorry, Maxie, but you have to see, that's their problem,' continued Philip. 'I can tell this is really taking its toll on you but it's not your responsibility. Let the police do their job.'

'It *is* my responsibility!' Maxie cried out, turning towards him. 'I could have tried harder, I could have taken leave to focus entirely on this, I could have begged her to go to the police, I could have done ... *anything*, anything to stop it ending like this.'

'You didn't kill her, Maxie,' said Philip. 'It's horrific what happened, but she didn't exactly help herself in all of this – she's the one who refused to report it and refused to tell her parents despite what you and her landlady advised. It's truly sad but what could anyone have done?'

The kettle boiled and steam filled the air between them. Words and emotions tumbled angrily around her head but she couldn't will them out. Her lips were tightly closed and she breathed furiously through her nostrils, like a bull ready to pierce the matador stupid enough to get into his pen. She walked calmly back over to the laptop and started typing, trying her best to ignore her husband. Every move he made as she sat there was like nails on a blackboard. He stood and watched her for a moment then started clattering around, clearing up dishes. Maxie turned away from him. She had to focus.

In her quest to get as close to Georgina's life as possible, Maxie had built herself a fake LinkedIn profile matching every job, college and school Georgina had ever been to. The website had then helpfully made suggestions of people she might link up with, people Georgina might have known. Maxie had gone through all the work and college contacts but she'd left the old school connections until last, guessing that many of these hadn't been in touch for years. Maxie scrolled the pictures of people who'd been at school with Georgina all those years ago – there were a lot of faces to investigate. It looked a daunting task but with Philip breathing down her neck, she wasn't about to show the despair she felt. She would conduct a preliminary search on each person and see if she could shorten that list.

'Who's he?' asked Philip as the search engine listed some results on the first name.

'Someone I need to talk to in connection with the case,' Maxie replied calmly.

'*In connection with the case*? Maxie, for Christ's sake, we've just talked about this. You have to let it go.'

Maxie stood up and stared straight at him. 'No, *you* talked about it and I don't have to let it go. What's more, I won't until the person responsible for attacking and then killing a young woman is caught.'

'Do it your way then. After all … what would the police know about investigating a murder?'

It would have suited her mood better if Philip had stormed out and stayed out, but throughout the day he reappeared every couple of hours, tutting at her as if she were a tiresome child, then doing whatever he'd come in to do as loudly as possible.

Maxie turned down offers of lunch and a suggestion that they go out to dinner and ploughed on. Philip made a few scornful remarks about Miss Marple before storming up to bed after the news. She continued to ignore him and concentrate on the results. Maxie wanted to find the link she needed now and ram it down her husband's throat. Her findings weren't promising; one old friend was now a record producer in London. She clicked on the link to a video of the rap star he managed, wondering whether his songs had any lyrics about rape or violence. She found one of the tracks on YouTube. The video wouldn't be winning any prizes for gender equality, but the rapper was eulogising about money rather than sex. Moreover, the producer lived too far away and he was quite famous so she was sure he would have appeared in the photographs if he'd been anywhere near the wedding. Surely, he had to be local?

'Think woman,' she quietly scolded herself. 'Whoever did this had to know she was going to that wedding. Is there anyone who knew both Georgina and Penny?'

She pulled up Penny's profile and cross-referenced those still living or working around the county who also knew Georgina; this was a much shorter list and one face stood out. She recognised him from the funeral; he'd arrived late and snuck out early so she hadn't had the chance to question him. And it was definitely him.

Nathan Hadley was a good-looking guy, the kind you don't forget and from the content of all these articles about him, you'd have thought he was a saint. Maxie skimmed through features of him coaching the football team of a local school. It was exactly what she needed. She didn't need Andrew's or anyone's permission now. She pulled up Nathan's Facebook page and sent him a private message, asking if he would give her a call. She debated making up a cover story, but she knew he knew Georgina and there was a chance he knew her name too if he'd heard about the podcast. She could see by the green dot against his profile that he was online and therefore he'd get her message straight away. Maxie waited, expecting an immediate reply but nothing came. She sent another and waited, still there was nothing.

'You might as well reply,' Maxie said to his profile picture. 'I know where you work and the gym you go to. I will find you.'

After waiting and watching, a notification finally came through. He'd accepted her as a friend even if he hadn't responded. Maxie realised the muscles in her face were doing something unfamiliar. They were pulling it into a smile and her brows were lifted as if opening her eyes fully for the first time in days. She was going to meet this guy and it would lead somewhere, she knew it, otherwise why would he friend her? Tomorrow she'd make real progress, she was sure of it but right now she was ready to call it a day. She stood up to make some camomile tea. Opening the cupboard she laughed out loud and reached into the back. She pulled out a mug she hadn't used in months; the mug that Karl had given her as a Mother's Day present many, many years ago. The mug that said "If at first you don't succeed – ask my mum to do it".

Surely that was a good omen.

# Chapter Twenty

Maxie waited impatiently as the traffic lights seemed to take an age to move from red to green. She really didn't want to be making this journey but had no choice. She needed to go into work this morning. She'd far rather be tracking down and interrogating Nathan, or checking on Rachel, but she couldn't do either yet. She was still the main breadwinner in the house, and they couldn't afford for her to lose her job too, not with a son going to university in the near future. Besides which, she actually loved her job and criminology fascinated her. Before her sister's death, she'd been considering a career in the force itself, but after they failed to find any leads, she knew she couldn't work within the limitations they faced. She joked to anyone who asked why she hadn't taken that path that she'd always had a disregard for authority, toeing the line, and uniforms for that matter.

But that wasn't the full picture. Staying in academia had been the safe option at the time, like marrying Philip and getting pregnant with Karl quickly afterwards. They were a cocoon when she'd needed it. However, as the years passed by, her research was more than just a safety net. It kept her looking at the big picture, able to make connections between cause and effect, motivation and method, and she found it all fascinating. The criminal mind was continually coming up with different ways of wreaking havoc on society and she and her research could help. Maxie had often asserted that she thought the most innovative minds in history hadn't belonged to poets or artists but to criminals. She stopped short of admiring any of them; even those who began with good intentions, like robbing the rich to feed the poor, inevitably stepped over the line and eventually harmed an innocent. That's why the Applied Criminology Unit was so important to her – she could actually do some good in this world.

Even thinking the word "innocent" brought Georgina's face to mind. Maxie looked out of the window at the blue summer sky and sighed with sadness that the young woman had never seen this day and that even the brightness of this sun wouldn't cheer those close to her. There had been a small local news story about her funeral but nothing more. The world was now getting on with life and in all likelihood, Georgina would be forgotten.

'Not on my watch you won't,' Maxie called out as she turned into the campus car park.

The undergraduate students had all left, but the research students were still around and the department heads were now concentrating on future plans and funding options. McAlister had approved the first draft of her proposal so it just needed tidying up and would be good to go to the University Board. Maxie knew the chief was speaking at a policing conference in the autumn and would want this working relationship close to finalised so she could unveil it then. That was good. It was finally going to happen, and today she was looking forward to updating the faculty with her progress.

The faculty meeting was being held in the conference room, a box nowhere near as grand or roomy as its name suggested. It had probably been designed to force people into short meetings – not that it seemed to be working today. As she'd driven in this morning, the temperature reading was already showing twenty-six degrees and it would be absolutely unbearable in here if this talking shop went on for more than an hour.

Maxie looked at the wall clock and watched the sixty-third minute tick by; she wondered how much longer the deodorant and perfume could hold back the charge of sweat cells that just wanted to burst through this stupid jersey dress she'd picked out this morning. What the hell had she been thinking wearing jersey in this weather? It had felt like a soft hug when she first got up and the air conditioning of the car had fooled her into believing that it wasn't such a bad decision. Now the heat of this July day, and the room full of sweaty academics convinced her that her wardrobe choice wasn't so much a hug as an exercise in asphyxiation.

A team took the floor to outline a proposed five year research study into the environmental and sociological causes of "tribal road rage" as they'd labelled the ongoing cyclist versus motorist battles. Maxie slumped in her chair, knowing the debate would go on for far longer than the topic had merit, purely because of all the cyclists in the room.

'Won't we all be in driverless cars in five years?' she contributed. 'Can't you just programme them to avoid cyclists?'

Her facetiousness was ignored, and the waste-of-time debate continued. Maxie drifted off for a moment until finally her place on the agenda was called out. She leant into the table and started speaking.

'In this room we have experts in every area of criminology. We know pretty much everything there is to know: protocol, investigation techniques, profiling, psychology, jury bias, and sentencing – we should be using all this knowledge. We are a huge part of this community and we could be doing much more with that extensive knowledge. Think about it, if each of you could say that the work you'd done had not only contributed to the knowledge our society relies upon, but had also solved a crime or enabled a family to get justice, wouldn't you be as proud of that as you would be getting an academic prize?'

Maxie started walking around the tiny room, stopping to put her hands on the shoulders of some of her colleagues.

'Your work on reducing knife crime, or yours on methods to improve the conviction rates – wouldn't you like to see them in action?

'As you all know, I've been working on a proposal to create an Applied Criminology Unit to raise the profile of the faculty; a team who work alongside the police, enabling the police to draw on the work we do to support their investigations. I've had discussions with our local chief inspector to try to get this off the ground and we've made very good progress.'

'Did you want to be one of Charlie's Angels when you were growing up?' The call was followed by laughter. Maxie laughed and nodded.

'Actually … I wanted to be Charlie.' She smiled before getting back to her point. 'Chief Inspector McAlister and I hope to finalise the proposal for the next academic year. If anyone is interested in joining me, I'd welcome your input.'

After the past few weeks, Maxie knew she wanted to head that Applied Criminology Unit more than anything; it seemed the best of both worlds, using her knowledge and instinct without being bound by the budget cuts and bureaucracy she knew hindered the local force. Perhaps a new role might invigorate not just her career but also her marriage. She'd have to hold meetings at the station, meeting people with "real" jobs as Philip called them; they'd live less in a purely intellectual space and perhaps, just that injection of a new rhythm and different conversations into their lives would surely perk things up and get them back on track. He might start taking her enquiries more seriously at the very least.

The room was enthused by the idea but raised the usual questions about budgets and priority. Maxie quelled the hubbub, asking them to email every question they had so she could consider and address it properly. She was sure they wouldn't think of anything she hadn't already and left the meeting in a better mood than when it had started.

Buoyed with the thought of this reboot to her life, Maxie went back to her office and dug out the good-intentions sports bag that stayed in her cupboard but had never been used. In it she found a pair of leggings and a baggy T-shirt and decided to throw off the shackles of that dress immediately. This might not be the traditional garb of a professor, but it would be infinitely cooler. She strolled down to the campus sports centre with the sun on her face and when she came out she was showered, freshly dressed, and seeing the world as a place of possibilities rather than problems. In this mood, Maxie went back to her office and checked her Facebook messages. There was still nothing from Nathan.

Maxie sent another giving her phone number and email, begging him to get in touch. To her absolute joy and delight, she got a thumbs up in return. That simple message, and the certain knowledge that this would lead somewhere, fired her up enough to focus on the launch of the new department, the ACU as it already existed in her mind.

Why should the police and the university work together? What would excite and motivate the two very different cultures? Two heads are better than one would seem to be the simplest line to use but she could imagine both the university and the force arguing they had the best minds for the job. Maxie studied the curricula of other universities, after all this was a competitive game and if the ACU couldn't attract students and high calibre staff, it would fail before it had even got going. There were definitely gaps in the justice system; gaps that angered the public. When Maxie thought about what was missing from current procedures, the vigilante tendencies of her students came to mind. The justice system hadn't kept up with the empowerment of consumers within society, and while she couldn't advocate mass involvement in criminal cases, there had to be some robust method of victim involvement. She'd hated the times she'd been told to "leave it to the experts" over the past few days and could certainly imagine the ACU taking more time with victims and their families and finding ways to involve them in the process.

These were her own crusades and if she was to get this up and running, she had to prioritise what McAlister wanted, where she felt her teams were under-resourced. Maxie left her desk and stood in front of the electronic whiteboard, rubbing it clean of all the notes she'd made during an end-of-term tutorial. Picking up a black marker pen she took the lid off and took a great big sniff of that glorious smell: a mixture of paint, thinners, and childhood. She knew they didn't actually make you high. No health and safety authority worth its salt would let them into schools nowadays if they did, but they were certainly doing something to fire up her brain.

She began mapping out the police process from the report to the conviction, drawing a separate box for each stage, including the evidence collection, the questioning, the arrest and the trial. Stepping back and looking at her diagram she could see there were so many opportunities for things to sway one way or the other. No wonder acquittal rates were so frustratingly high. Picking up a blue marker pen she began to parallel each of the police processes with an existing academic study which might just swing the balance for them; psychological profiling, improving eyewitness accounts through the type of work Leo was developing, and identifying subconscious bias in juries.

The day flitted by as Maxie covered the whiteboard in blue ink – this could really work. When Leo popped his head in to see if she wanted to go for a coffee, she was shocked to see she'd been writing for hours. She rubbed her eyes and stretched out her body, suddenly aware of how stiff she'd become and how much her arm ached from reaching up to the board. She'd blocked out the murmurs and footsteps in the corridor that would have told her people were heading to the canteen for lunch, but now it was as if someone had turned the volume up and most of the academic teams were emerging from the cubby-holes that were their offices. The volume had also been turned up on her stomach, which now rumbled loudly, insisting that she join them. She locked her office door and smiling, followed Leo towards sustenance.

'I thought what you said about applying our knowledge was interesting,' said Leo as they queued for a tray at the canteen. 'I'd be keen to work on this with you.'

Maxie nodded. She'd already thought that if she were to get this new function off the ground, she'd ask Leo to join her team and build on the interview technique research. This was something that could be applied easily within police training sessions and would be a great example of the two bodies working together quite quickly. The only issue she could foresee was that Leo, being a pure academic at heart, would probably want to study the technique for several years before venturing to suggest it worked. That was the line she'd have to tread, as many of her colleagues simply weren't happy with the ambiguity of real life.

Reaching the serving point, there was little left because

they'd missed the main lunch hours. Maxie opted for a jacket potato piled high with melted cheese and carried it to an empty table while Leo waited for his toasted panini. She opened the lid and let the food cool down, the steam drifting up in front of her face and the smell of cheesy-carby comfort as good as any aromatherapy spa; Maxie inhaled deeply, full of anticipation. She hadn't eaten properly for days and took one forkful, rolling the soft creaminess around her mouth before swallowing it. It was so good.

Her eyes were closed in heavenly appreciation of the food when the call came through. She'd zoned out of the moment and didn't notice the low-pitched buzzing coming from her bag.

'I think you've got a call,' said Leo as he arrived with his tray of food.

It wasn't a number she recognised, and her first instincts were to let it go to voicemail. Seconds later she was extremely glad she hadn't.

'Professor Reddick?' asked the voice on the other end of the line. 'You wanted to speak to me? My name's Nathan Hadley.'

# Chapter Twenty-One

Nathan had to be on duty later that evening but arranged to meet Maxie at six o'clock outside a bar under the arches of the promenade. As she stood waiting for him, alone and with no one knowing where she was, it crossed her mind that the community-minded football coach could be a front and she might be about to come face to face with a violent criminal, one she'd given her number to and one she'd publicly taunted on the podcast. She decided to play safe and took a picture of herself outside the meeting point and sent it to Leo.

'Just in case I go missing,' she texted without explaining herself any further. She got no reply and could picture him with his head in his books not noticing his phone buzzing. It would be just her luck to be kidnapped and tortured, only for Leo to realise three weeks later that he'd known where she was all along. He'd have to do. She wasn't going to worry Karl with this and she imagined Philip would be furious if he knew what she was up to. He probably wouldn't come to her rescue out of spite.

'Professor Reddick?'

She swung round in the direction of the voice to see the exceptionally handsome man from the funeral standing with his hand held out to her. She shook it without speaking, just nodding and then smiling. There was gorgeous and there was Nathan Hadley. In a couple of seconds, she scanned him from head-to-toe, hating herself for doing so but completely unable to stop herself. Like most beautiful people, although he was dressed simply in jeans and a T-shirt, he looked as if he'd be equally at home stepping off a yacht in the south of France. His clothes didn't warp over man boobs or struggle with a muffin top.

They sat down at a table on the outside terrace of the bar nearest to them and he raised his hand to attract the attention of the waiter and asked for some water. It arrived promptly and he poured Maxie a glass before pouring one for himself.

'I saw you at Georgina's funeral.'

He blew his cheeks out and nodded. 'Yeah, I heard about it on the radio and she didn't deserve that. I kind of had to pay my respects. I knew her back at sixth-form college but not very well. It was a huge place and if you didn't take the same subjects, you didn't really meet up. I was mainly into phys ed and sports and she wasn't really that type – she was quiet, always into her religion.'

'You knew Penny too – were at her wedding?'

'I was invited to the evening do, but was knackered from work. It's really horrible though, what happened,' continued Nathan. 'I saw the pictures he posted, the ones the media got hold of and if they were all like that, it's bang out of order. I mean it's almost as if this guy knew what mattered most to her, how he could really humiliate her. Like knowing someone wants to be a concert pianist and chopping off their fingers. She wasn't some party animal. She seemed like the type to keep her life so private and to do this to someone like her, or anyone really, it's just wrong.'

Sitting in front of her was a man who seemed to tick a lot of boxes: he knew what mattered to Georgina; he was local and looked strong enough to hold anyone down. He'd also been invited to the wedding and although he hadn't appeared in any photos, he could have deliberately kept out of them. Was this the man she was looking for? Was he sitting in front of her right now, calling her bluff? She had to stay calm and find out more.

'Have you seen Georgina since school?' she asked, slowing her breathing to try and appear relaxed.

'No, never. We all left at eighteen to do our own things – so that's nine years ago now. I only have contact with a few people from school. I'm not one of those reunion groupies. I mean, do you knock about with your old school friends?'

Maxie didn't and even though Philip was about to try to "mine" his for business contacts, she knew they'd find his call a bolt out of the blue. He wasn't a "reunion groupie" either. She was getting frustrated with the way this conversation was going.

'Is there anyone I should be talking to about Georgina's school days? Anyone who knew her better?'

Nathan shrugged and then leant forwards, lowering his voice. 'I don't know but me knowing Georgina wasn't my main reason for getting in touch with you.'

He paused and Maxie signalled him to continue. He reached into his pocket and pulled out a crumpled piece of paper.

'Some of the websites who got hold of the pictures, they said there was a weird phrase written in the church over the photographs – about being a harlot or something ...'

Maxie knew this detail had got out so nodded as she took the sheet and unfolded it; her jaw dropped as she read the single line inside:

The surest cure for vanity is loneliness.

It was a quote by Tom Wolfe.

'Where did it come from?'

'It was just stuffed in my jacket pocket when I left the gym. I thought it might be a joke, but it's not the kind of thing my mates would ever think of and then I heard about what had happened at the church ...'

'And realising that you knew Georgina too, you called me. Why not the police?'

'And say what? That I'd had some quote shoved in

my pocket? I mean I don't even know if it's in the same writing.'

Maxie took the note and said she'd have it checked. But was this guy playing her? There was only one real way of finding out and that was by keeping him close. It was a connection and the first one she'd found.

'So, let's say there is a link,' she said to him. 'Is the only connection between you and Georgina, school?'

Nathan nodded.

'Okay, so was there a yearbook back then or class list that we could look through together? It's an extremely long shot but you might remember someone who had a grudge against you and maybe that person had a grudge against Georgina too.'

'Yeah, we actually did start a yearbook. Mine's probably still somewhere in the attic. I'll dig it out.'

'Could you bring it to the university, my office?'

'It'd be easier if you came to mine. I might have boxes of photos too when I start digging around.'

Maxie hesitated slightly as the image of a fly being slowly tempted onto a spider's web flitted across her mind; Nathan must have spotted it.

'Don't worry,' he said laughing. 'I live with my mum.'

'So did Norman Bates.' Maxie was nevertheless smiling as she took his address then said goodbye. In for a penny ...

Having dropped off the note at the police station, Maxie picked up a bottle of wine on the way home, partly as a peace offering to Philip and partly because she finally felt she was getting somewhere in all this. If she and her husband could have a balanced conversation over a glass of wine tonight, maybe he'd explain his new company to her and she could explain why this investigation meant so much and what had happened tonight, why she felt it had to be a lead. If they could get back to confiding in each other, then her home wouldn't feel like a war zone.

As she opened the door with a swing of the hips, clenching the bottle to her chest, she could hear laughter. Maxie unloaded everything she was carrying and called out in the direction of the laughter. The patio doors to the garden were open, but no one had heard her come in. She noticed one empty wine bottle in the recycling pile and another open in the fridge; a cheaper bottle than Philip normally drank. Nevertheless, she poured herself a glass and walked out into the evening sunshine to join the voices. Philip was sitting with his back to her while an attractive woman with an American accent talked; neither of them noticed her arriving.

'You just have to keep going and believe in yourself. You'll be awesome,' said the woman, putting her hand on Philip's shoulder as she spoke. He looked slightly drunk.

Their garden faced south-west and at this time of the evening, only a small section still had the sun. Their patio chairs had been specifically positioned so that she and Philip could take in the last of the sun's rays at the end of a working day. The woman turned to top up her glass and noticed Maxie standing by the doors. She nudged Philip who turned around with a big smirk on his face.

'There you are,' he said, staggering up to embrace her and lead her into the garden. 'Sorry, but we're talking shop. This is Christine, from the US office. Christine, this is my wife Maxie.'

The women nodded to each other.

'She thinks she's Sherlock Holmes,' Philip mock whispered to Christine, tapping the side of his nose. Christine laughed then Philip, wobbling a little, nudged one of the spare chairs towards her. It stood in the shade as he invited Maxie to sit down. He didn't wait for her to join them before getting back to the conversation with his glamorous new colleague.

Maxie stood for a moment, watching as the sun glinted off the pale golden wine in Christine's glass and her equally golden hair. Christine smiled and raised her face towards the light, taking deep breaths of this summer air. In the shadow of the house, Maxie felt a shiver go up her back. Philip chatted on oblivious, but Christine suddenly turned to her and started to get up.

'Gosh, I'm so sorry, am I in your seat?' she said.

'No,' replied Maxie calmly. 'No honestly, you're really not.'

# Chapter Twenty-Two

Maxie scanned the room – it all needed painting. Together they'd decided on a tasteful, gender neutral, pale grey when they'd decorated nearly five years ago but looking round her bedroom now, she wanted to go bold. The high ceilings could carry bold and so could she.

She felt different today. Her body was lighter, more agile as if a weight she'd been carrying for months now had been lifted and she could move unencumbered. She dropped her shoulders, her neck felt long, and her face was no longer scowling. She'd spent so long in a tightly closed almost foetal bundle of anger, frustration and despair that to realise she was now free of it, was both liberating and sad. She was free because she no longer felt the need to take care of Philip. He wanted to do it himself and she could see that now. She'd stayed up most of the night listening to her husband and his guest enthuse about the potential of the new business and for a while, she'd tried to join in, but every time she commented on one of their points, Philip dismissed it. He made it clear she wasn't wanted there and being the third wheel was never much fun so she'd left them to it.

Shedding Philip's woes and finding Nathan helpful had enabled her to sleep well. It was only 6.30 a.m. but the gloriously long daylight hours of July were already beckoning her back to the job and the investigation and, having had her full quota of REM for the first time in months, she couldn't bloody wait. Downstairs Karl was already in his sports kit and was mixing one of his moss-green protein shakes; it looked vile.

'Whatever happened to a strong cup of coffee in the morning?' she asked.

'This has caffeine in it and electrolytes and whey.'

'Sounds delightful. Pop some carb-loaded toast in for me while you're at it.'

Karl brought her a cup of coffee, a plate of toast and the butter dish.

'Can't imagine you'll want the sunflower spread.'

'You imagine correctly,' replied Maxie grabbing her son and planting a kiss on his cheek. She sighed in bliss as the first mouthful of coffee hit the spot. 'Is your dad still in bed?'

'Shouldn't you know the answer to that question?'

'You think I'd have him disturbing my sleep after a session like that?' she replied trying to make it light-hearted. 'Do you know what time Christine went home?'

Karl shrugged. 'Dunno. Maybe they're still out there,' he said. 'Yakking about how *awwwesommme* the business is.'

Maxie laughed and draining the coffee, stood and picked up her things. 'Well, let's leave dad to sleep it off. Do you need a lift?'

Karl said he didn't, so they parted company on the doorstep. Maxie got into her car but sat there watching her tall, handsome son striding down the road. Philip's situation and her mood had been tough on him, but they'd got through it and maybe soon, their home would be a little easier to come home to when university started. Maxie took a long deep breath in and blew it out, her cheeks enjoying the sensation of getting every last ounce of tension out of her body – it was going to be a good day.

The academics were finishing for the holidays after today so all that needed to be done at the university was to make sure she had her notes in order to complete the proposal.

While she gathered everything together a text came through from Nathan asking her to call when she could.

'You'd better not let me down now.'

Just in case she had to yell at him, Maxie took her things out into the university grounds to make the call. Not for the first time she thought how lucky she was to work somewhere like this rather than on some breeze-blocked industrial estate. The remaining students and staff lay chatting and relaxing on the grass which was now slightly parched yellow with all the sun they'd had this month. She spotted Leo at a bench and walked over to him; she smiled at his plastic container with his carefully folded wrap. He looked like the kid whose mother still made his lunches but who still hadn't made any friends to eat them with. As she approached, he looked up in surprise.

'You really were in a world of your own, weren't you?'

'It's a place we geeks are quite comfortable in,' he replied. 'At school I learnt that when you prefer discourse to football, it's either love your own company or enjoy continual rejection trying to get people to like you.'

'Well, I'm sure none of them are making as much of a contribution to society as you are now,' replied Maxie. 'He who laughs last and all that.'

'Too true,' replied Leo, suddenly animated and waving his plastic spork at Maxie. 'Now most people think Shakespeare invented that expression but actually, it was first found in print in the play *Christmas Prince* around 1608. And the original expression was "Laugh on, laugh on my friend. Hee laugheth best that laugheth to the end".'

Leo looked expectantly at her as if hoping for a round of applause.

'That's a good one to bear in mind for pub quizzes,' said Maxie, imagining Leo arguing with the quizmaster. He'd probably have known that Tom Wolfe quote too.

She excused herself and strolled to a seat out of earshot to call Nathan but frustratingly she got his answerphone. She looked back at Leo and thought about his seemingly encyclopaedic grasp of geeky facts. Recalling the words plastered across the church with the pictures of Georgina, she googled them on her phone and found them in a poem by William Blake. She also found discussion forums dissecting the poem but none of the pontifications gave her any more insight. She presumed the words were designed purely to humiliate Georgina by suggesting that she'd been a willing partner. They'd succeeded.

'The photos would have been enough to achieve that,' murmured Maxie to herself. 'So why the slogan?'

She switched on her voice recorder.

'Hiding behind quotes? Less intelligent than you'd like to be seen? Socially awkward and often ignored?'

She knew there had been several studies profiling people who loved inspirational quotes; they'd been found to be quite gullible people who believed in conspiracy theories as much as they believed in religion. Not just any religion, but all of them at once, particularly anything they thought was eastern or mystical. Then again, on the opposite side of the argument, she'd also read studies that claimed these quotes bolstered people, reinforcing their opinions. If saying "live for today" justifies you having to put off difficult decisions, then you're more likely to have it as your mantra.

'What does this say about the man we're looking for? Had he called Georgina a harlot because in doing so, he justified his actions? He can't be religious in the conventional sense or he surely wouldn't have desecrated the church?'

Maxie kept recording, the simple act of saying it all out loud releasing her thoughts; perhaps he was religious and didn't think Georgina was pious enough? Was it retribution in his mind? Maxie thought again that this had all the hallmarks of an act of revenge. She couldn't think of a motivation that fitted this crime better, so whoever did this had to know or believe he knew something about Georgina that she hadn't found yet. Had she rejected him before settling with her current boyfriend – hence the harlot label? If the quote Nathan had received was from the same guy, had Nathan rejected him too? A good-looking guy like him could have been one of the mean ones at school; he certainly wouldn't have been mingling with geeky types, the likes of Leo for example. Maxie checked her phone but there was still nothing from Nathan. She was desperately hoping that in his yearbook they'd come across someone he remembered from their schooldays, someone perhaps he and Georgina had rejected. She desperately needed to talk to this guy again and the summer light was still fooling everyone into thinking it was still daytime when finally, her phone rang.

'Am I disturbing you?' asked Nathan.

Maxie reassured him that he wasn't.

'Mum thinks she might have some of my old school stuff in the loft. She's going to dig it out so if you want to come round tomorrow night and see if there's anything useful?'

Maxie was about to roar with frustration at having to wait another twenty-four hours.

'Couldn't we do it later on tonight?'

'I'm on a shift and it's no use if I'm not there.'

'Can you swap shifts or something?'

'I'm sorry I can't and besides, if you really think the attack was targeted at Georgina specifically, then the damage is done now isn't it? Twenty-four hours won't make any difference.'

'But what about the note you got? You might be in danger.' She knew from Andrew that the handwriting on the note had been carefully and slowly scripted to avoid any particular patterns that might be matched up. So they couldn't say one way or the other whether it was the same as that in the church. There were also no fingerprints that matched. Still Maxie sensed that there was a link here and was certain that there'd be something in his yearbook. She desperately wanted to look through it and she wanted to do it sooner rather than later.

'Nah, I've been thinking about that stupid quote and I'm probably reading too much into it. It was probably just a note some crazy person was handing out on the street.'

'We don't know that. We shouldn't be wasting any time.'

'I'm sorry, there's nothing I can do – we'll see you tomorrow.'

Maxie stared at the phone as Nathan ended the call; she'd been itching to start searching online for the yearbook and pupils who'd been there with Nathan and Georgina but had so far resisted, knowing the wasted hours that could lead to. There would be hundreds of ex pupils so it would be far more efficient and effective to wait one more day and let Nathan guide her through the people who'd known them both. But her fingers were now impatient, poised to type and if she didn't do something with them, then they would definitely start that search on their own. She typed the name of Philip's new company into the search engine.

The level of relief Maxie felt when she found their website on the first page surprised her. Deep down she'd feared that the company might not really exist but here it was and although it wasn't a well-known organisation, the website looked professional enough and explained that the company provided a "network of contacts for the experienced consultant". The photographs used were of older, greying men and women still smiling with their perfect white teeth in beautifully tailored suits. Maxie's heart murmured with a little sadness and guilt as she read about the company's purpose. It was just as Philip had explained and spoke of a world where experience was being cast aside by large corporations, where an employee's loyalty counted for nothing. She could imagine her husband reading this and it hitting home. The website went on to say that if everyone with twenty years of experience pooled their contacts – the people they'd worked with over the years – they could create a network of consultants and business contacts. The consultants were people like Philip who'd been made redundant and were now looking to start up on their own. Maxie sighed. It was a hopeful vision but she couldn't help thinking that having a contact wasn't the same as getting the contract.

She clicked on the website tab labelled "Meet our Team" and saw Philip listed as the MD of the UK operation.

'Managing Director?' she asked his picture. 'Did you tell me that?'

Christine's picture was also there and she was listed as the European Business Development Director. The UK office was a relatively new offshoot of this much bigger American concern. Maxie's first thoughts were that, as an American owned private company, she had no chance of looking up their finances to check on their stability. She really hoped Philip hadn't put his faith in something that was going to collapse – after the bank she couldn't bear the idea of him having to go through all that again. How the hell could she ask him about it without revealing she'd spied on him? She couldn't think of a single way to introduce the topic in polite conversation without fear of attack and incriminations. Maxie closed down the website and slouched forward on the bench with her head in her hands; she wished she hadn't looked them up as now she simply wouldn't be able to let it rest. The weight she'd thrown from her shoulders only this morning seemed to have found her again and now it seemed even heavier.

# Chapter Twenty-Three

'Anyone home?' called out Karl as he thudded a ton weight of sports bag on the wooden hallway floor. He picked up the post lying on the doormat and listened out to the hollow silence of the house, knowing that there was no one in but him. He'd come to expect this now; his family always seemed to pass each other by these days with each person heading somewhere different, and when they were together, it was just plain awkward. Walking into the kitchen he opened the fridge door; the cool blast was blissful after the heat of the gym. He grabbed the milk and glugged straight from the bottle, managing to empty it without coming up for air. As he drank, he watched a fly head-butting the window time after time, buzzing frantically trying to escape. He threw the empty carton into the recycling bin then picked up a magazine lying on the worktop, and with one well-aimed swat, put the frustrated creature out of its misery.

Karl grabbed the biscuits from the cupboard and carrying the full packet with him, wandered around the empty house, demolishing the biscuits and leaving a trail of crumbs as he went; even in her current state of total distraction, his mum would kill him for that. The whole place felt eerie. It was as if a plague had destroyed all human life but with still a few signs left behind to show that his family had actually existed: in the living room his dad's TV glasses were on the arm of the chair, and the blanket his mum wrapped her feet in, even when the weather was scorching, was piled on the footstool. He kept walking. In the study, his dad had left a tell-tale whisky tumbler smudged with fingerprints on the cabinet and, as if this silence was determined to give up all his parents' secrets, Karl spotted an empty bottle clumsily hidden under scrunched up paper in the bin. He picked it out and shook his head; did his dad really think his drinking would suddenly be invisible if he rammed a couple of sheets of A4 on top of it? His mum had to have noticed it. She never missed a thing. His mind wandered back to a few months ago when his mum had asked, 'So, it's serious then, with the new girlfriend?'

He hadn't even mentioned having a girlfriend let alone how much he liked this one. He remembered gawping at her.

'Clean jeans every Saturday for the past month means you're not wasting the night on *Grand Theft Auto* with the boys,' she'd said.

He held his hands out to say "you got me" and she'd continued, 'This Sunday you've told us you're out again, and tonight you're using a knife and fork rather than shovelling it all down like a Neanderthal. I'm guessing she's invited you round to lunch to meet her parents so you're practising your table manners. How did I do?'

'What colour is her hair?' he asked smiling.

'Dark,' she replied instantly.

'How the hell did you know that?'

'Coz you'd only ever date a girl who looked like your own dear mamma, wouldn't you?'

He'd thrown a bread roll at her which annoyingly she didn't give back but ate instead. It seemed like that was the last moment of genuine laughter in the house. Nowadays they all tried really hard, putting on this fake cheerfulness but there was always one of his parents who wasn't in the mood and it inevitably fell apart. It was insane. Absent-mindedly Karl picked up some of the ripped-up sheets of paper from the bin and started piecing them together like a jigsaw puzzle.

'What the hell do you think you're doing?'

The papers were snatched from his hand before he had time to look at it, not that he'd even planned to. His dad pushed past him and stood in front of the desk, the bin, and all his possessions as if guarding this territory from a predator.

'Nothing, I ...'

'Out of this room now,' his father instructed, the tone less angry and more anxious now. 'These papers are private. You wouldn't like it if I rummaged around in your stuff, would you?'

'Honest, Dad, I wasn't ...' Karl retreated out of the study, grabbed his bag, and ran up the stairs. He heard the study door slam behind him. He slammed his own door in response and threw himself down on his unmade bed; his heart was pounding, not through fear but anger and confusion. What had he done? He hadn't been prying, not really. He didn't give a toss what was stuffed in his dad's bin. He felt his eyes prick with the onset of tears and feeling ashamed of himself for almost crying, swallowed them back.

'Prick,' he cried out, but not loud enough for anyone to hear, then pressing his headphones firmly down, he blocked out the world.

He must have fallen asleep because the next thing he knew, his mum was shaking him.

'Have you seen your dad?' she asked lifting a skew-whiff headphone cushion from his ears.

Karl briefly recalled the scene in the study and didn't care where his dad was now. He shook his head and lay with his arms folded as she wandered round his room picking up dirty clothes and stuffing them into his laundry basket, then collecting the discarded cups and plates that lay on pretty much every surface of the room.

'I'd wondered where this lot was. You'd never know from looking around the kitchen that I actually had a full set of crockery – it's all up here.' With her arms full, she nudged the door wider and stood waiting for him. 'Come on then, I'm putting a curry in.'

He was still hurting from the row with his dad and his instinctive reaction was to lie there and sulk, but his mum had noticed his mood. Maxie sat down on the bed beside him.

'What's wrong?' she asked, and he shrugged. She put the back of her hand to his forehead like she used to when he was a kid. 'Hmm, no fever but it's obviously something very serious if you're getting a waft of those magnificent spices and lying here as if you don't care – still, more for me.'

His mum left his room and as if taking a stage direction, the smell suddenly was like a magic flute to his belly and it rumbled loudly in response. He dragged his body up and slouched down the staircase after his mum, listening to her wittering on about absolutely nothing; she was doing that fake cheerfulness again.

They were eating in the kitchen, propped up on stools at the breakfast bar. His mum brought the cartons out of the microwave, got out a couple of napkins, and handed him some serving spoons for him to do the honours. She reached into the fridge and pulling out a couple of bottles asked, 'Cold beer? I'm celebrating my end of term.'

Karl had felt pretty crap about the row with his dad but his mum was doing her best to try and cheer him up. He guessed she'd noticed how he was feeling even if she couldn't possibly know the cause.

'Have you seen your dad tonight?' she asked again, taking the tops off the beer bottles and handing him one. He nodded sullenly. 'Ah, so I'm guessing you two had a row?

How could she know? Karl hung his head and kept chewing the food he had in his mouth, hoping she'd change the subject, but he might have known that she wouldn't. She waited without saying a word until he'd finished eating and had to lift his head to get another spoonful. As he reached out towards the serving spoon, she put her hand on his.

'I know it's hard right now but losing your job is a big thing when you get to our age and then setting up a business is difficult at any age. We have to cut him some slack.'

'We've been doing that for months now.'

'I know.' She squeezed his hand a little. 'But once he's settled, things are bound to be *awwwesommme*.'

Despite himself, Karl snorted. Pulling his hand away from his mum's, he placed it round the beer bottle and left it there. The cool perspiration ran between his fingers calming the blush of rage and also embarrassment he felt smouldering through his body. He'd acted like a stupid kid but then his dad shouldn't have shouted like that. He wasn't doing anything and hadn't even seen what was on that paper.

'Is it going to work, this business of his?' Karl muttered.

His mum wrestled some naan bread and having conquered it nodded at him.

'I think so, but it'll be hard work. Why do you ask?'

'It just doesn't feel right, and he never wants to talk about it. He could be doing a *Breaking Bad* for all we know.'

'Well, at least we'll all be millionaires soon if he is.' His mum smiled. 'Look, you know what it's like when you just want to process things yourself before telling the world. You were like that with your exams, wouldn't tell us how things were going, and we knew better than to ask. I'm sure everything is okay. It'll just take a while to settle.'

That was true although his mum seemed to have forgotten how distracted she was during his exams. Still he knew she'd taken note of what he'd said when she changed the subject.

'I met the head of computing earlier this week. He asked about you.'

'I bet he didn't.'

'He did, said he was looking forward to hearing from you when your results arrive.'

Karl shrugged. He'd had to accept the offer from Lonsdale or his mum would have found out and at one time, staying close to home had seemed the right thing to do. But now ...

'You won't get room service like this in halls of residence,' his mum said. Then looking at the curry leftovers added, 'Although, the cuisine might be remarkably similar. Seriously though, you'll save a fortune being at home and our departments are on opposite ends of the campus so we'll never see each other except here. And it's a good university.'

Karl just nodded; he'd heard the arguments before as well as the glowing endorsements from his mum. Why did everything feel so difficult right now? The thought of coming home to this atmosphere every night for the next three years almost choked him, but if he went somewhere else they'd be devastated, at least his mum would be. He felt like a boxing referee who'd ended up in a cage fight and didn't quite know the rules. He wiped his mouth with the napkin and stood up. Kissing his mum on the cheek, he told her he was going out.

'I'd have a swig of mouthwash before kissing anyone with that vindaloo breath,' his mum shouted after him.

Maxie cleared the debris and sighed; she'd been stupid to think that Karl wouldn't be affected by what had been going on between her and Philip, no matter how much she tried to gloss over the difficulties. Why was he asking about his dad's company? It was a bit of a coincidence it had happened on the same day that she'd looked them up. She'd brought her son up to question everything, so she supposed the arrival of Philip's colleague had had the same impact on him. Maxie crossed the hall to the study and reached out to the door handle. She edged it down slightly but then stopped herself. She couldn't do this; she couldn't spy on Philip. She'd ask him to talk her through the company and his appointment as MD. If he was doing that well, they should be celebrating it and besides which he couldn't go through the whole of the rest of their married life blocking her out.

Maxie noticed the pile of post sitting on the hall table and picked it up, taking it back to the kitchen. Most of them seemed to be long thin envelopes which promised statements and bills, so she wasn't in a hurry to face them without cheering the place up first. Maxie flicked through the stations on the digital radio until she came to the one she was looking for, the one that reminded her of her youth and dingy nightclubs. Totally 90s radio; with the volume up, she'd been hoping for a bit of Oasis or Blur but what she got was an even better fit to her mood – The Spice Girls.

She bellowed the words to "Wannabe" across the kitchen. Trying to remember some dance moves she wondered how and when she'd completely lost her sense of rhythm. It had to have been stolen at some point over the past twenty years. Seriously, otherwise how could it have just vanished? The station fortunately moved on to the very mellow "Killing Me Softly" by the Fugees next, so Maxie sat down, giving up any attempt to dance. At least she could still manage to sway along to gentle music.

It was a beautiful song that she'd always loved but as she listened now, the lyrics "killing me with his words" had a new meaning and her mind flicked back to that line by Blake and Georgina's final week. How did guys like Andrew cope with this day in day out? They were just normal people, how could these crimes not get to them and start infiltrating their home lives, their families? She'd always thought herself quite tough, but if she wanted to work closely with them, she'd have to be able to switch off better than she had so far.

'By focussing on catching the criminal,' she said to herself.

There was nothing that she could do about that until she met with Nathan so she went back to the unopened post and started sorting through. She stacked one pile of mail for Philip and one for her. At the bottom of an uninspiring collection there was one addressed to her that had been hand delivered. She noted it was a good quality envelope and as she ran her index finger along the top to tear it open, she got a paper cut.

'Ouch,' she yelled as her blood smeared over the folded letter inside. She put her finger in her mouth and sucked the small wound clean. The letter wasn't on good quality paper, it was just the type you'd find by university photocopiers or any other copier for that matter. She opened it up with her good hand; in the centre of the page, typewritten, were just five words:

Mind your own business Bitch.

Shocked, she held it out at arms' length as if it would bite her. Pulling herself together, she ran upstairs to get a pair of tweezers from the bathroom cabinet. Back in the kitchen, she picked it up by the corner of the page and checked both sides. Then she did the same with the envelope, but there was nothing on either which gave any clue as to who'd sent it. She pulled a new ziplock bag out of the drawer and carefully put both bits of paper inside. Her heart was pounding. It had to be from him and this time he'd typed it to disguise himself; first Georgina, then Nathan, then her. But why? He must know that she was involved, that she was investigating. Had he heard her on the podcast provoking him? He must have known he'd left no clues and the police were no further forward. Maybe he thought that without her persistence, they'd close the case. It might go the way of seventy per cent of crimes in the county, closed without a result. He was trying to scare her into giving up, but it wasn't going to work. She took a long deep breath and looked at the contents. It was just a piece of paper – it couldn't hurt her.

Her nostrils flared with a determination that the letter was not going to put her off. In fact it would spur her on even more.

She walked to the window and looked out at the park opposite where the evening shadows made everything eerie. The trees and bushes were in full foliage and someone could be hiding there right now, watching her. He knew where she lived; where her family lived. It wouldn't have been hard to find out, but he'd made the effort to track her down. Maxie strode round the house triple-checking every door and window was locked. She'd just asked herself how the police coped letting crimes infiltrate their personal lives. Well she was about to find out.

# Chapter Twenty-Four

*Friday, 10 July*

'Jeez,' said Andrew examining both sides of the letter as she'd done yesterday. She'd gone to the station immediately the next morning. 'I did ask you to stay out of this.'

'Again, someone else gets blamed for something he's done,' protested Maxie. 'I'm at fault now because he threatened my family? That's not how this should work.'

'Nevertheless, I'll have a squad car drive past your house later,' said Andrew.

'Please don't,' replied Maxie. 'I won't feel like a prisoner in my own home.'

Andrew sighed. 'You're bloody stubborn, aren't you? I'll get these processed and see if anything matches what we found at the crime scene. He's typed this one but you never know.'

'Was there anything useful on the photos at the church?'

Andrew shook his head.

'Makes sense. No one would be stupid enough not to wear gloves and this guy likes people to think he's intelligent,' said Maxie.

'What makes you say that?'

'That quote – it's quite obscure and by Blake, a poet particularly admired by intellectuals.'

'Yeah, we know it's Blake – so you think he might be a bit of a geek, our guy? Have you pissed off any of your students recently?' asked Andrew.

'Constantly,' replied Maxie, 'besides which, just because he wants us to think he's intelligent doesn't mean to say he is. Pseudo-intellectuals love quotes. You can quote me on that.'

Andrew said nothing but Maxie watched his eyes stare upwards as if he were constructing a speech. He had the look of a boyfriend who was about to dump you, but wanted you to guess what was coming; she'd seen the look enough times in her youth to know it.

'What's the matter?' she asked as the silence between them went on.

'You know sometimes we don't want to look too close to home in case we don't like what we see,' said Andrew. He shuffled some papers then sat up straight, resting his forearms in front of him in a calm professional manner.

'I know that, but I really don't believe any of my students dislike me that much or would have done anything like that to Georgina. They're too young to know her or mix in her circles, anyway.'

'Still, I can't advise you strongly enough to lie low, and not provoke this person further. No more baiting him on that podcast. Whoever it is knows where you live, and he may have got that from the university. And Stanmer had a lot of students working as temps although we've found no leads. I'll look into it and let you know if we find out who sent this.'

'Good,' said Maxie. 'But don't expect me to stop or lie low.'

'Why is this so important to you?' asked Andrew. 'You didn't know Georgina, did you?'

Maxie looked directly at him. 'No, I didn't. I had a sister. She died ... was killed ... I'd just graduated. The police told my mum to let them do their job and we trusted them. But they let us down. They didn't find who did it. Someone killed my sister and walked free and I did nothing. I will never make that mistake again. I won't let Georgina down like I let my sister down.'

'I'm sorry, I didn't know that, but it's a big responsibility to bear.'

'I've got broad shoulders.'

'Seriously, don't make this personal.'

'It's already personal,' she said. 'And I will keep going even when you stop. No one is going to convince me that I should stop looking – he deserves to be hung drawn and quartered for what he did.'

Andrew sighed and got up to signal the meeting was over. Maxie got up but stood firm.

'Although you didn't find anything on that other quote I gave you, I'm convinced there's a connection even if you aren't. Two people from the same school and two weird quotes?'

Andrew moved round to her side of the desk and took her gently by the arm.

'Those quotes are everywhere,' he said. 'Open up any social media and you'll find another one.' He moved her forward, like a sheepdog, slowly but surely rounding her out of the office. 'I'll get back to you with the results of the letter but until then, please leave this to us.'

'I can't,' Maxie called out as he let the doors between them fall firmly shut.


Maxie kicked the dustbin outside the entrance causing a pile of cigarette stubs to collapse and rain over the pavement.

'I bet you'd get me for littering though,' she shouted back towards the reception. A couple of tired looking constables walked past the crazy lady shouting but simply nodded politely; they probably saw this every day. She had to keep going but knew it might all be too little too late. If Andrew actually had any leads she was sure he would have said something to encourage her but he hadn't. Finding the guy was the first problem but what if they couldn't get enough evidence to get a conviction? What did she actually plan to do if she did identify Georgina's attacker without a shadow of doubt? The vigilante words of her students came to mind, and she wondered how far she'd go to ensure the person was punished in some way. She simply couldn't let this go.

She hadn't told either Philip or Karl about the note and although she'd turned down Andrew's offer she needed to check that they were both still safe. Karl answered her call quickly, and just as quickly told her he was with friends and had to go. Maybe she'd get a conversation out of her husband.

'Hello, stranger,' she said as jauntily as she could. She'd been surprised to actually get any answer at all, given that he'd be able to see who the caller was.

'Hi, yeah, been busy, haven't we?' came the distracted answer.

'That's what I thought. Look, I have another late meeting tonight but I have a couple of hours to kill and just wondered if you fancied a coffee, or a quick bite, or a drink, or a quick chat, or …' She'd run out of suggestions and he hadn't reacted positively to any of the ones she'd made.

'No can do,' Philip replied. He was speaking like this all the time now and it was almost like hearing an old man trying to get "down" with the kids. 'Burning the black stuff myself, getting new investors on-board.'

Maxie stared into her handset, glad that the grimace she was pulling couldn't be transmitted; it was just as well she hadn't used FaceTime. Who was this man who was suddenly burning midnight oil – or it could have been Guinness for that matter? He hadn't wasted any time picking up the American corporate lingo.

'Where are your offices?' she asked realising that she had no idea where he was right now, but if they were around the corner she'd drop in on him whether he wanted her there or not.

'We have a primarily flexible base to keep overheads low. Big offices are old-school vanity.'

'I'm not one of your potential investors you know. You don't need to talk to me like that. Where are you actually sitting right this very moment?'

'I'm near the airport, in a hotel conference room ... with Christine.'

The hesitation made her nervous. Maxie couldn't get to the airport and back in time to meet Nathan but now, she definitely needed to know what her husband was up to. She wished him luck with the investors and said goodbye. Looking around at the buildings nearby, Maxie pinpointed The Midland and headed towards it. She needed somewhere with good free Wi-Fi and even better coffee. If the most expensive hotel in the city couldn't offer them, then the world really had gone to the dogs.

The atrium of the hotel housed a grand piano and behind that, two sofas which no one seemed to have noticed. They were empty and secluded, just perfect. Maxie signalled a waiter and asked for some coffee to be sent over then made herself at home, spreading out her belongings to ensure no one felt comfortable joining her. She kicked off her shoes and perching herself lengthways along the sofa, put her feet up and pulled out her tablet. The waiter brought the tray of coffee, which to Maxie's delight came with complimentary shortbread, and gave her the Wi-Fi code. She didn't plan to leave this sofa until she knew what the hell her husband was up to.

She pulled up the website she'd visited before and clicked on a tab labelled "join us"; an advert flashed up to tell her she was in luck, there was an investor conference near her today. Ordinarily, she hated the Internet's ability to pinpoint her location but today it was extraordinarily useful. If this was the investor conference Philip was talking about, then he'd lied to her, it wasn't near the airport at all, it was being held in a hotel opposite the bay and started in the next half an hour; she had plenty of time to get there before meeting Nathan.

She packed everything up hurriedly and popped her shoes back on. Then leaving enough money for the coffee and a tip, ran out.

She arrived at the marina with five minutes to spare before the start of this investor meeting. As Maxie parked up, then stepped out into the blue sky and breeze, she realised she didn't have a clue what she was going to do next. She'd envisaged walking into something similar to the academic conferences she attended – big, anonymous events where you could easily hide at the back unnoticed. The hotel she was standing in front of was unlikely to have rooms big enough to host anything like that. It was a small but stylish place and would probably instil confidence in any would-be investor, but the meeting spaces here were more likely, at the most, to host thirty people rather than three hundred. Still, if you were trying to attract an exclusive investor base, this place was ideal.

'Well, I'm here now,' she murmured to herself as she approached the automatic doors and they swished open to beckon her in.

Although both the hotels she'd been in today were aiming for an upmarket but welcoming atmosphere, this place wanted to say contemporary rather than traditional. Maxie looked around her to work out how they were doing it with just an empty space and some sofas. The sofas were aged leather rather than upholstered, the music was ambient jazz rather than soft classical and the staff had sleeves rolled up to reveal tattoos which she very much doubted ever happened in The Midland. Maxie mentally congratulated Philip on his choice of venue; this place definitely said new beginnings.

She walked up to the noticeboard where today's events were listed. There were only two: a WSET wine tasting course and an Investors Showcase as it was called. She noted the room it was in and went up to the reception.

'Hi, I'm thinking of holding a team meeting here,' she said. 'Can you tell me how many people the Lanyard Suite holds?'

'Twenty around a table and forty-five with the seating in a theatre arrangement,' the receptionist replied without a moment's hesitation. 'I can give you a leaflet about all our suites.' She tucked a single page into an envelope and gave it to Maxie.

'I'd rather see the room now as I'm here.'

'I'm sorry. It's occupied at the moment but it's due to finish at seven, if you'd like to come back.'

'I might do. Is it set up with a table or theatre arrangement right now?'

'It's theatre style and we have refreshments for thirty booked.'

Maxie knew she couldn't hide in a room of thirty so thanked the receptionist and said she'd come back later.

Checking the layout of the hotel and the location of the meeting suite, Maxie saw that she'd be fairly well hidden if she sat in one of the stylish leather porter's chairs in the corridor. She could see the room and the toilets from there so if anyone came out, she could pounce. She had a plan, so settled back into the seat with its high back and hood hoping that she didn't fall asleep in it before she could find anything out. She sat idly scrolling through her work emails. There were significantly fewer of them now that term was over but now was as good a time as any to get through them. She was surprised to see a response to her second draft proposal for the Applied Crime Unit from McAlister; was the quick response good news or bad? Maxie opened it and was delighted to see that she liked what had been proposed so far and was inviting her to discuss it further and hopefully finalise it. Reading the email in full she saw Andrew would be at the meeting too.

'Seems we're going to be seeing a lot more of each other,' she said to herself. 'Poor you.'

The meeting room door opened and a man carrying a prospectus barged past into the Gent's. Maxie positioned herself ready to accidentally bump into him when he came out.

'So sorry,' she squealed as she stage-managed the collision and dropped her bag with Oscar worthy acting. 'I was trying to get into this meeting, but I think it's started.'

'It has,' grumped the man, bending to pick the bag up and hand it back. 'But I wouldn't bother if I were you.'

'Really, it looked interesting. I've just been made redundant.'

'Me too, but this feels like a con. Trying to get their mitts on your pay-off.'

He nodded a goodbye and walked away. He wasn't carrying the prospectus he'd had when he'd walked out of the room, so he had to have left it in the Gent's. Maxie checked both directions and headed in, calling out to check if anyone was there. She grimaced as the unmistakeable smell of badly-aimed urine reached her nostrils. How come even in a nice hotel, gent's toilets smelt like this? She couldn't see the prospectus lying around so walked over to the bin beside the hand dryer and stood cautiously on the pedal hoping that the prospectus would be laying on the top with nothing more than a slightly soggy hand towel soiling it. Fortunately, her prayers were answered, and she pulled it out with the tips of her fingers. She heard the outer door open and rushed into a cubicle where she had to wait and listen to the peeing and whistling of a stranger for longer than anyone should. She heard him walk out without washing his hands and hoped that the guy who'd been handling this prospectus hadn't done the same.

Concerned by what that guy had said about it all being a con, Maxie decided not to even try sneaking into the conference. She had to read this brochure and understand the business model before she saw Philip again. She had time to get home and do this without being disturbed. Maybe that guy had it all wrong.

Back in the daylight, the breeze had dropped, and the bay was baking hot. She walked towards her car with sweat dripping down her back – probably as much due to her anxiety about being caught spying on her husband as the heat. She'd have to change before leaving for Nathan's. As she unlocked the car door, a food delivery guy sat on his moped in full leathers and helmet only a few yards from her.

'You must be scorching,' she murmured as she climbed in and thanked God for air-con.

# Chapter Twenty-Five

What the hell are you up to now? Do you think you could just stop interfering at some point? This isn't your cause. It wasn't your life they ruined with their sanctimonious behaviour and I won't be diverted from this course of action by anyone. I *will* get justice for what they did to my brother and although I have no gripe with you, if you get in the way then that's on your head not mine.

I could try to warn you, but you wouldn't listen. I can tell you're not the listening type but you should be and one day maybe I'll tell you why all of this had to happen. You'll want to hear my story; it's not that different to your own. You'll understand. You can put me on your podcast and if people knew why, then I'm sure they'd do the same in my situation. Maybe not with the precision or skill of my plans but they'd do their best. They might copy me; I might inspire a generation of people ready to seek justice for themselves. Because that's what it's come to. Ordinary people having to do what the system won't. That's why I'm still free, because deep down, the universe knows that I've acted justly. I took no more from that harlot than she deserved.

Tonight, I need to concentrate. Some people think they're untouchable and the police might even try a little harder with their investigations when the public outrage starts, as it will for this one; you see there are double standards in life and some people are deemed more worthy than others. It doesn't matter. They won't find anything. What would anyone report? Another anonymous interchangeable employee? Just one of thousands in this city; you brush arms with them every day and you don't even notice them.

And now, as a complete stranger with a flat box in my hand, every door in the city would open to me, no safety chain, no fears. It's ridiculous how easy this is. That's what you should be investigating. The public aren't even safe in their own homes and that's the real crime here. Don't pester me; I'm just putting some of my own things right.

# Chapter Twenty-Six

The woman who opened the door to Maxie was probably a decade older than her but had obviously spent those years in a yoga studio rather than slumped over a desk. Maxie smiled in response to the genuinely warm greeting being extended to her.

'Come in, come in. I don't often play hostess to a professor ... especially not one who's an internet star too. I'm a bit of a podcast junkie, I'm afraid.'

She beckoned Maxie into a living room that bore all the signs of having recently been cleaned: tramlines in the carpet pile where the vacuum cleaner had been dragged back and forwards, the TV remote stacked neatly on top of the listings guide rather than scattered across the room, a whiff of air freshener, and the photographs on the mantelpiece in a completely symmetrical display. Maxie's smile widened and she wondered whether, if like herself, this woman did more tidying in the ten minutes before a guest arrived than she did for the rest of the year.

'You have a really lovely home,' she told her host.

'Oh, thank you. Now, I've pulled out everything that I have from Nathan's sixth-form days and laid it out on the dining-room table so you've got room to work.' She led Maxie towards the stack of photo albums then stopped. 'I'm sorry, Professor, I haven't even introduced myself. I'm Laura – obviously Nathan's mum, and if there's anything he doesn't know then just ask me. I probably remember more of his childhood than he does.'

Maxie knew she could probably say the same about Karl, and her mum could say the same about her; you only appreciated how fleeting youth was when you were watching it from the sidelines.

'Please, call me Maxie, and I know exactly what you mean,' she said. 'Is Nathan here?'

'Upstairs getting changed. He's just finished his shift. Have a seat and I'll bring you in some tea.'

Maxie started leafing through pictures of people she didn't know; it took her some time to even recognise Nathan.

'I looked pretty different, didn't I?' he said as he walked into the room, drying his still damp hair with a towel. He was wearing glasses now and could have been modelling them for a magazine.

'Just a bit,' replied Maxie. 'The specs suit you.'

'I wear contacts most of the time but they start grinding after a full day.' He sat down beside her and swivelled the album so they could both see it.

Nathan in his early teens was as good-looking as the man in front of her now. This wasn't an ugly duckling story; he'd obviously been blessed since an early age.

'I bet he was popular with the girls,' said Maxie, addressing Laura who was walking back into the room with a tray.

'They were always hanging around,' said Laura. 'But I taught him to show respect and never lead anyone on if he wasn't interested in them as a person. Never get sidetracked and always paddle your own canoe.'

Nathan shook his head in mock despair. 'She did indeed. She always said, know where you want to go and keep looking forward, no matter what others say.'

'So, you always knew you wanted to become a nurse?' asked Maxie.

'At first, I wanted to be a PE teacher, but I got an injury and I couldn't take up my place. Then I dreamt of taking off to Australia or New Zealand and they always need nurses, so it was a means to an end. I still want to do something with sport but things drifted – I started going out with my ex and I put it on hold; that's why I'm at Mum's – we split up and I came here while we sell the flat we had.'

'So you can start following your dreams again now,' said Laura as she started pouring the tea into cups; the liquid was a very pale green colour and Maxie sniffed at it before she had the chance to stop herself.

'It's peppermint,' explained Laura. 'Trust me you'll like it. You're about to work your brains and nothing stimulates more than mint. It's fresh from the garden. The cake is carrot, but the mention of a vegetable is just an excuse to have the frosted icing. Enjoy.'

'Thank you.'

With that, she left them, and Maxie picked up her cup. It really did smell fresh and clean and whether she was imagining it or not, the aroma seemed to head straight for her frontal lobe and give it a shake.

'I've never really been a herbal tea person, but this is good,' said Maxie to Nathan. 'Now, tell me about everyone you went to sixth form with and let's see if we can find some link. You never knew Georgina before then?'

'No, we all came together from different schools into one college. It was quite a new set-up and pretty prestigious back then.'

Maxie knew the college he was referring to. It had opened with the goal of excellence and did maintain a fabulous academic record at one point but also a reputation for not standing by any pupil who didn't pull their weight and therefore risked ruining the school's enviable position in the rankings' tables. It changed after the first head left, and started to go downhill.

'What A levels did you study?' she asked.

'Biology and sociology,' replied Nathan. 'I guess I was destined to be a nurse with those choices.'

'Or maybe pharmaceutical research. I think they make a lot more money.' Maxie smiled. 'I know from Rachel that Georgina took marketing and psychology – did you ever cross paths with those areas?'

Nathan shook his head. 'Not in classes, but maybe in the canteen and probably at some parties I guess.'

Georgina wasn't in any of his personal photographs either: field trips, school events, or parties.

'Ah, she's in this one. It's a group pic taken by a friend – not very good quality though,' Nathan said, handing her the only picture that actually contained both Nathan and Georgina. 'That's me. That year the college got the best A levels in the county. I think ninety-eight per cent of us got an A-star in one of our subjects.'

'Impressive,' replied Maxie looking at the photograph but seeing only a blur of teenage faces. 'I don't think I'd recognise my own son from this. You said there was a yearbook?'

Nathan pulled out a glossy hardback which had much clearer images with smiling faces peering from the pages in alphabetical order. He flicked to H. 'That's me ... bad nineties haircut and all.'

He flicked to P. 'And that's Georgina.'

Maxie touched the picture gently. 'She was so pretty. The boys must have been interested.'

'Possibly, but you said she was quiet and shy too. Let's face it, at that age, with the hormones going haywire, you want someone who's going to put out without you having to work that hard.'

Nathan shrugged to say he wasn't proud of what he'd said, but it was just a fact of life. Maxie couldn't be critical. When she remembered back to her late teens, she knew she'd ignored the quiet sensitive guys in favour of the party animals every time.

She turned the book back to the letter A and asked Nathan to take her methodically through everyone listed, telling her anything and everything he remembered about them and their relationship with either Georgina or himself. She started recording as he spoke and simply listened and looked at the faces, hoping that some clue was hiding in these pages. Nathan began to give comprehensive descriptions and anecdotes about everyone he knew, although there were many in the book that he simply hadn't been friendly with. Maxie learnt about their prowess on the sports field, their supremely successful careers and the practical jokes that went wrong – but there was simply nothing that seemed to have any bearing on this case. Still she listened intently hoping that she wouldn't have to go back to Andrew with the finding that there was simply no link between Nathan and Georgina other than having both been brought up and schooled in the same county. As the evening went on, Nathan started to skip the commentary and simply said of each picture "Didn't know them" or "unlikely suspect" and that seemed to cover everyone.

They were nearing the end of the book with only seven letters of the alphabet left. They turned the page to surnames beginning with T and Maxie tapped one of the photos immediately.

'Leo Turner. I know him, and he studied sociology so you must have known him too.'

'Oh my God, Leo the cowardly lion. How do you know him?'

'He's completing his PhD in my department.'

'Always was a brainbox and I'm not proud of it, but the guys did take the piss out of him back then and I didn't do much to help him,' said Nathan. 'There was this one time we were at a magistrate's court as part of the course and this no-hope was up for aggravated burglary. His family were in the public gallery alongside us. It must have looked a complete circus. You had us, all wide-eyed and innocent, taking notes next to a bunch of Manson family lookalikes. The court was full and Leo had the dubious honour of having to sit beside the suspect's mother – a bulldog of a woman. Anyway, part way through, Leo made one of his intellectual comments, straight from the sociology textbook, something about the guy's upbringing. What the hell was it he said?'

Nathan raised his eyes to the ceiling trying to remember while Maxie could just imagine Leo having absolutely no social skills at that age; he had pitifully few now.

'Oh God, it was something like ...' Nathan put on a high-pitched nasal voice that sounded pompous but really nothing like Leo. '"It's highly probable that there is a dominant matriarchal figure and he is completely subservient to her", or pretty close – so studenty.

'And the mother turns around slowly, like that kid's head in *The Exorcist*, and barks really loudly at him. Just barks and barks, right in his face. She was removed from court, but he was still shaking even after she'd gone. After that, poor kid, he was always plagued by someone shouting "woof" or "down boy" in the corridor.'

Leo had once told her he was more of a cat person. Now she knew why.

'Did Georgina take part in all of this?'

'No, she wasn't there, and it didn't last very long, anyway. The college really wouldn't tolerate anything like that back then.'

Maxie felt slightly sick thinking back to Andrew's words about not wanting to look close to home. It was a tenuous link, but it was a link and it wouldn't be the first time a person had harboured hatred against his school bullies and only acted out several years later. It really didn't seem like the Leo she knew but she'd have to follow it up. He'd been at college with Georgina and Nathan and he certainly knew enough about the law to have a stab at defying it.

'I'll talk to him tomorrow,' said Maxie. 'I'll see if he remembers anything you don't. Can I take this with me?'

Nathan nodded. The doorbell rang and they heard Laura yelling, 'I'll get it,' and striding down the hallway. Maxie picked up the yearbook and edged it into her bag, ready to leave.

'Nathan,' yelled Laura. 'Why have you ordered pizza? I told you I've got some bolognese that I can heat up. It'll be much healthier than this.'

Maxie heard her politely add, 'No offence to you,' which she presumed was directed at the delivery person. Nathan held his palms upwards in confusion.

'I didn't. They must have the wrong address,' he yelled back as he got up.

'No, he says it's definitely addressed to you.' Laura appeared in the dining room. 'The guys from the hospital won't have done that thing where they have hundreds of pizzas delivered to you over the course of the night will they? I thought that was just on stag nights. It's such a dreadful waste of food when so many ...'

'No, Mum, they won't have. I'll sort it out.'

'They sent him a load of Valentine's cards earlier this year – hundreds of them,' Laura told Maxie as Nathan headed out. 'I was recycling them for weeks.'

Maxie smiled, picturing the scene and imagining Laura was probably delighted to know her son was popular enough to warrant a practical joke. They wouldn't have sent cards to Leo.

The next thirty seconds seemed to last an eternity and yet no time at all. She heard Nathan explaining that he hadn't ordered anything, asking to see the delivery note then calling back to his mum to ask for some change. There was a moment of silence and then a scream. A howl of agonising pain that didn't stop. Maxie and Laura rushed to the cries and saw Nathan doubled over on the doormat, his hands and the side of his face blistering. On the path outside, a pizza box and a plastic bottle had been discarded and the delivery guy was already on his bike, revving up to escape.

'Water,' yelled Maxie. 'Clean, fresh water, lots of it and a clean towel now!'

Laura wanted to go to her son, but Maxie pushed her towards the kitchen. She was back in seconds with the washing-up bowl full and a pile of towels. She knelt down beside Nathan, wrapping his hands and gently tried to cool down his burning skin. Maxie ran back to her phone and called the ambulance and Andrew. She returned to Nathan and taking another towel starting draping them everywhere the acid hadn't hit so it couldn't spread any further while his mother was laying a soaked towel around his face, gently removing his shattered glasses. It was a sad state of affairs that Maxie knew to do this because of the utterly horrific and very recent assault on a three-year-old boy in a supermarket. "How to deal with an acid attack" had become one of the most googled questions in the days afterwards.

The ambulance arrived within minutes and Andrew wasn't far behind. Laura left with Nathan and Maxie promised to join them later. She gave Andrew the details of what had happened but frustratingly could tell him very few details. For year she'd imagined that were she ever the victim of or witness to a crime, she'd take more notice than the average punter. She'd be able to say more than "he drove a blue car". But in the frenzy of the moment, she'd seen nothing but a leather-clad delivery driver in a full-face helmet speeding off on a black motorbike. It could have been the same guy that she saw down by the marina for all she knew; they all looked the same in uniform. She didn't get any of the registration number and wouldn't have even caught the name of the pizza company if it weren't written on the box. It just hadn't been her priority in those few seconds of opportunity.

Andrew moved on to organising door-to-door enquiries as neighbours started to appear in their gardens, summoned by the blue flashing lights, to find out what had happened. Maxie took the towels and bowl back to the kitchen sink then soaked one of the clean towels, pressing it against her forehead. It was so cold. What if it had been Karl? What if he'd answered the door to someone like this? What if it had happened when she wasn't there to help him? Her hands went instinctively towards her face as she pictured the raw blistered skin bubbling on Nathan's face. She buried her head in the towel and her whole body started shaking. She sank to the floor and tried to scream but her cries stuck in her throat and choked her just as surely as if someone was squeezing their hands around her throat.

# Chapter Twenty-Seven

Andrew insisted that Maxie get a lift to the hospital in one of the squad cars. She'd done a sweep of the house, making sure the hob was switched off, the windows closed, and the back door locked. She doubted Laura would be coming back here tonight, but she wanted her to feel safe if she did. Maxie also bundled up all the photographs they'd been looking through together, now absolutely sure that the cases had to be linked.

'It's a completely different MO, so more likely to be someone with a grievance against him,' Andrew had said to her as he helped her to the car. 'But we won't rest until we find the bastard who's done this and when we do, we'll see if there's someone with a sexual assault charge in the background.'

Maxie thanked him. She knew the investigation would be completely thorough for a nurse. The police would regard any member of the emergency services as one of their own, and while it might well be a completely different modus operandi as Andrew had said, Maxie knew it was the same person. However, tonight wasn't the night to protest the link to Georgina, tonight was about making sure that young man, and his mother, had everything they needed. Then she needed to go home to the men in her life and hug them like there was no tomorrow; because if this summer had reminded her of anything, it was that tomorrow was never guaranteed.

The neon strip lights of the hospital were a shock to the senses, not because of their harsh glare, but because of the way they lit up the pain and grief on everyone's faces. It was impossible to hide your feelings in this place. Maxie was taken to the waiting room where Laura paced, biting her knuckles. Some anxious-looking men and women, whom Maxie assumed were either Nathan's off duty colleagues or gym buddies, stood awkwardly watching her, trying to think of a way to comfort her; one six-footer tried to put his arm around Laura and make her sit down but she shrugged him off – all five foot two of her – and he retreated. Maxie walked up to Nathan's mother and simply stood in front of her.

'How is he?' she asked.

Laura reached out and hugged her, burying her face in her shoulder.

'They said it could have been a lot worse,' she whispered before beginning to weep and clinging on to Maxie even tighter. 'Apparently, it was a good job he had his glasses on when he answered the door.'

Maxie hugged the broken woman as closely as she could; Laura's whole body rose and fell with each sharp sob. Neither of them spoke, and the men in the room seemed to signal to each other as one by one they left them alone. Eventually Laura pulled herself away and wiped the back of her hand across her eyes. She nodded a thank you. Maxie handed her a pack of tissues from her bag and they sat down on the plastic chairs.

'They gave him something for the pain,' said Laura stumbling over that final word but catching herself and putting her hand on her chest to stop the tears starting again. 'And to make him sleep.'

'That's probably for the best.'

Laura nodded. 'At least while he sleeps he isn't hurting.'

They sat holding hands and the next thing Maxie knew, a doctor was shaking her gently; she realised they'd both fallen asleep on each other's shoulders. Laura jumped up.

'Is he okay? Can I see my son?'

The doctor put a reassuring hand on her shoulder and told her that he was awake but groggy.

'The liquid hit the side of his face not his throat and you did the right thing with the cold water so this helped minimise the potential burn damage,' the doctor explained. 'You can see him, but I must prepare you that it will still look quite upsetting. The burns are dressed, and you mustn't touch his upper body.'

Laura nodded as he spoke and Maxie could imagine she'd nod to anything whatsoever if it just meant she could get to her son's bedside as quickly as possible. Laura turned to her.

'Will you come with me please?'

The women held hands along the corridor. Nathan was lying in a private room. His face and hands were bandaged, and gauze lay across his shoulders and chest. A cannula in his arm led to a drip and a heart rate monitor showed a steady sixty-three. Laura let go of Maxie's hand and went to the bottom of the bed. She uncovered her son's foot and kissed it. Maxie brought a chair to her and Laura sat down, never letting go of her son or taking her eyes off him.

'I'll leave you two in peace,' whispered Maxie, easing the door open and closing it after her as quietly as she could.

Andrew was walking down the corridor as she turned to leave.

'The doctor says he'll be okay. His face must have been turned sideways when the liquid was thrown so there'll be no lasting damage to the airways or vocal cords,' he said to her. 'The attacker wasn't completely on target, thank God.'

'That's a relief. He looks dreadful right now.'

'What were you doing at his house?'

Maxie explained that Nathan was the man with the quote and he'd offered to take her through his old photographs to see if they could find the link with Georgina or if it prompted any recollections.

'And was there anything? Anyone labelled "most likely to murder" in the yearbook?' Andrew shook his head in apology immediately after he'd spoken. 'I'm sorry, that was completely uncalled for.'

'It's okay, this is getting to me too. I feel as angry as you do, and I've only known Nathan for a few days. Did you get anything useful from the house to house?'

Andrew shook his head. 'Pizza delivery guy in black and riding a black bike. We have the box but he escaped down an alley way and there was no CCTV on the streets or houses.'

'What about the pizza place, do they know who placed the order?'

'There was no order. It was an empty box just used to hide the bottle. He probably picked it up out of someone's recycling.'

Nathan's attacker knew that anyone would open their door to a delivery guy; any other complete stranger in full leathers and a helmet would have at least been greeted with a security chain and some caution.

'But we'll get him,' Andrew continued. 'Do you need a lift home?'

Maxie turned to face him directly and grabbed hold of him by the sides of his arms.

'I know we're not finding the evidence we need right now but I really do believe that this is linked with the attack on Georgina. I feel it.'

'Because of the quote?' asked Andrew.

'And the school link and the nature of the attack, the specific method chosen. Look, I know you're coming to the meeting with McAlister about the ACU, does that mean you're interested in working together?'

'I'm not sure yet.'

'Then meet me tomorrow,' Maxie asked. 'Give me one hour at any time of the day, or night, that's all I ask.'

'Why?'

'I want to convince you that the attacks are related.'

Andrew nodded slightly. 'Okay, one hour. I'll call you in the morning.'

Maxie turned down the offer of a lift, saying it was more important for Andrew to visit Laura and Nathan right now. She walked out of the confines of the hospital and into the real world; it seemed to have kept turning, oblivious to the extremes of pain and joy taking place inside that building. As she stood watching the ambulances arrive and despatch their latest casualties, a random thought struck her that at this very moment, families across the whole of the city were at home watching celebrities make fools of themselves trying to ballroom dance; some of them had even ordered pizza not knowing who would deliver it. She knew this guy wasn't picking random strangers to attack but she still screamed out loud across the car park, forcing the frustration and anger out of her body. She needed to be back with her own family right now.

She dialled Philip's number and to her astonishment, he picked up.

'I'm at the hospital,' she said. 'Don't worry, there's nothing wrong. I'm here for a friend but I could really do with a lift. Are you anywhere close?'

'I can be there in ten minutes,' he replied.

Maxie sat on a bench near the entrance with the smokers and vapers. On this occasion as she watched them, she didn't have the energy to feel the sense of dismay she usually did. Smoke yourself to death if you want, she was thinking.

'Might be dead soon,' she said, startling one of her new companions.

In less than ten minutes she spotted Philip's Audi approaching the entrance, so she stood up and waved him to a spot away from the ambulance entrance. The luxurious heated leather passenger seat hugged her, and she sighed. 'Bad day?' asked Philip.

'Horrendous,' she replied then turned to stare out of the window; she couldn't talk about it yet.


'Mum, have you heard what's happened?' exclaimed Karl descending the stairs two at a time as they walked through the door. 'A nurse has been in an acid attack.'

'I know – it was awful.'

She kicked off her shoes and beckoned him to her, hugging him and kissing him on the forehead.

'Is that why you were in the hospital?' asked Philip and she nodded.

He took out his phone and searched for details of the attack while Maxie walked into the living room and slumped herself down on the sofa. Karl went into the kitchen and came back with a bottle of wine and two glasses. He poured hers first. Philip's eyes skimmed left to right as he read the story lighting up his face.

'Jesus,' he said, 'and you were there? Why?'

'There might be a link between the nurse and the other case.'

'For God's sake, Maxie! You mean to say you still haven't dropped this? It doesn't sound like the other one. Please don't tell me you're interfering in something new,' yelled Philip. 'You shouldn't be hiding things from us like this. It was obviously dangerous, and you could have been killed. What if you'd opened the door?'

His comment about not hiding things would have normally made her lash out and ask him about his own deceptions, but tonight she didn't have the energy.

'It was someone else's house,' she murmured. 'I wouldn't have answered their door.'

She drank her wine letting its warmth melt through her as the men watched a continuous loop of local news reports from outside Nathan's house. There was no new news, just a succession of anchor men and women repeating the facts, trying to make them sound different each time. They'd obviously found no one with any video footage and although Andrew had told her the neighbours hadn't seen anything, it wouldn't have been surprising to find someone with a video of the whole thing withholding it from the police, but selling it to a news channel. The anchor woman was interviewing a neighbour now, but all they had to say was how shocked they were, what a nice guy he was and how they'd "never thought it could happen in a quiet street like this". Maxie thought for a moment that they could have superimposed that interview onto any TV crime scene in any suburb across the world, everyone said the same thing. It was as if the public had been media trained; everyone said "our hearts go out to the family" too. It might even be worth someone doing a study on public response at some point. Even now she couldn't take her mind off the job.

'I need a soak,' she said draining her glass, refilling it, and taking it with her.

She just couldn't subject her skin to her usual red-hot bath after tonight; instead she filled it with lukewarm water and bubbles, letting her skin cool and mellow. Afterwards she massaged in some heavily scented body lotion, as if showing her thanks to whoever had made sure her body remained unblemished tonight. Philip had been wrong; it couldn't have happened to her. Not only because she'd never have had the cheek to answer someone else's door as she'd said, but it had been intended for Nathan only. He'd been the only target. Putting on a light silk nightshirt she was aware of the soft fabric brushing softly against her thigh. Nathan would probably lose some of his sense of touch. He wouldn't know if it were a feather or a knife being held against him without looking.

Maxie took her glass of wine to bed and putting in her headphones, pulled up an easy-listening album to try to calm her down. She closed her eyes. She felt someone sit on the other side of the bed then get in beside her. She tensed then looked over to check it was Philip.

'I didn't mean to disturb you,' he said putting his hand around her shoulder.

Maxie took the headphones from her ears. 'You didn't. I was just trying to come down. Tell me about your day. How did it go with the investor meeting?'

She wasn't trying to catch him out and didn't really care what he said but she needed to change the subject and it seemed like a moment of truce; he'd found out how involved she was with the case and maybe he'd now feel more comfortable telling her what was going on. There might be one good thing to come out of today.

'Good,' he said. 'The journey to the airport was a nightmare as you'd expect, nose to tail traffic all the way round the motorway. I thought I was going to be late but got there with ten minutes spare. Just as well, the place was packed. We'd been worried that we'd hired too big a room but in the end, it was just right.'

Philip looked over to her. 'Are you asleep?'

She moaned a little to suggest she was getting there; she'd turned her back on him after the word "airport". If there was to be any truce between them, she had to tell him what she knew and convince him to tell her the rest. This farce had to end.

# Chapter Twenty-Eight

*Saturday, 18 July*

Maxie sent a text to her husband and son letting them know she'd gone to her office at the university so when they eventually woke up, they'd get it and not worry about her.

Even the postgrads weren't here at the weekend and although she'd come here for the peace and quiet, as she wandered through the empty corridors today it felt like something more, as if the whole place had gone into mourning. She had played the good citizen all week, answering every question the police had about the night of the attack then spending each night at home pretending all was well. But it wasn't and she had a choice. She could succumb to the sadness that resulted from Georgina, Nathan, and Philip or she could do something about it. She wasn't a succumbing type of woman.

'Is the link the wedding or sixth form?' she asked the pile of notes and photographs as she sat ready to go through them all again.

Now that Georgina's case was out in the open, she'd been able to question Penny and ask the bride about her guests. Both she and the police had spoken to every single one and had come up with nothing. Did this mean that the link was definitely college? Whereas previously Maxie would have said that the attacker had to have been a stranger or Georgina would have recognised something about them, now, having been through the trauma of a crime first-hand, Maxie doubted she'd have known if it were her own husband under that bike helmet.

Maxie raised her hand to her forehead, suddenly feeling nauseous; Leo had a moped. She couldn't believe Leo might be involved in this but he'd been at school with Georgina and Nathan, he'd been bullied and he could probably be at any party without being noticed. There were too many links to him now for her to ignore it. She had to speak to him as soon as possible.

She logged on to his online calendar and slumped in her chair, seeing that he had left for a summer conference shortly after they'd spoken. He hadn't mentioned it when they'd discussed the ACU but if he left on the Thursday evening or Friday morning, it meant that he was miles away when the attack on Nathan happened. Although a conference could be a very convenient alibi. Manchester was only a couple of hours drive away. He could easily register his attendance and come back up on the Friday night. No one would notice. At least she could check whether he had checked-in and get a list of other attendees. If it came to it, there were also ways of finding out whether he'd been there for the whole time. She couldn't believe she was thinking this way about one of her own students.

Rolling her shoulders to relieve the tension, she clocked the time and as it was finally a respectable hour to start making phone calls, she dialled Laura's number.

'Did he have a good night?' she asked getting a "as well as can be expected" in response. 'And what about you, have you had any rest at all?'

Hearing the weary response Maxie just wanted to be with Laura right now. It wasn't surprising that she felt that way. Maxie knew it had been well-documented that human beings in times of acute stress look to bond together and she understood these research findings on a personal level right now. It was known to academics as the "tend and befriend" phenomena, when people, usually women, who'd been through the same ordeal needed to stick together, to share their vulnerability and look after each other. No one else completely understood the emotions they were experiencing and that's exactly how she felt. Maxie closed down her PC and locked away the yearbook and photographs; they'd still be there in an hour or two.

On her way to the hospital, Maxie stopped off at a supermarket and bought all the things she thought Laura might need right now. She knew Laura hadn't left Nathan's bedside since the attack and probably wouldn't until she was prised out by the hospital staff so picked up some fresh toiletries, a tracksuit, a pack of knickers, and a huge selection of fruit and nuts she could snack on. Laura would be able to pick up chocolate and crisps from the hospital vending machine but Maxie imagined she'd be grateful for something healthier if she could ever bring herself to eat. Thinking about Nathan she picked up cartons of juice with straws built in and finally, some peppermint foot cream.

She saw Laura in the waiting room with Andrew. No one had been allowed in to see Nathan until now, so she guessed that the detective's presence was good news but braced herself just in case. Laura turned as she opened the door and to Maxie's enormous relief gave her a big smile and an even bigger hug.

'It's so good to see you. They're just changing his dressings,' said Laura as the two women risked crushing each other with the weight of the embrace.

Maxie showed her the contents of the bag and Laura thanked her.

'Didn't I tell you she was thoughtful,' Laura said turning to Andrew. She picked out the foot cream. 'He'll enjoy this.'

Maxie sent Laura to freshen up in the toilets, promising to come and find her when the nurses had finished.

'Mrs Hadley tells me you were the one who kept their head when the attack happened, that you knew what to do,' said Andrew. 'It could have been far worse for Nathan if you hadn't been there and kept your cool.'

'One hour,' said Maxie shrugging off his compliment. 'That's all I'm asking for.'

Andrew nodded and when Laura came back looking slightly refreshed, they said their goodbyes, promising to come back later.

'I want you to get to grips with the motives of the person we're looking for,' Maxie explained as she and Andrew drove to the university.

'How is this going to be any different to the psychological profiles we get?'

'It's similar but right now, you don't really believe we're looking for the same person and I don't blame you for that. Rapists tend to stick with rape and we only have a penchant for obscure quotes to link the crimes but Georgina and Nathan have a connection, no matter how tenuous it seems, and I need to show you why I strongly believe it's the same person.'

'So, tell me how it works.'

Maxie talked him through. 'If you want to know a person, goes the old saying, walk a mile in their shoes,' she explained.

From the look on Andrew's face as he exhaled through his nostrils, he was starting to regret promising to give her this one hour of his time. She had to make the most of this.

'Let's walk into the grounds,' she said as they parked up. They walked out into the sunshine and landscaped lawns of the far end of the campus boundary walk. Maxie looked around and spotted a quiet spot which would be perfect for this. She briefed Andrew about what she wanted him to do; Maxie was going to stroll down towards this quiet area and Andrew had to attack her. He frowned and dropped his jaw in disbelief.

'I can't do that.'

'It'll help, honestly,' Maxie reassured him.

Andrew looked around to check that no one was watching and nodded for her to start. Maxie started strolling and muttering a commentary.

'You saw me at the wedding, and you recognised me, but I didn't even look at you. You see me leave and you follow me. What are you thinking?' She noticed Andrew holding himself tall and pulling his shoulders back.

'You haven't even noticed me,' he replied in a lazy self-satisfied voice.

Good, thought Maxie, he's getting into it.

Maxie stopped at an empty patch of grass and following the description of what happened from Georgina's letter, Andrew instantly "bouldered" into her, knocking her off her feet and onto the ground. The speed and ferocity of it shocked them both. Maxie lay rubbing her back where it had slammed onto the solid turf, Andrew was about to check that she was okay but Maxie frowned at him to continue.

'This part *was* pure frenzy,' said Maxie gasping for breath. 'A spontaneous, intuitive act. No matter what planning had taken place, this was his animal instinct taking over. This is the assault written about in journals, the pure act of violence.'

Andrew eased back.

'The first attack would have been over quickly,' continued Maxie, 'but this guy didn't leave, he didn't flee through fear of being caught and the rest of his behaviour wasn't so consistently frenzied. He relaxed like you are now. He attacked her again, then sat back and took some pictures.'

Maxie looked up at Andrew and saw an emotional response in his eyes. 'Close your eyes,' she instructed. 'Now bottle the way you're feeling right now, bring it into yourself. Give it a colour, a shape, a name. Put the fingers of your right hand around your left wrist and squeeze tightly, now make that feeling bigger, more colourful. Squeeze. Now let go.'

Maxie had anchored the emotion so he could recall the power of it and when they came to the next re-enactment, he would be able to recall it. He stood and held out his hand to pull her up.

'That was intense,' he said blowing out his cheeks.

They needed a front door next so walked towards the groundsman's hut hoping that no one would be in; they were in luck. The door was locked but Maxie could appear from the side of the hut and it would work just as well. Maxie started the commentary again, but Andrew stopped her.

'Let me do this one,' he said. 'So, Nathan, I know you. I've watched you. I know where you live, I know your shifts, and I know you'll be home tonight. I've been to this street before to check it out. I've seen the respectably middle-aged neighbours dutifully draw their curtains at night and I guess that many of them will be asleep in their chairs within the hour. This neighbourhood washes its cars on a Sunday and sees crime on the news but never thinks it'll happen to them. They don't need CCTV because they look after each other. They've got their useless little Neighbourhood Watch. It's perfect.'

'Good, keep going.'

'Have I seen you at the gym? Do I know you fancy yourself a bit?'

'Don't analyse him, just be him,' instructed Maxie.

'I've seen you, not a hair out of place. Always perfect. You make me sick. The men and women look at you when you walk into a bar, but they don't even see me. They don't fawn over me the way they do to you. If only they knew.'

Andrew started walking slowly towards the hut and Maxie retreated so she couldn't be seen.

'I can't do this on the street, there are always too many people with bloody mobile phones taking pictures and anyway, I'm clever aren't I? You won't be expecting it on your doorstep and in the panic, I'll be able to get away. And there will be panic. This is the crime of the moment, the one everyone dreads but it's so perfect for you. Those men and women will be staring at you for a completely different reason after this.'

He reached the hut and holding one hand out flat as if it were a pizza box, knocked loudly on the door. Maxie appeared, pretending to open a door and Andrew thrust his hand towards her, throwing the contents of his imaginary bottle into her face over and over again until it was empty. Maxie doubled up onto the ground and Andrew ran.

He ran and ran reaching the edge of the field before bending over, his hands on his knees, gasping for breath. Maxie subconsciously wiped the imaginary liquid from her face. The ferocity of his actions had again taken her by surprise and once again brought home how fragile life was and how quickly it could be destroyed. Andrew walked towards her and apologised.

'Professor, I'm so sorry if I got carried away. Are you okay?'

'Don't worry, that was the point of it,' said Maxie. 'How did it feel to be him?'

'Good,' said Andrew. 'I had no regrets. It didn't feel wrong. I felt ... satisfied. If that makes sense? As if finally ... justice had been served.'

'Exactly,' replied Maxie.

# Chapter Twenty-Nine

'It doesn't bring us any further forward does it?' Andrew continued as they entered Maxie's office. 'Knowing he enjoyed himself makes me want to punch his lights out, but it doesn't tell me who it is.'

'I didn't expect it to on its own but if you'll accept for one moment that the person who attacked Georgina might just be the person who attacked Nathan, then we have other details.'

Andrew nodded for her to continue.

'He knew them both and the only time I can see when they spent time together was at sixth form. They didn't attend the same secondary schools beforehand or the same colleges afterwards. I've drawn a blank on the yearbook. Nathan didn't know of anyone who bore either of them grudges but your guys could do a more thorough background search.'

Maxie realised she'd stood up and she was leaning closer and closer into Andrew and he was responding by arching backwards. She smiled and apologised, taking a seat opposite him and giving him the safety of a desk between them.

'And he took a balaclava to that wedding. It was probably the type you wear under bike helmets as we now know he rides a moped. How many of the guests or staff at the wedding were former pupils of the sixth-form college? Do any of them match Georgina's description and do any of them have a motorbike licence? Did any of the casual staff they didn't check arrive by bike? Now we know what we're looking for, could you go back to that crime scene and see what was missed? There is so much to go on if you accept that they're linked.'

Maxie paused and watched Andrew starting to take notes. She continued, 'I know it's a long shot that any DNA from the church matches the pizza box or the bottle but it's worth a try isn't it? He also had to have staked out Nathan's street beforehand so maybe we widen the crime scene?'

Andrew sighed. 'I honestly don't think DNA is going to solve this one. The crime scenes have been a mess but it won't do any harm to go over things again with a fresh perspective.' They both fell into a slightly awkward silence.

'This feels a bit odd doesn't it?' said Maxie needing to fill the void. 'A bit like the Christmas truce in no man's land.'

'Something like that, but isn't this what you wanted? The police and the university working together more closely.'

'It is and I think we'd be good for each other, but this is just like the first date isn't it? We barely know each other.'

'So, go on then, I'll buy you coffee and you can tell me what you do,' said Andrew.

Maxie held her hand out and they shook on it. She walked him to the canteen which was closed but still housed the only decent coffee machine on campus and Maxie talked about the research they conducted, her vision for an Applied Criminology Unit, and all the areas they could link up.

'My specialism is motivation,' she said. 'Understanding why someone would commit a crime, what they're getting out of it because there has to be something in it for them.'

She noticed he was about to protest but held her hand up to stop him.

'I know what you're going to say, that evidence of the suspect having the means and opportunity weighs more heavily for the CPS, but understanding motive can help you in every aspect of the investigation from narrowing down suspects to knowing the questions that will hit a nerve in interrogations.

'It wouldn't just be investigations where we could help. We could offer training for your officers or a sounding board whenever you needed it. I'm particularly keen on techniques to help victims recover details without distressing them further and also helping them get over the incident. I know you don't have time for that at all.'

Andrew listened as he sipped his coffee, but Maxie's went cold, untouched. She had someone willing to listen to her ideas and found the words just flowed and she meant every single one of them. Eventually she stopped and came up for air.

'What do you think?'

'I've never really been sure about the value of police consultants if I'm honest, but you know you stuff,' said Andrew. 'And having a sounding board ... it always helps doesn't it?'

'It does.'

Maxie led him back to her office and gave him her proposal for the unit and the names of all the people he'd promised to check. As she watched him turn the corner out of sight, she punched the air with both fists. He was definitely hooked, and she was determined to reel him in no matter what it took.

Maxie knew that by the time he arrived back at the station, briefed the team and begun the searches, she would have reassured herself about the one name she hadn't given him, the one that was bothering her – Leo Turner. She went back to her office and pulled up the name of the conference venue and hotel he was staying at. Maxie looked at the schedule listed online and according to that, it was finishing today, and he should be in a panel discussion until the end of the day. She rang the hotel and was assured that he'd checked in on the day of the conference and had now checked out with no extras added to the room. The conference organiser also confirmed that he'd registered and collected his name badge. No one could tell her that he'd stayed there for the whole time and sounded very uncomfortable even being asked about it.

Maxie was aware that she was the one sounding like a criminal, a stalker, or a jealous lover right now. She asked for a call to be put out to the delegates for him to contact her immediately. She could have called his mobile again but that wouldn't prove anything because he could tell her he was anywhere. If the only message he got to call her came through the conference itself, then it had to prove he was there right now. It wouldn't tell her whether he'd left the hotel that night and driven the two hours to Nathan's house but it was a start. She still couldn't imagine that earnest face of his being involved in either of the two horrific crimes she was investigating, but if the shoe was on the other foot and someone was saying to her, "honestly, he may have been ridiculed at school and been a guest at the wedding but he's just not the type", she knew she wouldn't put much store by their word alone. And it wouldn't help reel Andrew in if she was prepared to investigate everyone except university employees and students.

Although Nathan hadn't remembered the courtroom incident as anything significant, Maxie knew that teenagers often underestimated the impact of their actions, especially on other teenagers. Attacking his tormentors would certainly be a way of proving he wasn't cowardly any more. She remembered Laura saying that she knew more about Nathan's school days than he did and decided to go back to the hospital on her way home. Home, the word alone made her shoulders drop in despair. It was Saturday night and Karl was guaranteed to be out with his friends but she really didn't want to be alone in the house with Philip, pretending to believe his lies. She couldn't face up to it yet so made a little bargain with herself; she'd call Laura and if she could meet her tonight, then she'd go to the hospital, otherwise she'd head home and face the music. She rang Nathan's mother quietly pleading with her to answer, but it went to voicemail. Maxie knew she had no right to pester this woman right now so just said that she hoped things were okay and that she'd speak to her in the morning. Philip it was then.

Maxie could hear her husband talking on the phone as she walked into the hallway and softly closed the front door. She wanted to listen to the call almost as much as she didn't want to. In the end she did what she considered the right thing, standing in the doorway of the study to let him know she was home then disappearing into the kitchen. She went to open a bottle of wine and saw there was one already open, she poured a glass for herself and took a mouthful of courage. Philip appeared within ten minutes holding an empty glass.

'You've started already,' said Maxie as he filled his glass up. He didn't respond.

Maxie sat down and took a deep breath; she wasn't going to pussyfoot around him any more. 'That investor's meeting you had, was it really at the airport?'

Philip looked straight into his glass. 'Why do you ask?'

Once she'd started, she couldn't stop herself, she had to go for broke. She explained how she'd been interested in what he was doing so looked up the company, then she'd found out the real venue of the conference and gone there. She told him she knew it had been quite a small affair but left out the part about one of the delegates calling it a con. She watched Philip trying to remain expressionless to begin with but then seeing his nostrils flare and his chest starting to rise and fall rapidly, she guessed his response wasn't going to be balanced.

'You did what? You fucking checked up on me and then followed me? Who the hell do you think you are? Am I one of your *cases* now?'

'Please, don't get angry, I was just interested, honestly,' she pleaded. 'I want to understand and if we don't talk to each other now, then we never will. Please, talk to me before it's too late. Tell me how it all works.'

Philip stood up and towered over her. 'You won't understand.'

'Please, just try me.'

Maxie watched his eyes darting in all directions and could tell he was constructing his narrative. He was choosing how to tell her whatever he had to say.

'You know the plumber we had last year, the one we found through Trusted Tradesmen?'

Maxie nodded.

'Well, the plumbers pay to be part of that service. They're vetted so the ratings are reliable, but they still have to pay.'

'Like being in the local directory or something?'

'Exactly,' said Philip relaxing his stance slightly. 'They not only pay to be listed but they pay to take the job. So they look at the description of work and decide they'd like to bid for it, then they pay a fee to get the client's details.'

'So, you're the Trusted Tradesmen here?'

'Yes,' he said enthusiastically. 'For the professional world. At our age we have so many contacts in companies all over the world but we're still too old and too senior for most of the vacancies. We can't escape the fact that a younger guy would do the job more cheaply.

'So, we gather the contacts, recruit trusted consultants, and try to match them with jobs.'

'People pay you to find them jobs? That doesn't sound so bad, why the secrecy?'

'It's a new model in this country and it's going to take some time to take off. I wanted it to be a success before telling you.'

Maxie put down her glass and stretched her hand out across the table, holding Philip's hand and squeezing it. She could see a hundred things wrong with the business model and was sure Philip had thought of them too but he'd obviously made a commitment to give it a go.

'So, I'm guessing when you said it's new to this country that it's successful somewhere else like the US?' she said and Philip nodded. 'And have they given you an idea how long it usually takes to build the business?'

'The model has me turning a profit within a few months.'

'That seems very quick. And after that, if it's not working, what happens?' Maxie asked cautiously, dreading Philip being made redundant again in such a short space of time.

'It's a franchise so I keep working until it does,' Philip replied quietly and then lowering his voice further, added, 'Christine develops the European arm and I own the rights to build the UK business.'

'Own them? You have to buy franchises, don't you?' Maxie kept her voice and gaze steady but the goosebumps lining her arms were showing her real fear. 'How much was it?'

'I did tell you I'd taken some money out of our joint account,' Philip replied.

He had, and she hadn't thought anything of it. She certainly hadn't checked how much was gone with everything else that was going on.

'You did,' she said struggling to keep that even tone. 'How much?'

'It was mine too.'

'Philip, I know it was and I can check for myself quickly enough but right now you're scaring me. How much have you invested in this?'

'Forty thousand,' he replied.

Everything they had; Karl's university fund, their safety blanket, their daydreams, and bucket list, it was all wrapped up in this now. Maxie's eyes blurred as she went dizzy for a moment. She dropped her head into her hands. It was surreal. He hadn't lost anything yet and it might make them a fortune but whatever happened, her husband had made a unilateral decision to risk everything without telling her. She looked up and grabbed him by both wrists; this time the squeeze was not affectionate.

'How could you?' she hissed. 'That's our son's future you've gambled with.'

# Chapter Thirty

If she'd had any choice in the matter, Maxie would have hidden in her room all day but she didn't because she had to get to the recording studio for this week's special edition podcast. She simply couldn't face the men in her life, could no longer pretend that things were okay. All week she'd been acting tough, ever since Philip had told her what he'd done but as the days passed, that's not at all how she felt. She was scared.

When she eventually heard both men leave, she got up and started to get dressed. Did couples come back from something like this? Was it worse than finding out he'd been having an affair with Christine or anyone else for that matter? It felt worse but she couldn't fathom why. If he'd had an affair, it might imply he no longer found her physically attractive but what he'd actually done suggested he thought she was somehow stupid or naïve – and maybe it was intellectual snobbery, but that hurt her more. He was gambling with everything they'd built together, in fact technically, he'd stolen from her. It wasn't all his money to use. She rubbed her eyes, dragging her hands down her face in despair. She couldn't imagine ever trusting Philip again and finally understood what it meant to have the rug pulled from under your feet.

She thought through everything she knew while she got dressed and put on make-up. Now that the doubts had started forming, she couldn't stop them. The business can't have been going well or he wouldn't be so secretive, surely? How long had he been working with them? It was the beginning of the year that he started talking about setting up on his own. Had he already had six months to make a go of it? Maxie began to wonder whether the visit from Christine had actually been a kick up the backside rather than a friendly flirtation between colleagues. She couldn't shake the thought that their savings were probably lost forever. She needed to have a thorough search of his papers. Perhaps she'd find that they'd deceived him into signing the contract or perhaps she could find a way to make it null and void. Maybe there was a get-out clause; she was clutching at straws to think of anything, just anything, to get their money back.

She ditched the make-up brush, rushed downstairs, and pushed open the door to the study. The silence inside seemed conspiratorial as if the room knew it was holding secrets and had no intention of giving them up. She sat at his desk and tried to work out where the crucial paperwork would be. The parent company might have needed a proper signature on the contract, so maybe he'd downloaded it and printed it out. There were foolscap files on the shelves above her, so she reached up and pulled one out. It was extremely heavy, too heavy. A cheap brand of supermarket bourbon was hidden inside. The sight made her sink back into the chair seething; she felt like pouring it all over his computer and ramming the empty bottle down his throat. She put it back in the folder. She didn't give a damn what he did now; he could drink himself to death for all she cared. It might actually be the solution to this hideous mess. She kept searching and eventually found the document she was looking for: the copy of a franchise agreement signed by Philip and Christine. If she took this to her colleagues in the law department, they might be able to help her understand their options. Of course, she'd have to confess her husband was a complete imbecile, but there was probably no getting away from that now. Maxie carefully put everything back the way she'd found it and closed the door.

She checked her phone as she got into her car but there'd been no response from either Laura or Leo yet. The former she could understand, but the latter worried her; she was, after all, his academic supervisor which was the equivalent of your boss calling you. She hoped it wasn't a sign that yet another man in her life was hiding something. There was no time to contemplate it now; she had to get herself into a better frame of mind.

At the university's request, this special was also being filmed for their YouTube channel. Her brief was to showcase the close working relationship between the police and the department so she and Craig had invited McAlister to discuss the rise of personal crime, like knife and acid attacks. The public needed reassurance rather than debate but she wasn't looking forward to trying to talk objectively about something she'd witnessed first-hand. She was also nervous about offending McAlister when they were so close to signing off on the ACU and hoped her co-presenter would go easy on her.

McAlister and Craig were waiting for her at the studio when she arrived. As they sat down in front of the mics, the chief inspector leant across and whispered that she'd heard Nathan had had a comfortable night; Maxie thanked her for the news and they both got into position. Craig kicked the recording off by introducing their guest and announcing that after recent events, they would be touching on the subject of acid attacks. He then began the discussion.

'Is it right that we've seen a seven hundred per cent increase in acid attacks in the past five years, Professor?'

Maxie nodded and was about to say something when Craig also turned to the chief inspector.

'Seven hundred per cent increase? Surely that's unacceptable. What are the police doing about this?'

So much for him going easy on her, thought Maxie as she watched McAlister put on her public-speaking face and wished she could have answered for her. The police and hospital staff often bore the brunt of budget cuts, public scrutiny, and the worse sectors of society together so they felt any crime against the other very personally; the chief inspector probably wasn't in the mood for a debate, but like Maxie, she had no choice.

'Any increase in crime is unacceptable but I do need to put the number you've quoted into perspective. There are still, thankfully, few attacks of this nature. Last year we had approximately five hundred attacks reported which means there were twice as many chip-pan fires in the UK but we don't get to hear about them.'

'Not exactly reassuring though. Professor Reddick, it's not a new phenomenon is it? Hasn't it been used for many years in some cultures?'

Sticking to the background of this crime helped to keep it at a distance but like McAlister, she had to watch what she said here. Acid attacks were often associated with South Asian cultures and with men deciding to disfigure a woman who'd rejected them, but that wouldn't help to find whoever had attacked Nathan, and it might just divert the whole conversation into a racial or cultural war. Maxie decided to stick to the British history of attacks.

'No, it's not new. In Victorian times one newspaper said that the only way to punish someone for committing an attack like this would be to cut off their arms so they'd never be able to do it again. Pretty harsh punishment but it shows that these attacks were happening back then.

It was called vitriolage back then, as the criminals were throwing vitriol which we British manufactured as part of the Industrial Revolution.'

'And isn't it known for use in so-called "honour" crimes?' Craig asked.

McAlister sat upright and slapped her palm loudly on the desk.

'No, and that's an enormously unhelpful line of questioning when a young man is lying seriously injured. There's a perception that this is a crime by men against women but last year, sixty-seven per cent of the victims of these attacks were male and forty-five per cent of them were white Europeans. Prejudice won't help us solve this crime.'

Maxie mentally spontaneously applauded the chief inspector then added her support. 'I couldn't have put it better,' she said as McAlister sat back in her seat and took a drink of water. It had been good to see the real person beneath that professional exterior.

'All very well,' continued Craig, 'but the crime isn't likely to be solved is it, Chief Inspector? Don't the vast majority of acid attacks go without any convictions whatsoever?'

Maxie knew it was true and as, in other instances, gang warfare tended to be behind the increase in attacks, it wasn't surprising. They wanted the notoriety associated with the crime and knew the public horror factor would ensure that the media would cover it. For gangs, these attacks guaranteed a moment of fame and little risk. After all, she'd been there at the very moment the attack had happened and she couldn't give the police any description at all. Moped gangs in their masks, balaclavas, and helmets knew this. All they had to do was ride away as quickly as possible. It's not as if their friends would give them up.

'And even if anyone were caught, aren't the sentences

pitiful?' he goaded. 'Why do these attacks carry lower charges than say, knife crime?'

McAlister paused and Maxie thought about that day in her office when she'd said how terrible it was to know the criminal but not have the evidence. She could see from the chief's downcast eyes that she was struggling to compose an answer.

'Can I tell you a little about the psychology behind these attacks, Craig?' Maxie asked hoping that by speaking, McAlister would have time to steel herself to reply later. Craig told her to go ahead.

'The person committing this crime wants the victim to suffer and live with the consequences. The outcome is often disfigurement which the victim will have to look at every day. A permanent reminder of what happened. This criminal wants to cause emotional distress. If he simply wanted to wound this young man, he'd have found a different way.'

'It's been two weeks now, do you actually have any leads, Chief Inspector? The identity of the moped rider?'

'Thanks to some work my officers are doing with the university, we know a bit more about this person and are pursuing a number of new leads.'

Maxie looked at her in surprise and caught a slight nod of the head; they were in this together.

'But let's be honest here, he's still out there. Do you think anyone else in is danger?' asked Craig.

'No,' Maxie replied quickly. 'Attacks like this are directed at a specific person as a form of punishment for something they're perceived to have done. We believe Mr Hadley alone was targeted. I will tell you something about the person we're pursuing though.'

Craig raised his perfect eyebrows for her to continue and Maxie shifted so that she was staring straight into the webcam.

'As much as I hate to disparage my own sex,' she said, 'the reason this type of attack was carried out often by women in times gone by is because it doesn't take any physical strength to do.'

She lowered her voice and made every ounce of fury she felt pour into the mic.

'The person we're looking for isn't strong. But it's not just lack of physical strength we're looking at here. I don't believe this man has even the brainpower to discuss his grievances like a rational person would. He didn't have the guts to have a face-to-face showdown. He ran off. This is a complete loser we're looking for, a bit stupid, and an absolute coward.'

With that, Craig closed the show, and blew out his cheek in delight as the producer leant in and told them that the social media posts about the programme were "off the scale".

'What are they saying?' asked Maxie.

'Doesn't matter,' replied Craig, looking delighted with the news. 'As long as they're talking about the show.'

With that, McAlister and Maxie were left to make their own way out of the studio.

'You really shouldn't have provoked him like that,' said McAlister. 'It could backfire.'

'With a description like black helmet, black balaclava, and tall, we're not going to get anywhere,' replied Maxie. 'Unless he gets riled and comes out of hiding or makes a mistake, we're never going to catch him.'

'As long it's not you he makes that mistake with.'

'You know what, Heather? I've had so much thrown at me this year I'd like to see him try. I'll be ready,' said Maxie. 'Nightcap?'

He turned off the PC and threw the can he was drinking

from against the wall. The sticky orange liquid fizzed up and stuck to the paintwork, staining it. Just one more example of how they'd all ruined his life and this bitch just wouldn't give up. He hadn't planned to hurt innocent bystanders, but if they stopped being bystanders then that wasn't his fault, was it? He'd studied crime shows and he'd planned this whole operation very carefully. The police always looked for the MO. Criminals stuck to one crime, they didn't change crime, and he'd been pretty much guaranteed to get away with the first one. They should be looking for someone with a sexual assault history and someone completely different with a grudge against that pretty boy. His masterpieces had absolutely nothing in common with each other and he'd taken such care to make the handwriting different that there was no way on earth those buffoons would be linking them through some stupid quote if it weren't for her. No, the professor had interfered in his business again, was insulting him across the World Wide Web. She didn't sound as if she'd ever give up. He had no choice. She had to pay.

# Chapter Thirty-One

McAlister walked into the bar and was immediately offered a table by the waiter; that one gesture had Maxie thinking, 'I bet your husband wouldn't dare gamble your family's future.'

She chided herself. She'd been furious with Philip not only for the risk he was taking but for not talking it through with her. For all she knew, the business plan stacked up but as he hadn't shared it, it was unlikely. They ordered coffees.

'Not worried it will keep you awake?' asked McAlister as the drinks arrived.

'I very much doubt I'll feel like sleeping any time soon.'

The chief nodded. 'It gets to you doesn't it? When you start caring about everyone involved in a case?'

Maxie nodded and they sat quietly, each in their own thoughts. Provoking this criminal on camera had been an instinctive move because she wanted him caught and soon, but now having calmed down, she hoped she'd done the right thing. If this guy really knew how to hurt his victims then the way to hurt her was through Karl. Maxie swallowed back that thought. Her son was always with friends now – surely there was safety in numbers? Maxie's self-doubt continued as she thought back to her first meeting with Georgina, the young woman's frailty and her belief that her attacker would never be caught so there was no point in trying; the best thing to do was to hope it would all go away. It hadn't gone away. Would Georgina be alive right now if she hadn't interfered? If Maxie hadn't picked at it like an open sore and made it worse? No, she physically shook her head to get that thought out of it. She had to remember what she always said to others – there was only one person to blame here. Whoever had decided to target Georgina had their own deep-seated reason for it and that reasoning included Nathan. Her only fault was in not working out who had attacked Georgina before he had the chance to commit his next crime.

'I hope you're not sitting there blaming yourself,' said McAlister. 'If you're serious about breaking through the academic world, you can't afford to do that.'

'So, you like the proposal? Do you think it could work?' replied Maxie, glad to have a slight change in subject.

'Perhaps with the right parameters in place.'

Maxie guessed this was probably about as positive as the chief ever got. Every sentence she uttered was probably nestled in a caveat of some sort. They sat for another fifteen minutes, sipping at coffees which had gone cold and talking about the practicalities of the unit: it would be based at the university but incorporate field days for both academics and officers to understand the needs of the force and the latest thinking in criminology. Maxie would focus resources around areas that would bring results to both institutions such as evidence-based policing and the practical application of their research. Although they were exchanging ideas about the subject closest to her heart, Maxie was waning, and she knew she was keeping the conversation going purely to avoid going home. Eventually McAlister stretched and said she had to be going. She signalled the waiter for the bill and Maxie stopped her.

'I'll get these,' she said. She reached down to her bag to pull out her purse and as she opened it, felt her phone vibrating. It had been switched to silent when they reached the studios. She paid the bill then checked her phone: eleven missed calls from Philip. Apologising and telling

McAlister she had to listen to her messages, she heard her husband's frantic voice.

'Where the hell are you? You have to call me NOW. There's been a fire at the house and Karl's in hospital. Wherever you are, call me.'

Maxie's entire being rocked at those words. She garbled the news to McAlister and ran off. She bundled her belongings into her car and, with her head feeling heavy and light at the same time, tried to focus on what she was doing. It was like an out-of-body experience. She took a couple of deep breaths and turned the Bluetooth on, calling Philip's number.

'Where've you been?' his voice echoed around the car. 'The show finished ages ago.'

'Why does that matter at all? What's happened? Is Karl hurt? Where are you?'

She listened to her husband telling her that when he got home, there was smoke in the hallway coming from the study.

'I didn't think there was anyone in but when I went upstairs, Karl was asleep on the bed with those damned earphones on. The smoke was starting to come up the stairs, but I got him out. Then as we walked past the study door, I just didn't notice it in time, but he reached out to try to open the door to put the fire out.'

'Oh, dear Lord, tell me he's okay.' Maxie had started to dry sob. 'Please, Philip, tell me he's okay.'

'He's fine, don't worry,' replied Philip. 'I got him away from the blaze. He's burnt his hand quite badly and has some smoke inhalation, but he'll be okay. We both will, they're just dressing his wounds.'

'I'll be there in ten minutes.'

McAlister tapped on the professor's window and mouthed that she'd heard the news.

'Can you blue-light me to the hospital?' Maxie asked. 'My son's there.'

McAlister nodded, hopped into her car then started the lights and siren going. Maxie fell in behind her and they sped to the hospital car park. The chief said she'd call in at Maxie's house and give her a call to let her know what had happened. Maxie waved a quick thank you as she ran into that neon-lit building yet again.

She found Karl and Philip quickly; Karl lying in a bed with an oxygen mask and his hand bandaged, Philip looking utterly exhausted. Maxie gently kissed the top of Karl's head, inhaling the smell of their burnt home. She didn't know what to say; she wanted to chide him for trying to open the door, tell him how much she loved him and make him promise her he'd never leave her sight ever again, all at once, but nothing came out. She felt as bad as Philip looked, completely spent. Surely this was the low point that would bond them and enable them to start building the family they used to have? With her home in tatters, her son in hospital and her husband – well just a complete mess, she couldn't think of a lower point.

She sighed and looked around once again at the staff and visitors scurrying around this place in the middle of the night. None of them wanted to be here. She shook her head getting rid of the self-pity that was threatening to lodge tight; she was lucky, her son had minor injuries and was drifting off to a peaceful sleep. He would recover. Her home could be repaired, and it probably was that bonding moment, the time that they all started to realise what was important in life. Out of the ashes and all that.

'I'll book us into a hotel for tonight,' whispered Philip. 'They'd like Karl to stay in overnight but it's just a precaution.'

Maxie nodded, glad that Karl would be here with all

these medical staff; her phone buzzed and she listened to Andrew asking her if she'd come to the house because he needed to speak to her.

'Would it be okay?' she asked Philip. 'I'll fetch some clothes and toiletries if I can.'

He shrugged as if he knew he had no real choice in the matter then nodded for her to go and they both stood for a while watching their son sleep. Maxie gently placed her hand on his bandages and promised to be back soon. The mother in her knew she should be staying where she was but the criminology professor wanted to know what had happened at her house and why Andrew needed her there. It could be a professional courtesy to signal a new working relationship between them, but she very much doubted that. The tone in his voice had suggested more concern than politeness.

Maxie drove slowly and cautiously. A mild tremor seemed to be running through her arms making them feel weak and somehow not connected to her body; exactly as if they were made of silly putty and she was trying to lift a heavyweight with them. She gripped the steering wheel willing herself to focus. The very last thing her son needed right now was for his mother to be joining him in the next hospital bed. As she turned up the hill towards her house, the flashing lights of the emergency services lit up her home. One fire engine was leaving, but another was still parked up and a little further up the road. She saw a police car and the BMW she knew belonged to Andrew. Her neighbours stood on the pavement opposite in hurriedly thrown on clothes and watched what was going on.

She pulled up and got out of the car. In a trance she watched the fire fighters and policemen, complete strangers, as they ploughed in and out of her home. It wasn't real; it was a scene from the news or a film. This wasn't the place she lived with her family. This wasn't the place she came to each night and kicked off her shoes. She wondered if the firemen had been upstairs. She'd left her bedroom in a complete mess this morning and if Karl were true to form then he wouldn't have flushed the loo after himself. Oh God, Karl. Breathe, breathe, he's not in there any more, he's in the hospital but he's fine, he's being looked after. Breathe.

She started walking towards the house; her next-door neighbour walked up to her and squeezed her arm, saying something about how worried they'd been and that they hoped the boys were safe. Maxie just kept walking until she reached the front path. She stared at the open door and froze; suddenly she was made of concrete. She simply couldn't will her body to take another step. Around her the emergency services rushed back and forth carrying somethings she recognised: a melted keyboard, a blackened chair; and others that she didn't any more. These more than the house itself stabbed her heart hard; fragile things destroyed, fragile like people. Christ this could have been far, far worse. The fear and hurt seemed to be snowballing in her chest, building and building but she didn't know how to release it.

'I'm afraid they think it could be arson.' Andrew's deep voice was behind her. It took her a moment to process what he was saying. Of course it was arson. That meant it hadn't started naturally didn't it? It wasn't a bush fire or lightning strike. How could it be? Her mind was as full of smoke as the building in front of her. No, that's not what it meant; it meant that it hadn't started accidentally. The boys hadn't left a pizza in the oven, she hadn't left the iron on, and it wasn't going to be added to the chip-pan stats McAlister had been talking about earlier. That would have been impossible anyway as they didn't have a chip pan. She was rambling; she didn't know what the hell to think.

'It wasn't an accident.' Maxie's throat choked as she said the words out loud trying to let their meaning start to sink in. 'You mean someone set fire to my house?'

She turned towards Andrew.

'Why?'

She didn't hear the words coming out of Andrew's mouth but could see that it was moving. A boulder hit her in the chest, and she stumbled backwards, her hands clamped over her mouth. Her thoughts went back to the podcast and she knew she'd caused this.

'It was him wasn't it?' She struggled to get the words out, picturing Karl in the hospital bed. 'He did this to me for calling him a coward. He could have killed my family. This is all my fault. I shouldn't have ignored that note.'

She bit down hard on her hand, needing to feel pain; needing to punish herself for her pride and stupidity. She felt Andrew put his arm around her and pull her away.

'Come with me,' he said as she allowed herself to be led away zombie-like.

The detective took her to the side of her house where crime scene officers were still working.

'It looks as if someone broke this window,' he said.

'It goes to the study,' said Maxie and then feeling the need to explain. 'It's where we all work but Philip, mostly.' She tried to peer around the work going on to collect evidence. 'It's the easiest way into the house but too small a window for anyone to climb through.'

'They didn't need to climb through it for this. It looks as if they smashed the window. This old Victorian glass might look good but it's easy to tap through quite quietly, and they threw a home-made device into the house.'

*Just like that*, thought Maxie. A tap of a window, a

squeeze of a bottle and the damage was done, just as it was at Nathan's.

'The room's full of paper and books,' she said picturing the shelves crammed with journals and academic texts that they hadn't touched for years. Would the carnage have been less if they actually cleared out the things they didn't use? She couldn't think of a single thing she'd miss from that room.

They were asked to move and walked back to the front doorway.

'There's quite a bit of smoke damage in the hallway and kitchen but otherwise your family called the fire brigade and got out just in time,' said Andrew.

In time; what time had it been? The first of Philip's eleven messages had been around the time she'd left the studio, probably a quarter of an hour after she'd taunted him. Instinctively, she started looking round at the faces watching the commotion; she knew most of these people.

'What was the device?' she asked still scanning the crowd to be sure there wasn't a tall man staring back at her from the shadows. She couldn't see an obvious suspect and, although she hated herself for checking for him specifically, it was an enormous relief not to see Leo out there.

'They're sifting through the debris now,' replied Andrew. 'They'll have more in the morning. You should get back to your family. You can't do any more here tonight.'

Maxie went back to the hospital and stood by the side of the bed, watching her son as he dozed. She'd almost forgotten about the hand-delivered note until tonight. It had seemed like an idle threat but now he'd decided to take the next step and actually attack her family. She didn't regret calling him a coward; this had been another cowardly act, going to her house when he knew she wouldn't be there, sneaking around and then running away.

'I'm going to get him,' she whispered to Karl.

'I know,' he murmured back, barely opening his eyes. 'Maxi-mum.'

She smiled at the nickname he'd given her as a child and kissed him as his head rocked back into sleep. Leaving his room, she walked to the ward where Nathan was and looked in at him and saw Laura asleep in a chair by his bed. Two mothers, three mothers – though she'd only seen Georgina's parents in the distance at the funeral; three mothers all hurting. As Maxie drove to the hotel, she reiterated the promise she'd made that she wasn't going to let any of them down now.

# Chapter Thirty-Two

Maxie peered outside the door of their room and was relieved to see the hotel manager had made good on his promise to dry-clean their clothes. She'd got back so late that she'd missed their usual deadline for overnight laundry, but she explained the circumstances and they said they'd try to have things ready for this morning. It felt like a good omen, that at least someone was on their side. It took a long shower using all the toiletries the hotel had supplied before she could convince herself that the smell of smoke wasn't lingering on her. She knew it was mainly in her imagination as she hadn't been in the house long enough for the ashes and carbon to shroud her, but she wouldn't wear any of it today.

Philip had booked them a twin room and although she was still furious with him about the money, she'd rather have her husband with her and know he was safe. She dressed and Philip stirred. 'I have a few things to do,' she whispered, sitting on the side of his bed. 'Will you give Karl a hug from me?'

Philip nodded. 'Don't do anything dangerous, promise me.'

Maxie nodded and began to lean over to kiss him goodbye as she usually did; she stopped midway and looked away from him. She couldn't do it, not yet.

Outside, the world was going about its usual morning routine, oblivious to her situation: deliveries were being made, joggers were jogging, and dog walkers were ambling along in that content space they always seemed to inhabit.

She needed air so took a bus to the seafront and then hopped off as soon as she could. Maxie took a deep breath of calm summer air and started along the promenade to Rachel's flat. Seagulls were fighting over the contents of a spilled packet of fish and chips in the top of a dustbin. If they didn't cause so much mess on the streets, she would probably have admired their strength and determination. They certainly didn't give up until they'd found what they were looking for.

Maxie arrived at Rachel's door and the young woman answered, still in her PJs. She waved the professor in and made her a coffee. They went to sit on the window seat where Maxie had first tried to coax Georgina into talking about her attack. Maxie realised that the memory must have been playing on her face when Rachel spoke. 'There's nowhere we can sit where you don't remember her, and what happened.'

They sat silently sipping their drinks for a moment.

'Do you think we did enough?' asked Rachel.

It was the question Maxie had been asking herself since Georgina's death.

'We still haven't finished,' she replied, wishing in some way that when they found this guy, it would bring her back. It wouldn't, but it might help those who loved her most.

Maxie remembered Laura's words; that mothers remembered more about their children's schooldays than they did, and she wanted to speak to Georgina's parents. She hadn't spoken to them properly at the funeral and asked Rachel for a more formal introduction. Rachel agreed and called them.

'We can go up this morning,' she told Maxie as she hung up the phone.

'Let's go and have some breakfast before we meet

them,' replied Maxie, anxious to get out of the flat and the memories that still clung to it. 'It'll do us both good.'

Georgina's parents were just as Maxie had expected them to be. Slightly older, quiet, and dignified, just as their daughter had been. Mrs Pickering introduced herself as Jenny and invited them into a gently traditional living room where photographs of Georgina throughout her life dominated the walls and mantelpiece: taking her first steps, in her first school uniform, on the beach with her parents and in her graduation gown. Maxie had the first three scenarios in her own house and certainly planned on that final picture joining the collection. Tears started to prickle as it suddenly struck home hard that at least she could still hope for that photograph. She'd put herself in the same place as Laura and this quiet lady in front of her; mothers who'd had their children threatened. She wasn't in the same place at all; at least she still had Karl and Laura still had Nathan. They'd both recover and there'd be more photographs taken but, for Jenny Pickering, this was it. There'd be no wedding photograph, no first grandchild, not even a thirtieth birthday celebration. Maxie had to turn away and take deep breaths to steady herself; it wouldn't help anyone if she broke down now.

'I heard on the radio that he burnt down your house for trying to find him,' said Jenny putting her hand on Maxie's arm and inviting her to sit down. 'That your son was hurt too.'

The local radio had played up the extent of the blaze but had tied it firmly to her confrontational comments on the podcast. Although the situation had been exaggerated, Maxie could see that this quiet lady also needed that bond with another woman.

'He's going to be okay,' Maxie said reaching out and holding her hand.

'That's a relief,' replied Jenny squeezing Maxie's hand and then releasing it. She sat up straight and looked directly at her. 'So, what can I do to help you catch him?'

Maxie explained the link with Nathan and asked if she remembered anything about Georgina's time at sixth-form college.

'Was there anyone who pestered her or that she complained about for any reason?'

Jenny blew out her cheeks and her eyes drifted upwards as she remembered back.

'She was always being asked out, I remember that,' she replied. 'She was a very pretty girl but never realised it.'

'Did she have a boyfriend back then?'

'No, she didn't. I did wonder whether she might be gay and be afraid to tell us. I remember having a talk and saying that both God and we would love her no matter what she wanted out of life.'

'And was she?'

Jenny shook her head. 'No. She said she just didn't like any of the boys at school in that way. I admired her strength of character at the time. There's always such a lot of pressure on young girls, isn't there?'

Maxie nodded, thinking back to her own school days – a different era but still the same pressures, although she'd been more than happy to succumb to every vice on offer in her own teens.

'And did she ever mention Nathan Hadley?'

'I know he was the chap who got attacked but I really don't remember the name.'

'Maybe if you saw a picture of him as a teenager?' replied Maxie bringing out a screenshot of the photograph from the yearbook.

'Gosh, he was handsome even back then, wasn't he?' said Jenny, her face smiling gently. 'I think he may have given an end of term speech once. I think it was quite a serious one, then again, it was so long ago …'

Maxie took out the picture of Leo next and asked about him. Jenny studied it and paused.

'Maybe,' she said. 'But again, she never brought any friends home. Perhaps the name Leo was mentioned. It's an unusual name isn't it?'

'In what capacity was it mentioned? Can you remember?'

Jenny shrugged. 'I don't know if she ever told me. She didn't tell me about the attack she's just been through and she's always been the same. She kept herself to herself.'

Jenny's face suddenly collapsed, and her body followed. 'Do you think something happened back then? Something I could have helped with? That might mean she was with me now?'

She was gasping for breath between words, hugging herself and beginning to rock backwards and forwards. Rachel and Maxie sat either side of her and held her tight, feeling every muscle in her body tense with the agony. Eventually Jenny lifted her head and Maxie reassured her that she didn't think there was anything she could have done. She didn't know whether this was the truth or not, but Maxie wished everyone would stop blaming themselves when they were the victims; she had to move on if she was going to find him.

'I have to keep looking,' she said to Jenny relaxing the hug. 'Is that okay if Rachel stays with you?' She looked over at Rachel who nodded her okay.

Jenny sighed and wiped away tears. 'Find him.'

'I will.'

Maxie left the two women and was about to head to the

hospital to speak to Laura when her phone rang. She saw that it was Leo.

'Hello, stranger,' she said. 'Where the hell have you been? I've been trying to get in touch with you for days.'

She listened as a sheepish Leo apologised and told her the conference had been so fantastic, he hadn't checked calls or emails and then he'd gone to north Wales for a bit of a break afterwards. It would sound a flimsy excuse coming from anyone else, but Maxie could very well imagine that he'd been engrossed and ignored all contact with the outside world. She asked him to meet her at the hospital canteen; it was neutral territory and she could progress the case as well as call in on Karl from there. It was fast becoming her new home from home, although she'd be very pleased when the day came that she never had to see those long white corridors again.

Karl was sitting up looking rested and a plate of barely eaten scrambled eggs was being cleared away.

'You have to eat,' said Maxie. 'You need to build up your strength again.'

'Relax, Mum, I'm not going to fade away just yet. I had some yoghurt which was easy on my throat and a lot easier to eat with one functioning hand.'

Maxie gently stroked the side of her son's face; if he was arguing with her, then he was most definitely on the mend.

'But that doesn't mean I want a crate load of yoghurt suddenly appearing,' he added quickly, causing them both to laugh. That's exactly what she'd been planning.

After they'd chatted for a few moments, Maxie got a text from Leo saying he'd arrived. Maxie told Karl she'd call back later and went to meet her student.

'I hear I've missed quite a bit of excitement,' he said as she approached.

'That isn't how I'd describe it,' Maxie snapped, and he apologised for his choice of words.

Maxie explained his connection with both victims and Leo nodded as she spoke.

'Obviously, I didn't know she was the woman who'd been attacked when we were discussing my research,' said Leo. 'But when I read about her death and then the attack on Nathan, the article said they'd both been to the same school as me.'

'Were you friends?'

Leo laughed. 'Hardly … Me, friends with a woman? I was the geek even then. They made fun of me most of the time. I didn't make many friends at all. School wasn't exactly the happiest time of my life.'

'I can understand that.' She smiled affectionately. 'Did you go all the way to Manchester on that moped of yours?'

Leo frowned at her as if she was stupid and then opened his mouth in horror.

'The person who attacked Nathan had a moped didn't he? Professor, do you think I had something to do with it? Is that what this is all about?'

In her heart, Maxie truly didn't believe he would be capable, but she had to rule him out and told him so.

'I can't believe you would think that of me.' He stood looking hurt. 'I sold that bike months ago if you must know.'

She watched him walk away without glancing back and regretted the clumsy way she'd dealt with him. Despite her misgivings, she'd have to check that he had sold the bike. Maxie got up and walked towards Nathan's room, hoping that Laura would be more helpful than either Jenny or Leo had been. Halfway there she found the pint-sized woman coming towards her.

'They're changing his dressing,' she said. 'He won't let me be there, says I make too much fuss.'

'These sons of ours don't know how lucky they are, do they?' Maxie smiled as they re-traced her steps back to the canteen.

Maxie explained that she'd spoken to Georgina's mother who thought she remembered seeing Nathan giving a speech at school.

'Oh God he gave loads of them. He went through a particularly earnest phase and began acting like he had to save the world and everyone on it. If there was an injustice to be addressed or a damsel in distress, then he just had to interfere.'

'How did he interfere?'

'He'd make a formal report to the student committee or tell a teacher or just stand up to whoever was in the wrong. I can imagine he was a bit of a pain in the backside when he wanted to be. I suppose it's my fault. I always told him to speak up if something was clearly unfair, to tell someone.'

Maxie listened as another mother blamed herself; one for not encouraging her child to speak up and another for doing the opposite. She'd always told Karl not to sit back and wait for others to make things happen; only now did she wonder whether that's what made him try to get into the study, so he could put the fire out before the fire brigade arrived.

'We can't win, can we?' Laura sighed.

'Doesn't look like it.' She pulled up the photos of Georgina and Leo on her tablet and placed them on the table in front of Laura. 'Can you remember either of these two people?'

Laura studied the photos but was shaking her head. 'I mainly knew his close friends, neither of these people came to the house but maybe he talked about them. Did they have any nicknames?'

'Leo might have been the cowardly lion, but I don't think Georgina had one – maybe Georgie or something like that? Her last name was Pickering.'

Laura looked up and tapped on the screen. 'George. I remember a George. Could that be her?'

Maxie shrugged.

'George was being hassled. That was one of his favourite words then. I remember it because I assumed it was a boy and wondered why he couldn't fight his own battles. Sexist, I know.'

'No matter, so Nathan interfered and reported whoever was hassling this George?'

Laura nodded.

'Do you know the name of the other person involved?'

'I'm sorry, I knew you would ask that, but I don't. It was at the start of the upper-sixth year. Term hadn't long started, and Nathan had just turned seventeen – an August baby.'

'And what happened? Can you remember anything else?'

They sat silently while Laura clasped her hands together. Holding them to her face she closed her eyes as she thought back. After a while she looked up, shaking her head.

'I'm sorry, I just can't remember. All I know is that whatever was happening stopped and Nathan moved on to another crusade.'

# Chapter Thirty-Three

Maxie needed to think; she left the hospital and headed towards the lush grounds of Stanmer Hall where she once again walked the path Georgina would have taken on that night. It was humid and the skies were filled with clouds waiting to burst. She wished they would and pictured her brain like a sunflower seed, the raindrops infiltrating it, helping it to spring into life and bloom brightly. She wasn't sure whether she was any further forward after her conversations; it was as if there were something lurking in the corner that she couldn't quite see but she knew was important. She sat on the grass and lay down, closing her eyes.

'What do I know about you?' she said out loud then took a quick glance either side of her to check she really was alone; she was, so she continued to voice her thoughts.

'I believe you took revenge. These attacks were personal and specifically targeted. You think they're completely justified don't you? Georgina had a reputation for turning men down, so you took her against her will. She must have turned you down publicly and you didn't like that, so you humiliated her in return. Nathan is bloody good-looking, so you ruined that for him. Did he get all the girls when you couldn't? You choose your methods carefully but that's no reason to kill, surely?'

Maxie sat up and looked around her, recalling the details of the original assault. He had taken his time over that attack; he seemed to have enjoyed himself too much. Also, there were the quotes – destroying Georgina's virtue and making Nathan unpopular.

'It was about ruining their lives wasn't it? Humiliating

Georgina in her church, her sanctuary and making Nathan's friends desert him. Maybe the way they deserted you?'

Her department's research had shown time and time again, that acting out a revenge fantasy gave the brain a pleasure hit in the part of the brain known as the caudate nucleus, a bit like taking cocaine; it was where the expression "revenge is sweet" came from. The problem was that after the initial rush, the thirst for vengeance returned like any other addiction. He had taken care not tó be seen during both the attacks, which indicated careful planning, so the anticipation of exacting the revenge on Nathan must have given him a real high. Maxie knew that in his mind, he'd done nothing wrong. He'd finally got the justice he thought he deserved, but for what?

Jenny had said that Georgina turned down lots of suitors, but it couldn't just have been that. Besides, if they had known each other back at school and he'd pestered her then, wouldn't she have recognised him? Even if he'd changed as much as Nathan had, there was always something familiar – a walk, an accent, a smell. You couldn't hide who you were completely. Maxie was convinced the core motivation for both attacks had something to do with the sixth-form college and that the wedding had just been the opportunity. She needed help from the one other person she knew who'd attended that college, but she wasn't sure he was still speaking to her.

'Leo, I'm sorry I offended you,' she said over the phone to him, 'but I need your help.' She begged and apologised as profusely as she knew how. Leo reluctantly gave in and she asked him to meet her at the university Faith Room.

The Faith Room would be empty during the holidays and it was one of the few spaces on the whole of the campus where you could be guaranteed silence. You could also lock the doors while in there, so they'd have privacy as well and Maxie needed both for what she was about to do. Leo hadn't enjoyed his schooldays, but she had to take him back there.

By the time he arrived looking both puzzled and slightly concerned to be meeting her here, Maxie had organised two armchairs facing each other and closed the curtains.

'What are you going to do?' he asked, taking the seat Maxie pointed him towards.

'I want to do some NLP that will help us both,' she replied. 'Some timeline therapy.'

Leo moved to get up, but Maxie put her hand on his arm, easing him back into the chair.

'You said school wasn't the easiest place for you, but you know that going back and confronting those thoughts will release you from them.'

Leo said nothing, but she saw his shoulders drop in acceptance of what she'd said. Although he wasn't a practitioner like Maxie, through his own studies in the use of Neuro-Linguistic Programming he would trust that what she was saying was true.

'And will this show you that I had nothing to do with these attacks?'

Maxie nodded. Although she hadn't said this to him, she was also hoping to establish whether there was a deep-seated memory that might be festering.

'I promise to take care of you,' she said. 'And I'll bring you out if there's anything too distressing.'

He nodded so Maxie started the process, getting Leo to close his eyes and relax. When she saw that his eyes had stopped darting around under his eyelids and his chest was falling and rising steadily to indicate a relaxed state, she began.

'I want you to picture your life as a timeline, lying along

the floor in front of your chair. With your finger, can you draw that line for me?'

In his semi-hypnotic state, Leo raised his hand and pointed out a line from his left to his right. Maxie could have guessed that's what he would have drawn. If he'd drawn his timeline from the back to the front of him, it would have suggested a more easy-going character, but his drawing from one side to the other was in keeping with an orderly personality. It also pointed to a tendency to retain negative memories. Maxie asked him to point to the past which was to his left and the future, to his right.

'Now I want you to imagine you're floating above that timeline,' continued Maxie. 'You're flying high, looking down on your life. You can see it all in the far distance and nothing that happened there can hurt you. Tell me some of the good things you can see.'

She watched as Leo, still with his eyes closed, scanned the imaginary timeline and smiled. 'I can see my graduation,' he said. 'I got a distinction.'

'That's good,' said Maxie. 'Now can we go back to before you went to university, to sixth-form college? Float back there for me, remembering that nothing that happened there can hurt you now.'

Again, she watched as Leo's face turned towards his left and therefore his past. His breathing became faster and his hands started twitching. He screwed his face up and tensed his body. This wasn't a good memory.

'What can you see, Leo?'

'Courtroom, people laughing at me, calling me a coward.'

Maxie knew he was referring to the incident Nathan had told her about and that this was the memory she had to free him from.

'Okay, let's float away from that. Move forward a little to a time, still at college, when you no longer feel bad.'

She watched his eyes move to the right and his body settle slightly but his hands still fidgeted.

'What's happening right now?'

'Not picking on me, ignoring me. Picking on some woman.'

'Do you know who?'

Leo shook his head and Maxie asked him to go forward again to a time when the threat was gone. She watched a very slight move of his head which suggested that the threat had been over quite quickly. He was relaxed and sighed.

'What's happened Leo?'

'They've gone.'

'How do you feel?'

'Liberated,' he replied.

Maxie mused over his choice of word. "Liberated" suggested someone had acted on his behalf.

'Can you look around you?' said Maxie. 'Is the threat completely gone? Has someone helped remove it?'

She watched Leo turn his head left and right then nod twice. His entire body was at ease, so she knew whoever had posed this threat to him was no longer in his life. There had been someone in his life who'd made things a complete misery, then moved on to a woman, and was then removed by a third party. Was this the link? Before rousing him into present day to see if his conscious mind remembered any of this, she had to take him back and eradicate that negative memory.

'Taking with you that feeling of being liberated,' she said to Leo, still in his trance. 'I want you to float back to that courtroom.' She watched until she could see from his facial expression that he was there. 'Knowing that you're safe, and only if you're able to, I'd like you to face your tormentor.' Leo's head turned and his nostrils flared. 'Knowing all the good things that your future holds, the liberation, your graduation, and the distinction, what would your future self now say to this person?'

Leo's face brightened and he lifted his chin. 'You can't hurt me. Get out of my life you dropout.'

Maxie guided him back to the present day and out of his relaxed state. He smiled at her and she marvelled for a moment at how effective it was to do something as simple as talk to your past life. The mind was a very strange thing. She imagined that Leo would want to get some air after that experience and suggested they go for a walk.

'I'd rather go for a beer,' he replied.

'Wow, you are feeling good,' said Maxie, reflecting that she could never remember him suggesting anything like this before.

Maxie waited until they were sitting with their drinks on the balcony of the bar before bringing the conversation back to Leo's sixth-form days. She'd brought the yearbook from her office and asked Leo to point out his tormentor.

'This was taken at the end of term,' said Leo, 'so he wouldn't be in here.'

'Why not?'

'He was expelled. He started picking on a girl after me and the guys rallied to get him thrown out.'

Maxie could barely contain the excitement she felt on hearing this; she calmed herself, asking, 'Were you involved in that?'

Leo shook his head. 'I wouldn't have dared.'

'Please, please tell me you remember his name.'

Leo rubbed his eyes, trying to remember. 'You'd think I would, wouldn't you? After all, he made my life hell. Jack something?'

Maxie knew that she could compare the college intake register for that year with the graduating names. There shouldn't be too many people to work her way through. It was a long shot that someone would take such violent revenge for being thrown out of school but it was a connection and her spidey-senses were telling her it was worth checking out. She was itching to speak to Laura but had to stay and talk university business with Leo for a while longer. She discovered his reason for being sheepish about the conference; he'd taken his new partner with him to enjoy the hotel break and they'd kept their phones switched off for the whole time.

'I didn't put any of his food or drink on expenses though,' he reassured her.

Maxie told him he was welcome to at least expense a bottle of wine. She was relieved to discover he hadn't been involved with this psycho who seemed to be acting out an age-old grievance and that his subterfuge wasn't anything to do with this case or wanting to leave the faculty. And beyond that, she was rather surprised to find out he had a romantic partner; people never ceased to surprise her. She clinked her glass against his and toasted "life" – it seemed worth celebrating.

With Leo and Maxie's first social outing over, Maxie tried Laura's number. She wasn't surprised to get her answerphone because they weren't keen on mobiles in the hospital, and it didn't really matter as she was heading there to see Karl now. But not before she'd stopped off at the supermarket to buy some yogurt.

Karl groaned affectionately when she opened the shopping bag but then took one of the pots and started eating.

'Dad was here earlier,' he said. 'He brought me jelly. I'm not a kid you know – I can eat solids.'

'Jelly and yoghurt – you've had a balanced diet then. Don't worry, all that will change when you're out of here. Have they said when that's likely?'

'Tomorrow,' he said. 'You're going to have to look after me from then.'

'The words every mother wants to hear,' she replied laughing. 'Her baby can't do without her.'

He stuck a yogurt covered tongue out at her.

'Where will we live?' he asked.

It was a good point. Maxie hadn't checked to see whether they could go back to the house and although she'd enjoyed her one night of luxury at the hotel, she doubted the insurance company would pay for that forever. She put it on her mental list of things to do after she'd spoken to Laura. A couple of Karl's friends arrived, and she took that as her signal to go.

Nathan and his mother were in the same room and Nathan was propped up. He nodded very slightly as she walked in.

'It's so good to see you sitting up,' said Maxie getting another nod and a throaty murmur. 'Will you be home soon?'

Laura told her that it would be another couple of weeks at least when they were sure there was no risk of infection from the wound.

'Then enjoy the rest while you can,' said Maxie before hesitating and then adding, 'I have a name I need to ask you about if you're up to it?'

Nathan signalled to his mum, who raised the bed so he could see better, then sat down beside him.

'The person who bullied Leo Turner,' she said. 'Was he the one who'd been picking on Georgina too?'

Laura shrugged but Nathan paused then nodded slowly.

'And did you lead a group of students to lobby to get him expelled?'

Nathan's tender eyelids closed as he nodded again.

'That can't be at the root of all this?' said Laura. 'It happened years ago.'

'It's the only link I can find,' said Maxie. 'And we don't know what happened to that boy, although Leo thinks he might have been called Jack. Does that ring a bell?'

Nathan mumbled something and Laura leant in to hear it.

'Jacko. He says he was called Jacko.'

'Was that his surname?' asked Maxie as Nathan nodded. 'Jackson?' Again, Nathan nodded. 'First name?' Nathan shook his head. 'And do you know what happened to him?' A shake and a grunt this time.

'Sorry,' translated Laura. 'He doesn't know where he went.'

Maxie told them she had to contact the college administration to find out the first name and then get this to Andrew. She thanked them and started speed-walking down the corridor full of hope and angst; hope that they'd found him, but angst that he was still out there. She wondered whether it was safe to leave Karl in the hospital after all. The attack on her home hadn't made sense at all. If this Jacko was really taking revenge for something that happened many years ago, then why firebomb her home? She had provoked him, but she hadn't been there when all this happened? And why a fire? It wasn't as personal or targeted as the other attacks. It bore none of the precision or planning of the other incidents but if she were being targeted, then perhaps he was simply going for those close to her; after all, hurting them was the best way of hurting her. She dialled Andrew's number and it rang many times before he finally answered.

'I've been thinking,' she said without acknowledging his "good evening" at all. 'If I'm a target of this wacko and he's already tried to burn down my house, then I should take you up on that offer of some police protection for my son at least.'

She finally took a breath and waited for his answer.

'I don't think you're going to need it,' replied Andrew. 'We have someone in for questioning about the attack on Hadley and there's something I need to talk to you about when your son is well.'

'You've found him? How?' Maxie was confused and if she were honest with herself, more than a little pissed off that they'd got to him first. 'I'll come down now. I know some of what happened, and I've got some new information so I can support the questioning. There's a new technique we're perfecting ...'

'No, Professor.' Andrew was emphatic. 'No, you have been brilliant, but this is now in our hands. Get some sleep and come down in the morning.'

He hung up before she could make any further attempt to argue her case.

# Chapter Thirty-Four

When she arrived back at the hotel room, Philip leapt up and poured wine into the bathroom tumbler.

'I wasn't sure what time you'd be back, so I just bought some supermarket sandwiches. If you get the room service ones, they're dog-eared before you know it.'

He picked up a carrier bag and emptied it onto the bed; packets of sandwiches, cashew nuts and bars of chocolate tumbled out. It was like a diet-breaker's treasure chest.

Maxie took a large glug of wine, plonking herself down on the other bed; when she came up for air she took off her shoes and reached across for the nuts. She hadn't realised how hungry she was.

'This is perfect,' she said. 'I couldn't cope with going out tonight.'

Philip reached out for her hand.

'I heard that they've caught him,' he said. 'We can relax now.'

Maxie nodded, but she wasn't ready to start making up and her mind was far from relaxed. She couldn't believe that it might finally be over; how could Andrew possibly have Jackson's name? She couldn't imagine Laura getting straight on the phone to him after she'd left and even if she had, Andrew hadn't had time to both track him down and bring him in for questioning. And he'd said he had someone for the attack on Nathan; he hadn't mentioned Georgina at all. Maybe that's what he'd be looking for during the questioning – the link between the crimes. Andrew shouldn't have turned down her offer of help. They really were working on interview techniques and besides which, she already knew the link – she could save him a lot of time.

'Come on,' Philip jolted her from her thoughts. 'Get into this. It'll make the world seem better.'

He was holding out one of the fluffy white bathrobes. Maxie went into the bathroom, stepped out of her clothes and into its cotton embrace. When she re-emerged, Philip was also in a bathrobe, holding out a refilled glass.

'A fresh start?' he suggested. Maxie could only manage a very slight nod, not at all sure how they'd achieve that.

They ate companionably but silently. Philip kept the wine flowing and as each packet of food was eaten, he tidied the debris away. Eventually, they'd eaten everything except a couple of bars of chocolate which neither of them could face. They sat back on their respective beds and flicked the TV on, scrolling through the channels until they found something that wasn't bad news, awful reality, or violent-crime solving. It took a surprisingly long time.

'Karl's coming out tomorrow,' said Philip.

'I know,' replied Maxie, letting the romcom wash over her but fill the potential silences in the room. 'We have to find somewhere to live until we can go home.'

Philip picked up the remote and turned the volume right down; he swung round on his bed to face her. Maxie watched his face as he chose his words.

'I had a thought,' he said hesitating, 'so I'll just say it and tell me what you think.'

'Go on.'

'It's a big house and there will only be three of us for a little while longer. Karl might stay with us for his first year at uni, but he's bound to want to flat-share after that. And it hasn't been exactly happy there recently. Why don't we see this as our line in the sand and move on? We could get somewhere smaller, maybe an apartment by the marina?'

He hung his head.

'The insurance will cover the repairs but I could probably do the bulk of them to save us money and we'd have equity which would cover the university fees until I recover the investment.'

Maxie didn't want to give him a complete get-out-of-jail-free card, but he had a point and maybe there was a case for second chances. Hadn't she regarded this as their absolute low point? She imagined the two scenarios: going back to that house and forever imagining what could have happened in the fire, or, waking up on the seafront, walking out onto a balcony every morning, feeling the breeze and seeing the infinite horizon. The latter was definitely more appealing. She reached out and squeezed his hand.

'It's a good idea, but let's talk it through in the morning.' She watched his face brighten as she spoke.

Maxie let go of his hand and got into the bed properly, turning off her bedside light and rolling over with her back to him as a signal that she wasn't going to talk any more tonight. Philip flicked off the TV and she listened to him getting under the covers and plumping up his pillow; the nightly routine she'd heard for twenty years now. He called out a hopeful goodnight and she murmured in return. He was snoring within minutes while she lay there unable to get that picture of the balcony out of her mind. It was a beautiful, peaceful scene and she'd felt completely at ease; but there had been a problem. No matter how hard she tried, as she stood there listening to the rigging of the sail boats clinking against the masts, she simply couldn't see her husband anywhere in that scene.

The next day, Philip woke her with a breakfast tray of fruit and scrambled eggs on toast that he'd had delivered to the door. 'Start as we mean to go on,' he chirped.

Maxie recalled their conversation yesterday and how

she'd felt as the day ended but smiled anyway. Perhaps all they needed was a bit of time.

'What are your plans for today?' asked Maxie through a mouthful of toast.

Philip picked up a notepad where he'd already been making a list.

'Get on to the insurance company to see where we stand vis-à-vis the hotel with Karl coming out, then speak to an estate agent and get a valuation with and without the repairs, then see if this place has two adjoining rooms or a suite they can move us to so we can all be together.'

'Sounds good.'

'What about you?' asked Philip.

Maxie felt slightly guilty that her thoughts were still on the case but she was justifying it to herself that the bastard had tried to burn down her home and hurt her son, so perhaps it wasn't just her ego urging her on.

'I have to go to the police station,' she said. When she saw the dismay on Philip's face she added, 'They need me to help put this guy behind bars. I need to know he's not still out there before I can ever have a fresh start. I promise I'll be back by the time they discharge Karl – we can go to the hospital together.'

She knew she was taking advantage of his eagerness to keep her happy and she guessed he knew it too, but he smiled at her and continued eating.

On her way to meet Andrew, the local radio station announced that the police were questioning someone with regard to the assault on the nurse. Was this it? Was this the day the culprit was caught, her son was pronounced well enough to leave hospital, and they all went back to how things were before? Not everyone obviously; Jenny Pickering could never go back and if they were only able to convict this guy of the attack on Nathan, then Maxie doubted she could ever let it rest. It wasn't how she thought she'd feel; she imagined feeling catharsis, satisfaction that justice had at least been delivered. Was that release missing because she hadn't apprehended him herself? She knew that was a vanity and she wasn't exactly proud of herself for feeling it.

She pulled into a visitor's spot in the car park and walked into the reception area of the station, remembering when she'd met Andrew initially. The frenzy of purpose still pervaded every movement of the officers rushing past her and she watched them, silently knowing that going backwards was no longer an option for her. Andrew appeared and waved her through the secure doors, down the corridor to an interview room where a file sat on the table. Maxie sat down and without waiting to be invited, opened it and read through the details.

'Is this him?' she said holding up the photograph.

'Could be, he's not speaking.'

Maxie read through the file. Burglary, mobile phone theft, aggravated assault at the A&E departments – yes, he had a background of moped attacks and had had the nerve to put in a complaint when Nathan restrained him during an attack at the hospital but this guy wasn't a planner. This was all seat-of-the-pants crime. Maxie closed the file and pushed it across the table towards Andrew.

'I don't think he's the one,' she said.

Andrew sighed and started counting out his rationale on his fingers. 'One, Nathan made him look pretty stupid when he restrained him at the hospital. Two, he was out on his moped on the night of the attack. We have him on CCTV not far from Nathan's home. And three, although he hasn't used acid before, his gang have and it wouldn't be hard for him to get hold of it; motive, method, and opportunity.' He'd run out of fingers by his last point.

Maxie pulled up her sleeves and started her own count.

'One, the crimes are linked. The person who attacked Nathan was also at the wedding and this person doesn't look as if he'd go unnoticed at a place like Stanmer Hall. Two, both crimes were planned meticulously to avoid capture and this guy hasn't even got the sense to take a route without CCTV. Three, the attacks were personal to each individual – he didn't know them and certainly there's nothing in his file to suggest that rape is part of his armoury. Four, the link is something to do with their time at sixth-form college and with all due respect, this guy wouldn't have passed the entrance. And five, I imagine you have his fingerprints on record? He doesn't look the type to remember to clear up after himself. Did you find his prints on the bottle or at the church?'

'It doesn't take a master criminal to wear gloves,' replied Andrew.

'I have a name,' Maxie pressed on. 'Someone who was ridiculed or scarred or whatever you want to call it by Nathan and Georgina when he was still at a vulnerable age.'

'Real life isn't like a psychology course,' said Andrew. 'People do things because they're off their heads on drugs, or because they need the money to get off their heads. These latent psychological desires are pretty rare, you know.'

Maxie opened her mouth to protest but then closed it before she could do any damage. He wouldn't be persuaded by her insulting him.

'What about the fire at my house? Is there any evidence to connect him to that?'

Andrew shifted awkwardly and paused before he spoke.

'That's actually what I wanted to talk to you about. We believe we have the source of the blaze. Come with me.'

He led her out of the room and down the stairs into a storage facility. He spoke to the woman on the desk and she brought back a box with a reference number on it. Andrew picked it up and took it to a table where they stood over it.

'It was a very simple device,' he said. 'Something that wouldn't have taken a master criminal to knock up and certainly took no planning.'

He reached into the box and pulled out a couple of sealed bags. He opened the first bag and showed the charred remnants of cloth Maxie recognised as an old nylon boiler-suit Philip had used for decorating years ago. How the hell did that get into the study? He hadn't mentioned anything about redecorating, had he? She knew that even if he had, during these past few weeks, she probably wouldn't have been listening. The second bag contained a tin of paint so maybe he was.

'Fortunately, the fire brigade got there before the heat had the chance to work on this,' said Andrew. 'Were you planning on some DIY?'

'Philip uses the room more than me. He might have been,' replied Maxie recognising the paint tin as a spare they had for the kitchen rather than anything new. The evidence was leading somewhere she didn't want to go. The officer opened the third bag.

'This is what set the whole thing off,' said Andrew holding the remnants of a glass bottle. 'The fabric was stuffed inside the bottle as a wick and inside the bottle was an alcohol and kerosene mixture – again neither of them difficult to source.'

Maxie's body rocked backwards, and Andrew caught her before she stumbled, guiding her towards a chair. The bottle was broken and blackened but there was absolutely no mistaking the cheap supermarket bourbon she'd put back into its hiding place the last time she was in that room. She dropped her head to her hands, thinking back to the conversation about fresh starts. She knew Philip had done this because he hadn't been able to see another way out. He wouldn't have known Karl was upstairs. He'd be charged with arson with intent to endanger life and if he'd made all the calls he'd listed this morning, then his intent to defraud the insurance company had already been acted out.

'It's quite an old-school device really,' continued Andrew gently. 'Almost as if someone looked up how to make a Molotov cocktail on the internet.'

He sat down beside her.

'None of the fingerprints we found at the scene were on our database but obviously I imagine the ones that are there will match your family, maybe even the sender of that note.'

Maxie pulled herself upright; she couldn't bring herself to look at him directly but could feel his eyes boring into her.

'I don't believe the person who attacked Nathan was responsible for the fire at your home,' he said gently but with purpose. 'Do you?'

'No.' She sighed. 'I will get the person who was responsible to come in but we're about to meet our son out of hospital and he's not going to do a runner. Can you give me a day?'

Andrew nodded and she squeezed his hand in thanks.

# Chapter Thirty-Five

He watched the news report as that policeman said he had someone in for questioning. What does that even mean? Have "someone in for questioning"? It's like "someone is helping us with our enquiries"; it means absolutely nothing. It means that they've got no fucking idea what they're doing but they need to pin this on some poor sap because nurses are somehow special. And if the police can't protect lovely precious nurses, then what chance do the ordinary people of this city have?

The professor doesn't think they've got the right person, I can see that from the way she's keeping out of the limelight. If she thought they had their man, she'd be mouthing it off like she was the other night. Oh, wait for it, they've asked her if she feels safer with this development – this should be interesting. Ha! I knew it. "I'm happy to let the police do their job." What kind of a response is that? She isn't usually happy to let them get on with it. She's basically saying "I had nothing to do with this and I think they've got it wrong".

I always liked you, you speak your mind and not many people do that these days. That doesn't mean to say I still won't come for you if you don't butt out of my business soon but I'm doing so well and they're evidently not even trying to catch the real avenger, so you're safe for now. That's what I am, not a criminal or a thug like the sucker taking the rap. I'm an ordinary man who simply wants justice and if people knew me, they'd understand.

I could sign up for one of your courses, Professor.

What's that thing you always talk about on the podcast? Walking in the shoes of the criminal? Understanding how they feel? You wouldn't have to do that if I were in your lecture hall, I could tell you exactly how I feel. You'd be welcome to walk in my shoes if you like but I think they might be a bit big. Ha. That's a good one – I could say that to the students. You know, I can empathise with those people who decide to write their life stories once they're locked up, or those who choose to appear on TV when they're released. Planning something like this makes you sharp, quick-witted, and far more entertaining than the masses in their brain-dead jobs. But pride comes before a fall; people who want their fifteen minutes of fame have to be caught first and that's not in my plans at all. No, I just need to bottle how alive I feel right now and use it to live my best life, that's what he would have wanted for me.

When this is over, I might have to let you go, Simon. I know it isn't healthy to live with all your stuff. I'll never, ever forget you, but avengers move on, they get justice and they move on, that's what I have to do. I'll keep the model of the Death Star though. Do you remember when we built it? It took us all day and then the next day, I painted it. You told me it was amazing; I liked that word. I liked it when you said the things I did were amazing. If you could see me now, you'd say this was amazing, I know you would. This isn't the original Death Star obviously; it's a new one that I made for you. He broke the one we built, said building models was for babies and homos. Stupid dick tried to fly it and smashed it against the wall. He had no right to touch my stuff. I got him back, though, didn't I? I knew they wouldn't find it suspicious, him overdosing with all that alcohol and Spice in his system. And when he was in charge of a minor too? Tut, tut, the authorities knew he was a waste of space. It's just a shame Mum didn't. She's gone now too. I don't know how but it wasn't me. They said she'd passed. Another stupid expression. I didn't ask how, and I didn't grieve. She should have looked after us. She should have backed you up, but no matter, I'm doing it now.

What's it like where you are? I imagine it's like that film, *Ghost*. I know it's a soppy girly film, but it gets them in the mood doesn't it? That's what you always taught me. I could sense you taking over my body like he did with that medium woman; you could feel what I was feeling. You had her, Simon. We had her together. Bitch didn't fight us off either, just shows how much she really wanted you. She was just playing hard to get back then; you knew that and so did she. She should have told them, shouldn't have let them do what they did to you. If she hadn't been so fucking prissy, you'd be here now. You two might even be married and I might be an uncle. That would be amazing too wouldn't it? I could build a Death Star with my nephew. Maybe you've met up with her where you are now; maybe you've forgiven her for what she did. That's your call, bro, if you two have finally hooked up in heaven then I'm happy to have been of service.

I didn't understand why you joined up, why you left me. I hated you for a while, leaving me with them, but I understand it now. You were fighting the enemy. You got them in your line of fire, and you destroyed them. You made the world a better place. I still have that letter you wrote me about the planning and strategy that goes into every operation. How the enemy don't have a chance if you keep your wits about you. That's what I've done. Kept my wits. You'd be proud of me.

He was the hardest to get for you. Operation Hadley took a lot more planning but that's understandable isn't it? Because a hospital can be like a fort can't it? They don't let you in and they guard their own, so I had to be smarter than them and wait till the moment was just right. Those war films we watched when you were on leave, the ones where the scared soldier can't take the pressure of the trenches and goes over the top screaming; you made me watch them for a reason didn't you? They were my training. You made me realise that sometimes in a battle you have to wait for the right moment. I had to wait to get him, but I did it. I enjoyed that one too. The women crying, just like Mum cried when she heard about you. Is it wrong to enjoy it? I bet he enjoyed snitching on you and getting you chucked out. I watched him for ages, looking at himself in the mirror when he thinks no one's looking – ha, well they're definitely looking now aren't they? You won't forget his face in a hurry now. He shouldn't have got involved at school; it wasn't his business. Not surprised he turned out to be a nurse; think they're saints that lot.

It makes me sad that the professor woman is standing up for them; I wish I could tell her what they did to us, how actions have consequences. I didn't set her house on fire, but she probably knows that; she knows I'm cleverer than that. It's a shame I can't meet her for a drink after all this is over and talk about it, tell her when she got close and when she was miles off. That would be fun; we might even have a laugh about it. I got all riled when she called me out on that show of hers but really I kind of enjoyed it. It was like we were opposites but still had respect for each other. I hope she knows it's time to back off. I hope she gives up now. I really don't want to have to keep her quiet. Collateral damage, that's what they call it isn't it, Si? Friendly fire? Getting caught up in something that has nothing to do with you. I hope that doesn't have to happen to her, but she's had a scare off someone now and she should give up. It's her decision.

I want to retreat into the sunset now, Si, like those cowboys who rode into town and did what they had to do. I hope you're proud of me. I know you'd probably take the piss out of what I do for a living but we can't all be soldiers and besides, it's karma isn't it? Everything happens for a reason and if I weren't doing this job, I wouldn't have found her would I? I wouldn't have seen her name on that table plan. I wouldn't have been able to have her for you, and then, I wouldn't have been inspired to get him for you too. There'd have been no justice and you wouldn't be able to rest in peace, but you can now, can't you? I hope so.

I wish you were still here though. If you had been, I might have been organising your wedding, to Georgina or maybe someone better than her. It would have been the best do ever and your army mates would have been here, maybe even giving you a 21-gun salute or something. That would have been cool. And then you'd have had my nephew. I'd have loved that, Si, being Uncle Josh. Now that would have been amazing.

# Chapter Thirty-Six

Exhaustion flooded her body as she sat in the hospital car park, readying herself to get out of the Fiat and put on a brave face. The veins in her eyes were filled with grit, and her eyelids felt as if they were scraping over sharp strands whenever she tried to close them, just for a small moment of calm; Maxie was utterly defeated. The clock on the dashboard told her it was time to go and meet Philip; to put on a happy face, at least while they greeted their son, but she wasn't sure she could do it. How could she link arms and play happy families after what he'd done? How could she look at her son's injuries, knowing they were caused by his own father's idiocy? The clock ticked another minute on. She didn't have time to think about this now. She had to take a deep breath and do what had to be done.

Maxie checked herself out in the mirror and applied some lipstick hoping the force of vibrancy would divert her boy from the angst written across the rest of her weary face. She'd wanted to buy a helium balloon declaring "Welcome Home" but couldn't help choking on the irony; well, there weren't any in the shop saying "Your father is a stupid bastard and you have no home".

Clutching a rather different balloon, and with a huge smile painted on her face, she met the men coming out of the hospital reception.

'Had to get you a gift,' she said hoping it excused her lateness. Karl looked at the mermaid shape bobbing above her head and laughed.

'No, Mum, you really didn't. Honestly.'

Maxie tied it onto his wrist nonetheless and planted a

big kiss on his cheek, leaving an almost perfect pout shape which he quickly rubbed off. She looked over at Philip who was looking to all the world, like an innocent man.

'So, where is home tonight?' asked Karl. 'Is the house okay to go back to?'

'Not yet,' replied Philip. 'Your mum and I have been staying in a hotel, but I've managed to get us somewhere bigger now you're back. I think you'll like it.'

As both Maxie and Philip had cars with them, they agreed that Karl would go with his dad and she'd follow on. She hoped to high heaven that he hadn't phoned the insurance company to get approval for this bigger place wherever it was. She got behind him as he led her down towards the marina and parked outside an aparthotel.

'We're in that one there, on the front overlooking the sea,' said Philip, pointing up at a balcony.

'Nice one, Dad,' said Karl.

Philip looked over at her for approval and she smiled faintly. He was obviously trying out the new life he'd talked about, and if she didn't know what he'd done, it would have been a perfect moment for them all. Maxie wondered what he was feeling right now; was he nervous that he still might get caught out? Or had he blanked out his role in all this? She knew some offenders believed so strongly that the end justified the means, that even when confronted with their wrongdoing, they truly believed they'd done nothing criminal.

'Would you like to do the honours?' Philip asked holding out the keys to her. She took them graciously and they walked the stairs to the first floor where she opened the door.

'It's two bedrooms,' said Philip rushing ahead, and opening the doors which led from the hallway. 'Both have en suites so no queuing for the loo in the morning and the rest is open plan.' He opened the final door with a practised flourish.

Daylight flooded towards them as they stepped into a stunning whitewashed living space where the balcony they'd seen from the street was now at eye level with the horizon. It was beautiful but the heartache of being here, and knowing it simply couldn't last, brought a lump to her throat and no matter how hard she tried not to, she started to cry.

'Mum, it's okay. I'm fine,' said Karl rubbing her arm.

'We all are,' added Philip pulling her towards him in a big hug. 'It's been an emotional ride but we're here now and things will get better.'

Maxie let herself sob into his shoulder for a few moments longer; she really had no choice in the matter. The heartache had to come out now or she knew it would when she spoke to Philip and that really wouldn't help. Emotionally spent, she pulled a handkerchief out of her pocket and blew her nose loudly and comically, breaking the awkwardness as everyone laughed.

'I'm sorry,' she said to Karl. 'I was just thinking that the balloon really clashes with the décor in here. Now is there any booze in this wonderful apartment or do we have to go out to celebrate the return of the prodigal son?'

Philip raised a forefinger to say "wait for it" and opened the huge American-style fridge, pulling out a bottle of champagne and three chilled champagne flutes.

'This place just gets better and better,' said Karl. 'Can we move in permanently?'

Philip raised his eyebrows knowingly at Maxie, but she gave a tiny shake of the head. Now was not the time to discuss it with Karl. In fact, it would be a very different conversation when that time eventually came, but Philip didn't know that yet. The three of them went out onto the balcony and Karl popped the champagne open. The cork flew over the balustrade. He looked out onto the street where it had fallen.

'Didn't hit anyone,' he told them. 'Do you think it's good luck to be hit by a flying champagne cork?'

'Doubt it.' Maxie laughed. 'It has to hurt more than bird poo.'

They toasted Karl's safe return, and new beginnings.

'What shall we do for dinner tonight?' asked Philip. 'Is there anything you particularly fancy after all that hospital food?'

'Don't forget the truckloads of yogurt,' added Karl getting a playful slap from his mum. 'Actually, what I really fancy is the biggest, meatiest pizza you can lay your hands on. Pepperoni, salami, prosciutto – the lot. Thick stuffed crust, pure heart attack city.'

'Sounds bloody good to me,' replied Philip pulling up the delivery app on his phone.

Maxie had a flashback to the night at Nathan's, and the delivery guy who wasn't.

'Make sure you're calling one of the proper delivery companies, someone who vets their drivers,' she said with a note of panic in her voice.

To the outside world the family of three sitting out on the balcony enjoying the fading sun and each other's company would have looked like something from a holiday brochure. You could photoshop out the bandages on the young man's hands, and maybe you wouldn't notice the reticence behind every one of the woman's smiles. She had to hold it together until Karl went to bed. The pizza arrived and, having insisted on seeing the driver's ID and the contents of the box before taking off the safety chain, Maxie brought it into the flat. Philip opened another bottle, but Maxie stopped him from pouring Karl another glass.

'You're on antibiotics,' she reminded him, forbidding Philip from giving him any more.

Philip refilled her glass which was still half full. She took a slice of pizza too but couldn't force either the food or drink down. Obligingly a seagull hovered, and she held up a piece of crust to it which it took.

'Don't encourage them,' said Philip. 'And if you don't want it, feed it to the gannet not the seagulls.'

Karl laughed and took the rest of the slice from his mum.

Eventually her son went to bed, and after waiting a few moments to make sure he wasn't coming back out, Maxie got up and made them both a coffee.

'This could work out, couldn't it?' Philip was saying from the balcony. 'Two bedrooms, much cheaper than our place to run, and no garden to look after.'

Maxie brought the cups to the table and sat down opposite her husband.

'Did you call the insurance company to arrange this apartment?' she asked.

'Not yet. I tried, but they put me on hold for an eternity, so I gave up. They'll be okay with it though – it's actually cheaper than the hotel.'

Maxie sighed with relief; at least that was one thing in his favour.

'Because it's an offence,' she continued, maintaining eye contact throughout. 'Arson with the intent to defraud.'

Philip looked at her, then away again quickly. 'I don't know what you mean.'

'Are we really going to play this game? For God's sake look at me. This is serious, Philip.'

Philip turned defiantly towards her, daring her to speak.

'They know it was you,' Maxie said. 'They found the bottle.'

'Why does that mean it was me? It makes sense to start a fire with alcohol, and it's not hard to get hold of a bottle of bourbon.'

'You evidently know what I'm talking about and anyway, it was the supermarket bourbon you had in the study.'

'Whoever did it wasn't going to chuck away the good stuff.'

'I know it was yours and I know that the last time I saw it, it was squirreled away in one of your foolscap files. It couldn't magically get out of there by itself, fill itself with fuel and throw itself through our study window.'

'What were you doing in my files? You had no right to.'

'For Christ's sake, Philip, grow up! This isn't about the bloody file. You've committed a criminal act and the police know it was you. Your bourbon, your overalls, your fingerprints – how stupid do you think they are?'

'Very, according to you when it suits. I threw those overalls into the bin outside and the bottle was only in the recycling – easy for someone to get out. And of course, my fingerprints are in my house. Yours will be too. Who's to say *you* didn't pick all that stuff up and do it yourself?'

Maxie sat back open-mouthed; was she really having this argument? Had she really been with this man most of her adult life? She clamped her hands over her face and stifled a scream.

'Fine, if that's how you want to play it,' she said when she emerged from behind her fingers. 'They can take us both in and test for residues. They have the letter too, so they'll be able to test that and you can add threatening behaviour and obstruction to your list of offences.'

Philip crumpled, putting his elbows on the table and burying his head down. His back rose and fell with rapid breaths. Maxie watched silently until the breathing steadied and he lifted his head up again, but his eyes faced downwards as he spoke.

'I thought I could make things right,' he whispered. 'I thought if we downsized, I could give you the savings back and we could get things back on track.'

'You didn't have to set fire to our home. You could have suggested downsizing.'

'I didn't think you'd go for it. I thought maybe a near-miss tragedy might bring us together and make us appreciate what's important in life.'

It was a completely flawed logic but in a way it had worked as she'd seen what was important in life as a result. Unfortunately, Philip wasn't part of it.

'The savings are gone,' he continued. 'I had to pay the franchise fee up front and it all seemed legit, it really did but they've gone bust and I'm just another creditor.'

'What about that American woman?'

'They've taken her money too. We're part of a long line of people who've been robbed.'

Maxie put her head in her hands. 'How much did they take?'

'Thirty thousand. I did research it, I really did and that wasn't unreasonable for a business consultancy franchise. They said we'd double our investments within six months. I guess if it sounds too good to be true ... They're the real criminals here.'

Maxie shrugged; she simply had nothing left in her. He was right in a way, and there were so many people they could blame for ending up here: the bank for making him redundant in the first place, society for being ageist and preventing him getting another job, the rogues at that franchise company, themselves for not being more frugal and never thinking this day would come, but the fact remained that none of them had committed a crime and her husband had.

'You need to go down to the station tomorrow,' she said calmly. 'I'll come with you.'

The metal legs of the chair scraped against the concrete floor of the balcony as Philip stood up and aggressively slung the contents of the coffee cup over the rail. Maxie got up and took the cup out of his hand before it could follow. She tried to rest her hand on his back supportively, but he shrugged it off.

'I'm not going. I've done nothing wrong. It was my house and it was an accident. I remember that now. I knocked over the bottle. There's no one hurt, so there's nothing to report. I'll tidy up the mess myself and we can sell up after that.'

'It's arson, Philip, and it's not your house. Technically it belongs to the mortgage company, so you've set fire to their property.'

'If no one tells them, they'll be none the wiser. What were you saying about that girl you were helping? No first-person report so the police couldn't do anything?'

Maxie couldn't help but snort. He had listened to something she'd said then.

'If I don't report this and you don't either then how can they investigate?'

'It doesn't work like that with arson, besides which, they're already involved.'

He turned towards her and stood with his face inches from her.

'Have you set me up? Have you already told them I did this?'

Maxie leant backwards feeling the spray of spittle on her face; she needed to get off this balcony right now. She dodged under his arm and strode into the living space. She tried to reason with him.

'I didn't need to. They worked this one out themselves. You're going to be arrested, Philip.'

'Will you give evidence against me? About seeing that bottle, in the file?'

Maxie knew that she should say whatever he needed to hear right now, but she hesitated, and it was all he needed.

'You will, won't you?'

She closed her eyes and tried to work out the wording.

'I will do everything I can,' she said. 'But you know I can't lie in a criminal case. It would be perjury and I'd lose my job, my reputation ...'

'Oh, your fucking reputation! Well excuse me, Professor, for damaging your reputation. Would having an arsonist as a husband help it then? Help you boost the listener numbers on the podcast? Talking about your first-hand experience of the criminal mind?'

'For goodness' sake!' she screamed. 'What can I say to get this into your head? *You* set fire to our house, our son was in hospital because of you, you tried to defraud the insurance company, and you've committed a crime that you will go to jail for. I spend all my life berating the police for not catching criminals. How could I ask them to let one get away? They wouldn't take any notice of me. I can explain that this is out of character and emphasise everything that we've been through, but I cannot lie for you. You know I can't.'

'All I know is that you *won't*. Not for me.'

To her relief, Philip grabbed his jacket and stormed out of the apartment. Maxie sunk down on the sofa and only then realised her whole body was shaking.

'Mum?' A quiet voice from the doorway made her look up. She tried to pull herself up, but he held out his palm for her not to come near.

'I heard everything,' he said going back into the bedroom and locking the door behind him.

# Chapter Thirty-Seven

*Tuesday, 28 July*

Maxie woke up on the sofa and immediately knew she was alone in the apartment. She hadn't closed the blinds when she'd surrendered to exhaustion here last night, and now the morning sunlight shone cheerfully across the room, completely at odds with her mood. Philip hadn't come back and sitting up she suddenly felt nauseous. What if he'd done something stupid? She chided herself for spontaneously thinking that everything he'd done recently was stupid, but it wouldn't be unheard of for a middle-aged man in his situation to believe he had nothing left to offer this world. She had to find him; they'd passed the point of no return last night, but he was still the father of her son and she needed to know he was safe, if only for Karl's sake.

The echo of emptiness told her Karl wasn't in his room, but she checked anyway. She hadn't heard him leave and guessed he'd been purposefully quiet to avoid any questions or explanations. What sort of parents were they to argue like that on the day their son got out of hospital?

'The type who put him in there in the first place,' she muttered to herself.

She guessed that Philip wouldn't pick up the phone to her but dialled his number anyway; it went straight to message. She dialled Karl's and he picked up.

'I think you two need some space,' he told her sounding more grown up than either her or Philip. 'I'm with a mate so don't worry. Do what you've gotta do, Mum.'

After checking the hospitals to make sure he hadn't

been brought in last night, Maxie called Andrew and told him that Philip was missing.

'He was trying to make things right again with the fire,' she said, trying to explain her husband's actions. 'It was bloody stupid, but he genuinely didn't know Karl was in. Will you go easy on him when he comes in?'

'If I don't have to waste resources looking for him, I'll think about it.'

Maxie thanked him and sent Philip a text begging him to go to the police station and promising that she'd come with him. She needed to try to fix what he'd done, so next up she called the estate agents who were doing the valuation; she asked them to send it to her then on to everyone who needed copies. She rang the insurance company and explained what had happened; the voice on the other end of the call-centre line was bizarrely unemotional and Maxie wondered whether getting an admission of arson was just par for the course in their world. She wondered how many of the calls they got were from wives snitching on their husbands. That's how it felt but if she didn't, she'd be complicit in the crime and then what would happen to Karl?

Having done all she could think of to put right some of Philip's wrongs, Maxie threw the phone down and sat back. Without her family she realised there was no sound whatsoever inside this apartment and she was completely alone. She walked across to the double-glazed doors and pulled them open, letting seagull cries and car engines fill the void. Is this what it would be like for her from now on? Silent and lonely? Maybe Karl would come to visit but after all this, she couldn't imagine him choosing to live with her rather than flat-share or halls of residence, no matter how much it cost. At least he would be close by and over time, they could perhaps repair the damage that had been done.

Could she ever learn to live with this emptiness? She doubted it. For eighteen years she'd had two men to take up her space and her time, feeding them, dressing them, cleaning up after them and loving them with all her heart. The gap was so palpable, it was like the day she'd woken up without a sister.

'Stop that right now,' Maxie called out to the empty room. She pulled herself upright. 'Think about Jenny Pickering and what she's still going through.'

She'd made a promise to that woman, and her stupid husband wasn't going to make her break it. Maxie didn't believe the police had the right guy so she had to keep going with her investigation. Maxie shook herself free of self-pity and tried to get herself back into the space she'd been in before all this chaos with Philip. What had she found out? What was she looking into? Conversations with Laura and Leo came back to her. Jackson was the name she had, along with his age, the area he lived in, and the sixth-form college he was admitted to, even if he didn't graduate. It wasn't a lot but better than a kick from a mule as her grandfather used to say. She could start searching online but as she looked at her laptop, sitting silently in this empty room, she couldn't bear the thought of being alone any longer. She'd go to the college at the centre of this and talk to the admin staff. She guessed they'd be in the building, handling pre-enrolment at this time of year. They'd be extremely busy, so she had to perk herself up and act like someone who meant business. Full-on Professor Reddick had to walk into that college no matter how wounded she felt.

The sixth-form college was quiet but not silent; it was the calm before the storm as staff members scurried through the corridors like ants in a colony, each knowing its own job. Maxie stopped one of the ants and told him she was working with the police – only a small fib – to locate a former pupil. She was directed to an office where she knocked briefly before walking in.

'Can I help you?' asked a woman with wild red hair, although her tone of voice was more "what the hell are you doing here?" She wore two pairs of spectacles perched on her head and pulled down one pair to read Maxie's ID.

'And to think people out there believe we get six weeks holiday,' said Maxie nodding at the paperwork all around and hoping to sound empathetic.

It worked. The mutual respect of another education sector worker came with a nod and the offer of a chair. Maxie explained she was looking for a former pupil in relation to a police enquiry. From the look in the woman's eyes, Maxie saw that she'd suddenly recognised her. 'It's about that attack on the nurse isn't it? What's the name you're after?'

'Jackson,' replied Maxie.

'First name?'

'Sorry, I don't know.'

'Year?'

'He would have started lower sixth in 2010, and he wouldn't have graduated.' Maxie hoped the whole unethical practise of off-rolling wasn't that common back then. With such pressure on performance, it wasn't unheard of for schools nowadays to remove students from their records to boost results.

'Different operating system back then but I should be able to access them from here.' The woman was murmuring to herself. She then looked at Maxie and asked, 'This isn't going to breach any rules is it? You are really working with the police?'

Maxie assured her that she was and gave DS Dawson's name and phone number for her to call if she wanted to check. Thankfully, and as anticipated, the woman took the offer at face value and simply nodded, resuming her search.

'I can tell you that a Simon Jackson enrolled that year but left the college shortly after starting upper sixth,' she said reading from the screen.

'Does it say why?'

'I'd prefer not to give that information at the moment but should the detective you mentioned need and ask for these records, we will of course fully cooperate.' She added, 'Suffice to say, I wouldn't be at all surprised if they did need these records. We don't condone this type of violent behaviour.'

She gave Maxie a knowing look and although it told her she could be on the right track, it would have been a lot easier if the woman would just tell her what she knew. Data protection was a huge issue for everyone though and Maxie doubted whether the university admin team would have even given away this much if they'd been asked. She thanked her for her help and said she'd be in touch if they had further enquiries. Maxie thought it made her sound more official.

Having the first name would narrow down the search. When Maxie had tried googling "Jackson – Lancashire", there'd been over ten thousand results but a quick check on her phone adding Simon had her potential trawl down to seven hundred stories.

The person she was looking for had committed two violent attacks recently but somehow wasn't on the police radar for any youth offences. Typical behavioural patterns would have started with a less serious crime – physical in nature but with extenuating circumstances and the offender would simply have been given a warning or fine. It could be something like a fight in a bar or an argument with a bouncer, the actions of a young man who'd simply had a few too many. She knew there was a chance that a warning given many years ago would have no record so decided to start her search with the local paper headlines, knowing they'd pick up on a minor fracas. Someone nudged past her causing her to drop her phone – the college corridor wasn't the place to do this.

Maxie got back into the car and called Leo, asking if he recognised the name. He said he'd blocked out anything from back then but offered to help her search for him. Guessing she'd get no answer, she called both Karl and Philip anyway to give them an update on where she was, just in case either men wanted to find her. Once again, every aspect of her life was a plate spinning precariously on the top of a long pole; there she was running from one to the other, giving it a quick twist and hoping it wouldn't tumble while she wasn't paying attention. If she could just find this Simon Jackson, she could hand that plate to Andrew.

Leo was ready and waiting for her with his laptop set up on the other side of the desk.

'Okay, boss, where do you want me to start?'

Maxie explained the mission. She began looking through the stories from present day backwards and he started from the beginning. They worked in a silence punctuated only by back stretches, yawns, and the occasional banter based on the headlines they'd found.

'There's a Si Jackson who's won a regional pie eating competition here; no wait, too old.'

Maxie was happy just to have the sound of another person in her day and couldn't imagine having to go back to the flat on her own. In some ways she hoped this search lasted into the night. It wasn't exactly cheery work, despite jibes about the local media covering mainly rescued kittens, and school sports days they reported their fair share of human misery stories: pensioners dying in blazes, children witnessing their father's overdoses, and mothers stealing to feed their families. Maxie hadn't heard of these people before today and yet their lives had been so miserable as to warrant an article. She did a silent prayer that the media wouldn't regard the recent events in her life as newsworthy but, given her profile, there was a very high chance that they would. Her phone rang and they both jumped. It was Andrew. Dreading news about Philip she answered cautiously then breathed with relief as he told her they'd released their suspect.

'I didn't think it was him,' she said, instantly regretting her words in case it sounded like gloating. She still needed this man to give Philip a break. She explained who she was looking for and he agreed to check the records for the name too.

'I'm presuming you haven't heard from your husband,' Andrew went on to ask. Maxie told him she hadn't but believed he just needed time to process what he'd done.

'The longer he holds out, the worse it'll be for him you know. Courts prefer to see some remorse and cooperation.'

Maxie knew this and promised she was doing everything she could to get him to come in but right now she hadn't a clue where he was. She genuinely hadn't a clue – he had no office to escape to, no home – where would he go? She had a sudden vision of him wandering the clifftops, afraid to come back and face her. She messaged both Karl and Philip, saying that she knew they all needed their space right now, but begging them both to just confirm they were safe. Within a few seconds both men had replied to tell her they were and yes, they needed space. Maxie wouldn't push Philip to give himself in right now; she was sure he would when he felt able.

Being busy was what she needed and getting back to her search, Maxie clicked on the link to a story about a Simon Jackson who'd been killed in action. He'd only been nineteen years old, but the photograph looked much younger; the poor boy was not much older than Karl now when he died. In fact, the photograph looked quite familiar. It was this boy's features, she'd seen them somewhere before. He was in his uniform and his hair was cropped but there was something about his eyes. It would come to her eventually. She had to focus on the search and a young man who'd died tragically in Afghanistan eight years ago certainly couldn't have been stalking a wedding at Stanmer Hall in May.

'Anything yet?' she asked Leo who shook his head.

'And I'm nearly done,' he replied.

'Come and look at this guy,' she said turning the screen towards him. 'I know it can't be him, but I recognise him from somewhere.'

'It is him,' said Leo instantly. 'I didn't remember the name, but that's the guy I went to school with. That's the bully.'

'But he can't be responsible for the attacks because he died eight years ago,' Maxie thought aloud, dismayed by the dead end they'd met, again. 'Could he still be our link somehow? Let's see what else we can find out about him.'

'We'd need a more specialised database than we have access to,' replied Leo. 'We could pay for births, deaths, and marriages?'

Maxie nodded and they pulled up the government websites that, for a fee, would give them access to the parish records they needed, without having to trawl around the county. They weren't the easiest of searches to use and more than once Maxie felt like hurling the laptop out of the window in frustration.

'How the hell do you decide to make a search this difficult, in an era when you have a best-in-class role model like Google?' She yelled at the screen.

Fortunately, Leo was far more patient and sent her out of the room to make them a coffee as he plodded on. By the time she'd returned, he had a triumphant look on his face.

'You've found him?' Maxie asked and he nodded.

'Simon David Jackson, born May 1994, died September 2013 aged nineteen. Informant, Julia Lovell.'

Maxie collapsed backwards falling into a cabinet then steadying herself.

'I should have seen it.'

'What's the matter?' asked Leo.

She rushed back to her laptop and stabbed the back key until she reached the story she'd been looking for.

'Here,' she said, and Leo leapt up to stand behind her, reading the screen. It was the human misery report about the young boy who'd witnessed his father's overdose. The son wasn't named, but the widow was: Julia Jackson had been the mother of two boys, one now deceased.

'I still don't get it.'

'Could you do some more searching for me?' asked Maxie without answering his question. 'You're looking for marriage certificates, birth certificates, deed poll name changes – anything to do with Julia Lovell.' She slammed shut the laptop and grabbed her things.

'That'll take some time. Where will you be?'

She reached into her bag and pulled out a business card, laid it on the table in front of Leo, and tapped firmly on the name: *Josh Lovell, Events Planner, Stanmer Hall.*

'To see this bloke.'

# *Chapter Thirty-Eight*

The phone wouldn't stop ringing with Leo trying to get through. Maxie knew what he was going to say and didn't particularly want to hear it, but if she didn't tell him that, he wouldn't leave her alone. She pressed the "accept call" button on the Bluetooth.

'Professor, if you seriously think this man is dangerous then you can't be going up there alone. I'm going to call the police.' Leo's voice reverberated around the car.

'Give it a go, but they won't get there as quickly as I can. And there's no evidence yet, just circumstance and I think I know what I need to look for,' she replied. 'What did the rest of the search tell you?'

Leo sighed and gave her the results she was expecting. She joined the dots in between and knew she'd found a familiar story; mother of young boys remarries and they all take the stepfather's name – Jackson. There are suspicions of domestic abuse and violent behaviour but no convictions; the eldest is expelled from school after an incident that the school covers up and joins the army to get away from his hideous home life. He's killed in action and the younger sibling blames everyone in the world for taking his brother away, especially the stepfather and the people who got him expelled in the first place. The father dies in suspicious circumstances or, more likely, is killed and the mother goes to pieces leaving the youngest son to find his own way in life. Survival and revenge were the oldest motivations known to man. Right now though, it was only a story; it gave motivation, but she had to find the evidence and make it a done deal.

'Are you still listening to me, Professor?' She tuned back

into Leo's pleading. 'I'm going to call your husband and let him know what you're doing if you won't listen to me.'

'Even better luck with that one,' replied Maxie turning the Bluetooth off and cutting him short. 'He's probably in custody by now and even if he's not, I think he'd send me into the lion's den quite willingly at the moment.'

Despite the bravado and adrenaline forcing her on, the professor was also quite terrified. She took a deep breath and wondered what the hell she was going to do when she got there. It was true, so far she had a story which would drive a disturbed young man to revenge but she had nothing to *prove* that he'd attacked either Georgina or Nathan. He hasn't a stupid man. He'd hidden his actions very well so far, but she knew there would be something he'd kept. The photographs he'd taken during the assault. He'd taken them for a reason besides humiliating the young woman, and putting herself in his shoes – she could see what it was.

'You want to show them to your big brother don't you, Josh? Show him what you did for him?'

She turned into the drive towards Stanmer and was slightly surprised to see notices all the way along announcing the wedding of Paul and Dani. She naively hadn't expected the hotel to be busy on a Tuesday, but she should have guessed summer was busy every day. Maxie knew there was no danger to the happy couple or their wedding party. Josh had taken very specific action against three very specific people, if you counted his stepfather, which she thought highly likely. In a way, he'd acted exactly as her students had said they would, by becoming vigilantes. He would probably never accept that he'd done anything wrong.

Maxie pulled into the car park some distance from the entrance and the celebrations taking place. She really didn't want to ruin this occasion for them and although she didn't exactly look like a cheery wedding guest in her black tunic, by adding the colourful scarf she had on the back seat of the car, she could probably, at a push, be mistaken for one of the hotel staff.

It was highly likely that Josh was here somewhere making sure the event went smoothly. Having achieved exactly what he wanted to do for his brother, he'd probably have gone straight back to work.

Maxie caught a glimpse of the happy couple as she walked towards reception and announced breezily to the receptionist that she was just popping in to see Josh. She wondered how the newlyweds would feel when they heard the news that their wonderful big day had been managed by a psychopath.

She reached Josh's office. It was at the back of the hotel, a quiet space away from the fracas. You would barely know there was anyone in the hotel from back here. She knocked lightly, waiting to hear if anyone invited her in. When they didn't, she turned the handle; the door was unlocked, which again demonstrated the behaviour of a confident man who felt he had nothing to hide.

Maxie crept into the room and closed the door behind her. She was almost instantly disappointed by what she saw – which was absolutely nothing out of the ordinary.

It was a tiny cupboard of a room with a desk that must have been a remnant from somewhere more grand because it really didn't fit, some metal filing-cabinets that recalled days before paperless offices, and a coat stand with a couple of dry-cleaned suits still hanging in their plastic bags. He lived in his office the way she did in hers. She didn't know what she was expecting but it would have been bloody handy if one of the walls were covered in photos of Georgina and Nathan with death threats scrawled over them like they always were in movies. Instead there was a neat year planner on that wall with coloured dots marking out the weddings and birthday celebrations taking place. He kept a desk diary with meeting dates and notes of schedules that seemed to bear no relation to anything but she'd decipher them later; she stuffed the diary in her bag. Beyond that there was nothing personal on display, no photographs or even the annoying desk toys that appeared every Christmas from suppliers. He was bound to get things like that, working in this industry, but there were none. He was a meticulous man.

Maxie started rifling through the drawers, again expecting to find nothing and fulfilling her own expectations. She wouldn't hide anything critical in a desk drawer so why would he? Where would she hide things? Where had Philip hidden them? He'd had a contract from that set of rogues, statements from the bank, and he'd had bottles of booze he was hiding from her. He'd hidden them in plain sight, in his rows and rows of boring looking foolscap files. There were hundreds of them in here and Maxie guessed that if he'd kept the photos of Georgina as she suspected he had, they'd be on a memory card somewhere. So that's what she was looking for in all of this. It was the modern-day version of the needle in the haystack.

'What would you have filed it under?' said Maxie as she opened the cabinet and flicked through the names staring back at her. 'Jackson? Simon?' There was no file under either name or any derivative of them. She moved to a cabinet with files listed in date order and found the details of Penny's wedding. There was a table plan with a tiny asterisk against Georgina's name; it showed he'd known she'd be there but nothing else. Maxie went through the pockets of the dry cleaning, then checked that nothing was sellotaped to either the back of the wall planner or underneath the desk. She scoured every inch of the office but could find no evidence.

'*Think*, Maxie. He's very careful and this is important to him. He wouldn't risk not being able to find it. It's not about being caught, it's about being respectful, being able to show his brother what he's done for him. He has to keep his trophies safe but accessible so they can share them.' She was speaking to herself as she looked around the room. 'Now, where would you keep something of Karl's?'

Maxie's thoughts went straight back to the first curl of soft hair cut from her baby's head; she couldn't bear to part with it back then and Philip had bought her a glass locket to keep it in. She'd been incredibly touched by his thoughtfulness until she'd found out it was known as a mourning locket and people kept the hair of lost pets or people in it. It felt completely wrong and, if she believed in all that garbage, it was surely tempting fate to store a keepsake from her son in something meant for the dead. Instead she simply wrapped the curl in a handkerchief and carried it in a pocket of her handbag before finally putting it safely at the bottom of her jewellery box. Her initial desire had been to keep Karl with her at all times and she was beginning to think that perhaps Josh would want the same. If so, that meant finding him and confronting him. There really was no other way as far as she could see.

Maxie left the room as she'd found it and asked for Josh's whereabouts. She was told that he'd gone down to the lake to tell the guests gathered there that the bride and groom were about to leave. The reception was filling with the chatter of expectation, but Josh wasn't among them. Maxie hesitated for a moment. There could be consequences to what she was about to do, but having come this far, she simply had to follow it through. She told the receptionist that she was going to find Josh and that if she personally didn't report back to her within thirty minutes, then the hotel was to send out a search party. She asked the receptionist to repeat the instructions she'd just been given and promise that she'd carry them out. The confused receptionist shrugged a lack of understanding but repeated the instructions, nonetheless. Maxie then sent a text to Leo saying the same. Hoping she'd covered her back a little, she started the walk down to the lake.

She saw him sitting on the grass with his back to her. He seemed very relaxed, leaning back on his elbows, in that spot by the hawthorns trees; the place she suspected he'd attacked Georgina only a few weeks ago. Her heart was thumping, and she felt no matter how quietly she stepped towards him, the sound of her fear would give her away.

'You found me then,' he called out without turning round. 'I wondered if you would. I'm just enjoying a peaceful moment with Si. He'd have loved it here.'

Maxie walked up to him and saw dog tags in his hand; he rolled the chain around them and stuffed them in his inside jacket pocket.

'He'd have loved seeing the girls all dressed up to the nines, having a laugh. That's why I took the pictures ... to show him. I leave them with him so we can look at them together and have a laugh. He was a bit of a ladies' man, my big brother.'

He turned to look at Maxie.

'That's how I know she was just playing hard to get. I was only thirteen years old when she made all those accusations against Simon – he told me how she'd made them up. No one ever said no to Simon. He could get any woman he wanted.'

'Taking any woman you want isn't the same thing.'

'They took her word for that. Simon would have got a fairer hearing if Nathan hadn't interfered,' he replied very matter of fact. 'Did they find out who torched your house by the way? It wasn't me but you probably know that.'

'I do.'

Josh got up and started walking away from her. Maxie glanced back up at the hall. She could see no one to back her up, but began following him anyway. She couldn't let him escape now, not without the evidence. He was getting closer to the edge of the lake but if he started running across the fields beyond, then she'd have no chance of catching him – hers was not an athletic build. He could have vanished by the time she got back to the hall and informed anyone. If she kept him talking, he might just let slip where he was keeping those pictures.

'I was wondering whether you'd be interested in telling your story to my students,' she said, hoping he'd fall for it. 'They'd probably have a lot of empathy with your decisions.'

He snorted. 'And how about interviewing me on that podcast? That would get the ratings up. There'd be more than an old codger and a scabby dog listening to it if I were on.'

Josh strode on, yelling at her as he walked.

'When they kicked him out of that school for *supposedly* assaulting that girl, my stepdad went mad. He told Simon he couldn't come back to live with us if he was just going to piss away his future. My mum didn't stand up for him either. Simon was furious. He always said he'd show them, that he'd come back a hero and we'd get a place together.'

'I understand why you did it, you know.'

'I know you do. I googled you, remember,' replied Simon, picking up the pace. 'I read all about your sister dying in that burglary and how the police found nothing.

We're the same you and me. It's no surprise you worked it out and not them.'

'You should still give yourself up,' she called out, breathless but still trying to keep up. 'I can explain what happened, explain how it feels to be let down by the system. The prosecution might be more empathetic given the circumstances.' Maxie had no intention of doing any of this but hoped it would keep Josh thinking they were the same.

He stopped moving and turned towards her, laughing hysterically. 'Nice try but you know as well as I do that wouldn't happen. They'd do the exact same as I have if they really understood the "circumstances" as you call them, but that won't stop them baying for blood. They wouldn't understand how it feels to be left alone with a dad who's favourite pastime is giving you or your mum a kicking. I was fifteen when Si died for Christ's sake. I lost everything because of those two people. *Everything!*'

His body contorted angrily as he screamed out that last word. He rubbed his eyes and Maxie took a few cautious steps towards him, her heart pounding.

'I know you did. I know that your brother tried it on with Georgina, but he didn't stop when she asked him to and she reported it. I know that Hadley got your brother expelled and I know he joined the army when he couldn't come home. I know he was killed in action and you never got that place together. I know and I understand, and I can help make others see that.'

'They don't know you're here, do they?' he said regaining his composure. 'The police? They don't believe your mad theories. I could see that from the statement when they thought they'd got the guy. They're always dismissing you as some lunatic, Professor.'

'They do know I'm here and they won't be far behind.'

She took another step forward and reached out, trying to put a hand on his arm.

In a flash, he was running along the small jetty and diving into the lake. Maxie rushed towards him.

'Come back! I can't reach you, I can't swim,' she yelled from the edge. 'I can't save you.'

'I don't want you to,' he said. 'Death or glory.'

Maxie watched in disbelief as Josh's head sank below the surface.

She turned towards the hall and screamed for help as loudly as she could but knew no one would be able to hear her. There was still five minutes until the search party would be sent out – and that was presuming the receptionist wasn't distracted by the wedding. Even five minutes was too long.

She had to do something right now, but what? Maxie couldn't swim. She looked quickly around the sides of the lake – there was no life buoy – surely there should have been? Maybe it wasn't that deep. Maxie took a deep breath and, kicking off her shoes, started to wade in.

Despite the sun, the water was cold as it swirled around her ankles, then her calves and her knees. She kept going, bending down and feeling down with her hands, hoping they'd find him soon. The water reached her thighs and reeds started tangling around her like weights, making her stumble and sink below the surface. She pushed herself back up into the air, gasping. She'd seen him. He was just ahead of her.

Ramming her fear to the pit of her stomach she waded on. The water was at her chest but she was within a whisker of Josh. She reached out and grabbed the edge of his coat, using every ounce of strength she had left to pull him towards her.

With the final fury of a man who had no more reason

to live, Josh lashed out. He pivoted around and kicked her hard in the stomach. The blow rendered her useless just long enough for him to wind her scarf around his wrist, tightening it across her neck. She felt herself tumbling and falling over the rocks on the lake bed, then the ground beneath her vanished and she kicked out, her feet trying to find a surface, something she could reach. There was nothing. The sun hid behind a dark cloud and the sky went black.

He was sinking deeper and deeper with her scarf wrapped around his wrist and the deeper he went the tighter it pulled. Maxie kept her mouth tightly closed but her lungs were bursting to inhale. She had to preserve the little air she had left inside them. Fighting every instinct she had, she stopped struggling to free herself and instead tried not to move. Josh's wilting body was still dragging her down; if she could just preserve her energy and stay conscious for longer than him. Air bubbles escaped her nose and she panicked. She'd have to breathe in soon: she couldn't hold this much longer.

Suddenly she felt the scarf go slack! She automatically opened her eyes and through the murky waters saw the shape of Josh floating, presumably now unconscious, and the bright-coloured scarf unfurling itself. She pulled it from her neck, kicked herself away from him and tried to push herself upwards.

It was too far away.

She needed to breathe.

She couldn't stop herself.

She opened her mouth. The water flooded her airways and lungs, her brain screamed out in pain. She saw a brilliant white light.

Then nothing.

# Chapter Thirty-Nine

'The grave.' Maxie jolted up then collapsed again, gasping for the air which scraped through her throat and lungs. A nurse gently but firmly lay her back down on the bed and replaced the torn-aside oxygen mask. Karl sat down beside her and took her hand.

'They know, Mum. They've got it. Get some rest.'

'Why does she keep saying that?' asked the nurse. 'Does she think she's still in danger?'

'It was something to do with a case she was working on with the police,' replied Karl. 'Evidence she needed them to find.'

'And did they find it?'

'Yeah – thank God or she'd have probably got out of bed and gone there herself, breathing or not.'

The murmured voices and their message soothed Maxie into rest; she was alive but so many questions were queuing patiently in her mind, all waiting to be answered that she could almost see them standing there jockeying to be heard first. She told them they'd have to wait. This time she simply couldn't fight the exhaustion that was creeping towards her, enveloping her as gently as an early morning fog.

The second time she opened her eyes she lay silently and, without moving her head, took it all in: a white room, bright lights, small hard bed. She could move her toes and fingers, could feel her legs, she was hungry, and her airways were finally no longer feeling like a rusty saw. Was her brain functioning? She silently quizzed herself. What year are we in? Who's the Prime Minister? Who wrote *Nature or Nurture: The Criminal Mind Revealed*? Where did Josh hide the memory card with those photos of Georgina? It was probably cheating to ask herself questions she knew the answers to, but she figured the fact that she was toying with herself also had to be a good sign. She lifted her head slightly from the pillow and reached out for the glass of water on the bedside cabinet. It alerted Philip, who was sitting in the corner of the room with his arms on his knees and his head slumped forward in his hands.

'I'll get that for you,' he said, rushing forward to pour her a fresh glass. 'Karl's just gone home for a change of clothes. How are you feeling?'

'Astonishingly good,' she replied, sipping cautiously.

'That'll be the rest and oxygen.'

She knew they had so much to talk about but couldn't bring herself to start. He stood up with his arms tightly folded and began pacing the room.

'I turned myself in. I'm only here under supervision.' He nodded towards the door. Leaning against the frame, trying to give them a moment of privacy, was Andrew. Maxie waved the police officer in, and Philip took it as his leave to go. He leant over awkwardly and pecked her on the cheek. As he was coming towards her, she wondered whether his touch would ignite anything, perhaps tenderness rediscovered after everything they'd been through, but there was nothing. A light wet touch that her synapses just responded to as if they'd come from an old friend. She watched Andrew instruct a uniformed officer to take Philip back to the station and as she did, sadness filled her heart. But not regret.

'We're doing what we can for him,' said Andrew, nodding towards Philip as he left.

'Thank you,' she replied. 'It wasn't the greatest idea he's

ever had but he did it for the right reasons. I will testify to that.'

'I know,' said Andrew.

'You came to Stanmer?' asked Maxie.

Andrew nodded. 'I set off as soon as I got the call from Leo and we got there not long after you started wading into that lake. I was shouting from across the grounds but you evidently didn't hear. I couldn't believe you were going in after him and that was before I found out you couldn't swim. What on earth were you thinking?'

'That I couldn't let him get away with it,' replied Maxie. 'Is he alive?'

'Yes. He was in a bit of a worse state than you. He'd inhaled a lot of water, maybe on purpose, but we got to him.'

'That's good. I wouldn't really want him to get away with what he did. He had his problems, but he caused more.'

'And you were right, all that semi-conscious rambling. There was a memory card with the photos and it was where you said it would be – with his brother. It was inside that little flower pot beside the grave. Fortunately, he'd wrapped it in a plastic bag so it was completely undamaged.'

Maxie nodded. If she'd thought of it before hitting the water, she could have gone straight there and wouldn't be lying here now.

'I knew he'd be keeping it somewhere close to Simon. He'd taken those pictures for him. It was a gift, proof that he'd avenged him. Were there pictures of the attack on Nathan too?'

'Yes, he was wearing one of those helmet cameras throughout the attack so we have the proof that he committed both crimes, when he's well enough to stand trial.'

They both sighed deeply at the same time. Maxie was thinking about Laura and Jenny. She hoped knowing that Josh had been caught would give both mothers some relief.

As soon as she was discharged, Maxie asked Karl to drive her to Jenny's house. She wanted to take her something but couldn't think of anything appropriate; flowers seemed too funereal, wine too celebratory, and cake too trite. She called Rachel and asked what perfume Georgina wore. Getting the name, she stopped on the way and bought a small bottle.

'I know she will always be with you, but I hoped this would help,' she told Jenny, handing it over as she and Karl entered the quiet house. The bereaved mother's eyes lit up.

'Thank you,' she said. 'People tend to avoid talking about her, thinking I'll get upset, but I want to talk about Georgina, to say her name, to remember her smile ... and her scent.'

Jenny sprayed a small amount on her wrist and inhaled deeply.

'He's going away for a long time,' said Maxie. 'There's absolutely no doubt about that.'

'I suppose that's something,' said Jenny. 'But the non-Christian part of me wishes you'd let him drown. I'm praying that I won't feel like that forever.'

Maxie squeezed Jenny's hand then nodded to Karl and they left, eventually turning the car in the direction of the apartment.

'I collected some more clothes and stuff,' said Karl as they walked back into their temporary home. 'The house is still out of bounds due to the damage, but I doubt you'd want to go back there, anyway.'

Maxie nodded; he'd thought right. She couldn't imagine

ever feeling ready to go back to that place. The fire-damaged house would be sold at auction for a fraction of its true value. When things had settled and she had the money from the sale, she'd find a small two-bedroomed apartment which Karl could at least come home to in the holidays. But that was a worry for the future.

Closing the door behind them, she took the turn that led her straight to her bedroom and she didn't protest for a moment as her son instructed her to get some rest. She changed into pyjamas and Karl brought her in a mug of tea before leaving her to sleep.

Over the next fortnight, Maxie responded to all the good wishes but turned down all requests for media interviews. Craig Johnston had told her to keep all "the juicy stuff" for the podcast but it wasn't that – she simply wanted life to get back to some sort of normal. Although this morning, Karl was acting anything but normal. He knocked on the door, bringing her breakfast in bed.

'To what do I owe this honour?' she asked.

'Just thought you might need your strength today.'

He left the room and she sipped the coffee, puzzled by his comment; why might she need her strength today? She picked up her phone and the headlines announced "A-level results: Record Year".

Of course! It was that time already. They had to go up to the school today and although the summer had been their own version of an annus horribilis, tonight she'd celebrate her son's results with him. Karl returned with the coffee pot, offering a refill.

'Buttering me up?' Maxie smiled, accepting the top-up. 'You're not worried about the results, are you?'

Karl assured her that he wasn't, but his emphasis suggested something else.

"*I'm* not worried" was how he put it.

The school was already crowded with students, parents, teachers, and the local media. The young people collected and shared their results, cried and celebrated with each other, and told their stories to the journalists. Their parents held anxious robotic expressions until they knew whether they were allowed to smile openly or whether they had to comfort their heartbroken children. Maxie stood where she was told to and waited for Karl to reappear with the all-knowing envelope. Another mother appeared at her side.

'Have you heard how Karl has done?' she asked, and Maxie shook her head.

'I was less worried when I was being drowned,' Maxie added.

Karl eventually reappeared and took his mother outside to a quiet part of the school grounds.

'Well?' asked Maxie.

'I got what I needed.' He smiled and Maxie hugged him, planting kiss after kiss all over his face and hair.

'I'm so proud of you, although obviously I never doubted for a second that my offspring would excel.' Maxie beamed. 'We need to call the faculty now and make sure they know you're coming.'

She pulled her phone out of her bag, but Karl took it gently but firmly out of her hand.

'Mum, wait.' He handed over the results letter. Maxie took it and read it, then read it again.

'I don't understand,' she said. 'These can't be your results.'

'They are mine.'

'But you need higher grades than this.'

Karl took both her hands and held them firmly.

'Not for what I've decided to do.' He spoke quietly and deliberately as if preparing her for bad news. 'I can't stay here. I've decided I'm not going to university. I need space, my independence, and besides which it's a lot of money.'

'But you don't have to start paying back the loan until you're working,' protested Maxie. 'And I'll help you as much as I can – you know that.'

'No, Mum, it's not just the money – I've already decided. I'm not going.'

'So, what's the plan?' Maxie's shoulders had dropped in defeat, fearful that she'd caused this decision but even more afraid that if she protested, she'd lose him forever.

'I'm taking an internship at a gaming company over in Manchester.'

'Manchester? How will you commute there every day? It'll take ages.'

'I won't be commuting, Mum. I'm moving there.'

Maxie stood, jaw dropped, as his words bounced around her brain, not settling and not making any sense.

'They have these flatshares for interns, so we don't have to pay full whack for accommodation. I'm moving in there.'

'But … I don't understand.'

'It's what I want to do, Mum.'

'Please, think about it for just a little longer.' Maxie was clutching at rapidly vanishing straws. 'Don't worry about the grades. I'll talk to someone. I was hardly there when you were taking your finals and your dad … Your dad was distracted by the business. It's our fault, I'll tell them that.'

'Mum, stop it. It wasn't your fault, and this is a good thing. I'm kinda looking forward to it. We both need a fresh start.'

'I just thought we might be making that fresh start together – at least for now.'

Her life had felt like a jumper unravelling for some time, but she'd thought she'd got to the end. Now someone up there had found that loose strand of wool and was giving it another bloody hard tug. They weren't going to let go until there was nothing left to pull apart.

'It wouldn't be right, Mum. Dad'll be locked up and everything has changed. You need to work out what you want in life as much as I do. It's better that we all do our own thing. I'd feel like I was picking sides and I don't want to do that. I still love you both.'

They fell silent. Maxie couldn't argue with that. Her son had shown more insight and honesty than her or Philip had done in a long time. Karl was being the grown-up in all of this. She knew he'd thought carefully about this decision and she had to respect it. She guessed that internships weren't easy to come by. She blinked back a traitorous tear and chivvied herself up, giving him a big hug.

'Still, it's only a few hours away so you could be back every weekend. Or I could visit – is there room for a sofa bed for your old mum in this flat?'

Karl rolled his eyes and she knew she sounded like the desperate clingy parent. Thousands of students left home at this time of year. She'd taken off around Asia after her A levels; at least he wasn't doing anything like that. She'd simply have to learn to enjoy the silence of her own company.

'Well, it isn't the celebration we were expecting to have,' she said, wiping tears from her cheeks. 'But it's still a celebration. Shall we go and empty a few champagne bottles on the balcony?'

# Chapter Forty

*May – One Year Later*

The significance of the date hadn't escaped her; a year ago today, Rachel had called and asked for her help. It felt wrong to be benefitting from that dreadful attack, but Maxie knew it had started the chain of events that had eventually led here.

If she hadn't stuck her nose in against police instruction, they wouldn't have known the connection when Nathan was assaulted, and they wouldn't have successfully prosecuted Josh. They'd presented the arrest to the media as a team effort, and that of course led to suggestions that the team effort be formalised. Maxie's proposal for the ACU finally had a proper hearing and after agreeing the terms of reference and getting some private funding, they were ready to cut the ribbon.

It had been a useful distraction. Philip had been convicted of arson and conspiring to defraud but with Maxie's testimony on all that was happening in their lives and Andrew telling the court that Philip had given himself up willingly, the custodial sentence was only six months. Maxie had visited most weeks and kept him up to date with the sale of their family home. Together they agreed that after they paid off the mortgage company, they would give Karl a chunk of money to help set himself up, and then share the remainder equally. They both realised their marriage was over and seeing the balance from the house sale in her account made it real. The past twenty years together had a monetary value and it wasn't a huge sum.

Philip moved away from the area when he was released

earlier in the year and Maxie hadn't heard from him since. She knew he kept in touch with Karl from the infrequent emails her son sent in response to her pestering him. Maxie could tell that he loved both his new-found freedom and the job itself. They'd even taken him on permanently so now he was being paid. He'd discovered the music scene the city was famous for and was living the kind of carefree life every young person should.

Then at Christmas, he'd stayed in Manchester to celebrate with his new girlfriend and her family. It was Maxie's first Christmas alone and when Karl Skyped her that morning, she put on her "everything's fabulous" expression and lied, telling him she was spending the day with old friends. But it wasn't true and it wasn't fabulous. It was still rather lonely and even though she spent every hour she could at the university, she had to go home eventually and when she did, it was just so quiet.

'You must be delighted,' said Andrew, pulling her out of her thoughts. 'After all the work you put into making this facility happen.'

Maxie smiled and told him it had been a team effort; that seemed the right thing to say.

'How's that son of yours doing?' he asked. 'It's a bit livelier there than here isn't it?'

'That's what he keeps telling me,' replied Maxie. 'And yes, he's really enjoying himself. Of course, I'd rather he were here. This year has been strange, to say the least, and now I seem to be suffering from empty nest syndrome. Too much time on my hands despite work and all of this.'

Maxie was trying to make light of it but didn't feel that way. They stood quietly as the ribbon was cut and the important people said important things. Maxie was called upon to take part in the photo for the press and after more handshakes the group went their separate ways.

'Can I buy you a drink?' asked Andrew as they left the university. 'To toast our new working relationship.'

'I've nothing else to do,' replied Maxie. Realising how ungracious that sounded, she added, 'Sorry, I meant to say thank you – that would be lovely.'

They drove out to a quiet country pub and settled in a couple of armchairs by the fire. Andrew returned from the bar with a glass of wine for Maxie and a bottle of low alcohol beer for himself.

'I wanted to say, back there ...' Andrew was stumbling over his words. 'You're looking fit ... Well ... I mean well.'

Maxie smiled at his awkwardness. 'I've been taking swimming lessons. I won't be caught out like that again.'

They both laughed at that and clinked glasses.

'To the end of the case and new beginnings,' she said.

'New beginnings,' replied Andrew.

They sipped their drinks and it was the detective who eventually broke the amiable silence and spoke up.

'You should feel proud of yourself, you know. This hasn't been easy what with Philip and the house, but you made a difference.

'Granted your detection methods were novel, getting inside the killer's shoes and all that,' continued Andrew, seeing that Maxie was still deep in thought. 'But they worked. You found him.'

'Thank you. Bizarrely, I enjoyed it. Not the deaths or near-death experience but getting justice for those families.'

'That's the whole point.'

Andrew's phone rang. He took the call then stood and grabbed his coat.

'Sorry, I have to go. There's been an incident ... unless?'

Maxie jumped to her feet.

'Just try to stop me.'

# Thank You

Dear Reader,

First of all, I'd like to thank you, dear reader, for choosing *One by One*.

I hope you've enjoyed meeting Professor Maxie Reddick as she will be back soon with another crime to solve. In developing her character, I wanted to create a strong, intelligent woman who would stop at nothing to get justice. Placing her outside the police force enabled me to give her freedom to investigate the crimes as she wanted. I hope that you were able to put yourself in her shoes and think about what you would do if you were in her situation and, most importantly, I hope I kept you guessing until the end!

If you've enjoyed *One by One*, please leave a review for the book on Goodreads or the website where you bought the book. You can also follow me on Twitter for news on my next book (details on the next page). Looking forward to hearing from you.

Helen x

# About the Author

Having failed miserably with every New Year's resolution that involved diets, one year, Helen Bridgett set herself a completely different goal – to write a novel and give it as a Christmas present. Having written one, she couldn't stop!

All Helen's novels feature strong female leads who are faced with situations that they have to resolve. Her goal is to create characters that you would want to get to know better in real life.

As well as crime, Helen also writes feel-good fiction. *Summer at Serenity Bay* – about a fictional village on the glorious Northumberland coast – was published in 2020 and the characters returned in *Christmas at Serenity Bay* in November 2021.

Outside of writing, Helen loves being outdoors walking with the dog and enjoying a glass of wine and banter with friends.

*To find out more about Helen, follow her on social media:*
www.twitter.com/Helen_Bridgett
www.facebook.com/HelenBridgettAuthor/

# More Ruby Fiction

## From Helen Bridgett

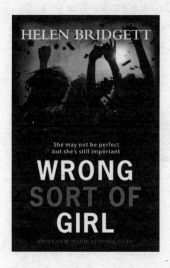

## Wrong Sort of Girl

**Professor Maxie Reddick Files**

**A young woman has gone missing. It's nearly Christmas. Why does hardly anyone seem to care?**

Kelly Ingles' case should have been one to tug on the public's heartstrings: a young woman missing in the run-up to Christmas. But Kelly wasn't perfect – she liked to party, enjoyed a drink, didn't always make the best decisions. And when evidence of her drunken antics appears online, it becomes clear that Kelly might not just have been in the wrong place at the wrong time; she might also be the wrong sort of girl to encourage public sympathy. It's a case that's right up Maxie Reddick's street. As a criminology professor, she's made it her mission to challenge unconscious biases within the criminal justice system – the sort of biases that cause girls like Kelly to slip through the cracks. But can she get the police and public on board before it's too late?

Visit www.rubyfiction.com for details.

## Summer at Serenity Bay

**What happens when you send a group of celebrities to a tiny seaside village?**

Advertising executive Chloe Walsh thought she was visiting her friend Roisin to get away from it all, but little does she know her kooky friend has a master plan to breathe some life into her sleepy seaside village through a new wellness retreat – and she needs Chloe's skills.

So starts a community effort to put the retreat, Serenity Bay, on the map. Everyone from Andy at the Surf Shack to Tony at the chocolate shop is involved – even Roisin's Gran has a few ideas!

But Chloe strikes gold almost too soon, attracting the attention of a major production company. Now a colourful group of celebrities are preparing to descend on Serenity Bay to film a reality TV show. Is the village ready for the fun and scandal that are bound to follow?

Visit www.rubyfiction.com for details.

## Christmas at Serenity Bay

**A peaceful Christmas in Serenity Bay? Think again!**

Chloe Walsh's skills as location manager for the beautiful seaside village she calls home have come up trumps again, and Serenity Bay is now the setting for cosy crime drama The Montgomery Mysteries, starring amateur sleuth Dominic Montgomery and his crime-solving dog, Agatha.

But Chloe is in a race against time. Filming has to finish before the village Midwinter Festival but schedules are tight – and a mystery saboteur is intent on slowing things down even further. Not only is Chloe facing problems with the shoot, she also has some personal conundrums to solve – a diva actor has commandeered her flat, her mum is having a late mid-life crisis, plus she has no idea what to buy for her Christmas-obsessed boyfriend!

Can Chloe sort out her life and save Christmas for an entire village?

*Sequel to Summer at Serenity Bay*

Visit www.rubyfiction.com for details.

# Introducing Ruby Fiction

Ruby Fiction is an imprint of Choc Lit Publishing.
We're an award-winning independent publisher,
creating a delicious selection of fiction.

### See our selection here:
www.rubyfiction.com

Ruby Fiction brings you stories that inspire emotions.

We'd love to hear how you enjoyed
*One by One*. Please visit www.rubyfiction.com and give your
feedback or leave a review where you purchased this novel.

Ruby novels are selected by genuine readers like yourself.
We only publish stories our Tasting Panel want to see in
print. Our reviews and awards speak for themselves.

**Could you be a Star Selector and join our Tasting Panel?**
Would you like to play a role in choosing which novels
we decide to publish? Do you enjoy reading women's
fiction? Then you could be perfect for our Tasting Panel.

**Visit here for more details …**
**www.choc-lit.com/join-the-choc-lit-tasting-panel**

### Keep in touch:
Sign up for our monthly newsletter Spread for all the latest
news and offers: www.spread.choc-lit.com. Follow us on
Twitter: @RubyFiction and Facebook: RubyFiction.

*Stories that inspire emotions!*